ROSE CITY KILL ZONE

DL Barbur

ISBN: 9781080212095

For all the cops, Coasties, Special Agents and soldiers I've known that have done the right thing, even when the people around them weren't.

CHAPTER ONE

I wanted to buy my girlfriend an ice cream cone but wound up in a gunfight instead.

Portland had been suffering under an oppressive heat wave for the better part of a week. It was a hundred degrees during the day and only cooled off to eighty-five at night. I wanted to hop in the car with Alex and go to the coast, maybe somewhere high up in the mountains, but we were currently hunting down a bunch of federal fugitives, so a stop for ice cream would have to do.

It was Portland, but I didn't want hipster ice cream. No vegan soy frozen yogurt for me, thank you. I wanted frickin' ice cream, made from milk from an actual cow, with plenty of artificial flavorings and additives I couldn't pronounce. I would give extra attention to any establishment where the staff didn't have facial piercings and make ironic comments. I'd been spending too much time downtown, and I needed a detox. Fortunately, we were in southeast Portland, and the hipster diseases hadn't spread this far.

"How about that place?" Alex asked, pointing at a burger joint down the street. It sat between a pawn shop and a nail salon. It wasn't part of a chain, and as we watched a crew cab pickup with a bunch of landscaping equipment in the bed pulled up and four hungry looking guys got out. The sign out front read "Shakes and Ice Cream! Beat the heat!"

"Perfect," I said.

Alex waited for the traffic light to change, then she gunned our Dodge Charger through the intersection. There were plenty of people out on foot, and quite a few of them gave us sidelong glances. The Charger was unmarked, but it had plain wheels and a couple of extra antennas on the roof, so to the attentive eye, it still looked like a cop

2

car. The glances weren't unfriendly, exactly, but they were wary.

We'd been driving around all day, looking for a guy named Francis Bloem. Until three days ago, he'd been a Portland Police officer, and he'd been dirty as hell. He'd been in cahoots with a human trafficking ring and had helped some guys nearly beat my former partner to death, and set me up to take the fall. For a while there, I thought I'd been headed straight to prison, but I'd managed to dig my way out, become a Federal agent, and now we had a warrant for Bloem's arrest.

Alex slid the car into the last available parking space, and we both hesitated for a second, reluctant to leave the air-conditioned comfort of the car and face the blast furnace outside. I gave first, glad to get out of the car and stretch. The Charger was a decent sized car, but I was well north of six feet, and sitting for hours had left me sore and tight. I tried to tell myself that being in my mid-forties had nothing to do with it, but these days all the things I'd broken, sprained and strained over the years were starting to catch up to me.

Alex was tall, almost six feet, and even though her hair was pulled back in a ponytail, and she was wearing a baggy shirt to cover the gun and radio strapped to her belt, she looked pretty good to me. It had been weird at first, working surveillance with my girlfriend, but after a while, I'd grown to like it.

I pointed to a sign in the window that said "1.99 soft serve special," and said, "I'll buy."

"Big spender," she said. "You sure know how to show a girl a good time."

We refrained from any public displays of affection while out in public, but we probably walked a little closer than a pair of plainclothes cops normally would. Hell with it. Life was short. I'd nearly died more times than I could count in the last few months, and I'd nearly lost Alex too.

Calling us "plain clothes" was being charitable. We both wore khaki tactical pants with all sorts of pockets, un-tucked rugby shirts to cover all the crap on our belts, and boots. If that didn't scream "cop" loud enough, we both wore plastic ear pieces attached to a curly cord to our radios. I'd long ago mastered the art of listening to radio chatter with only part of my brain while going about my business. Right now, Dalton, who had taken on the role of our dispatcher since suffering a nasty gunshot wound to the leg, was coordinating the other four cars full of agents in our so far fruitless search for Bloem.

I could feel the heat of the asphalt through the soles of my boots, and by the time we finished the twenty-yard walk across the parking lot, I was drenched in sweat. The inside of the burger stand was blissfully cold. The guy flipping burgers at the grill did a double take as we came in, and I gave him a nod and a friendly smile. I figured there was a fifty percent chance he was on parole and a fifty percent chance he was on probation, but I wanted him to know I was there for the ice cream, and not for him.

As we waited, I turned the current search for Bloem over in my mind. Three days ago, we'd been waiting for him at the Portland Police Bureau's East Precinct, all set to arrest him as he came in for his shift. The Bureau leadership hadn't been happy, but we'd promised to keep things quiet, and they played ball.

The only problem was he didn't show up. After an hour of waiting, it became painfully obvious he'd been tipped off by somebody. We hit his apartment an hour after that and found it empty. His wallet and cell phone were sitting on the kitchen counter, and the door to an empty gun cabinet was hanging open. You didn't have to be Sherlock Holmes to put all that together.

That's where Casey, our resident computer hacker came in. Fueled by Chinese takeout, and an unhealthy amount of Jolt! Cola, she'd started trying to find any digital footprints Bloem might have left. We had a couple of hours of digital surveillance footage of Bloem. Surveillance cameras were frequently hooked up to the Internet these days, and using a combination of facial recognition and gait analysis, Casey had managed to catch him at a convenience store right here in Portland.

We didn't have to lean on the store owner very hard to find out he'd bought a pre-paid cell phone with cash. From there Casey determined Bloem had made a phone call to a guy named Earl Maddox, an ex-con with links to white supremest groups and a penchant for illegally converted machine guns. We all thought that was an interesting guy for a cop to have in his contacts list.

Since then, we hadn't been able to get our eyes on Maddox, but Bloem had turned on his phone a half a dozen times, for only a few seconds each, probably to check for a text message. We'd never been able to refine his location better than a square mile or so but it was something.

We were next in line, and I was debating between chocolate, vanilla, or the further complication of swirled ice cream when Casey's voice came over my earpiece.

4

"Bloem just turned on his phone. It's definitely in South East Portland. I'm trying to refine the fix to an exact location."

It looked like ice cream was going to have to wait. I opened my mouth to say something to Alex when another voice broke in on the radio.

"I see Maddox's car. He just passed us headed east on Division. We're westbound, but turning around." It was Byrd, a young guy, barely thirty. He and his partner Drogan were riding in a car together. She was older, well into her forties. They were the two agents on my team I'd worked with the least.

In unison, Alex and I turned toward the door. If Maddox and Bloem were both active in southeast Portland, that likely meant they were trying to link up.

Dalton broke in on the radio. "Maddox's car is a black Chevy, license plate NTJ-891."

"Yep. That's it," Byrd said. In the backg round I could hear the engine of his car revving. "We did a U-turn and we're catching up.

"They're going to blow it," I said to Alex as we stepped out into the heat. I'd been worried about this. Our team had been chomping at the bit for days. People were tired, bored and ready for action. Drogan and Byrd should have kept driving and let one of the other member's of the team pick up the tail. Some of our cars were more discreet, but Drogan and Byrd were driving an unmarked Charger just like ours. I didn't see any way that Maddox wouldn't notice an obvious unmarked police car doing a u-turn behind him.

"He's speeding up a little," Drogan said over the radio. She had probably taken charge of the radio so Byrd could concentrate on driving.

"Shit," I said as we reached our car. Alex unlocked the door and reached to open her door.

"Hold on," I said. "Armor first."

I had a set of keys to the car as well. I popped the trunk and pulled out a heavy armored vest. I handed it to Alex.

"We need to get there," she said. The radio traffic was fast and furious. Bolle, our boss, and Big Eddie, his assistant were in separate cars, and they were converging on Maddox. Casey and Henry were driving the surveillance van, and even they weren't far behind.

"We need to not get shot."

She blew a strand of hair out of her face, something she'd done for as long as I'd known her and reached for the vest. She threw it on with a grunt and turned back towards the driver's door.

"Helmet," I said. She rolled her eyes, a gesture that never failed to remind me that I'd known her since she was a teenager, and planted the kevlar on top of her head. I threw my own vest on, then grabbed my own helmet and a guitar case from the trunk. I popped the back door and squeezed into the back seat.

"Why are you back there?" Alex asked as she slid behind the wheel.

"I can shoot out of the left side this way without sticking my gun in front of your face."

"Oh," she said as she backed out of the parking spot. "Good idea."

Once we were on the street, she stomped on the accelerator and my head snapped back. The chatter on the radio was growing more excited, and I was starting to have grave concerns about how this was going. I forced myself to be calm and deliberate. I resigned myself to the fact I was likely about to get into a gunfight in the next few minutes.

"He just stopped at a bus stop and picked up a male. I think it's Bloem," Drogan said.

"We're three blocks behind you," Bolle said.

There was quite a bit of communication, but very little planning happening over the radio. I resisted the urge to get on the air and start barking orders. That was Bolle's job, and if I stepped in right now it likely wouldn't go well. I just concentrated on owning my own little part of this developing cluster fuck.

I made sure the straps on my vest were tight, strapped on my helmet and put on a pair of amber-tinted safety glasses. Then I unzipped the guitar case in my lap.

When it came to guns, I was pretty old school. Assault rifles were all the rage these days, but I was still a fan of the 12 gauge shotgun. When I'd been with the Police Bureau, I'd clung to an old Remington pump that was older than me. Now that I was a fed with my very own government purchase card, I'd upgraded to a semiautomatic Benelli M2 with a 14" barrel. My one concession to modern technology was the compact little electronic dot sight mounted on top.

The shotgun was a thinking man's weapon. It could fire a wide range of ammunition, from less-lethal bean bag rounds, door breaching ammo, buckshot, and slugs. I pulled a box of the latter out of the gun case. Instead of multiple projectiles, this ammo contained a single giant bullet almost three-quarters of an inch across, effectively turning the shotgun into an immensely powerful short range rifle. The slugs were made by a company named Brenneke, and made of a specially hardened alloy. This fight was probably going to happen around vehicles, and I wanted to be able to shoot through stuff.

I fed the fat shells into the gun's magazine as we careened around corners, blew through red lights and passed a bus in the opposite lane. Alex was technically a Federal agent, but only in a consulting status. She was a forensic pathologist by training, but her hobby up until recently had been racing sports cars at Portland International Raceway. I'd ceded the wheel to her without hesitation.

"He's turned into a neighborhood and is making a bunch of random turns," Grogan said.

"Shit," I said again. That was an obvious sign Maddox was on to us.

"I'm right behind you. I can see you," Bolle said. "Eddie is right behind me."

So now Maddox had three cars behind him, following every random turn he made.

"This is going to be bad," I said to Alex. I chambered a round in the shotgun, made sure it was on safe, and slapped an elastic card full of buckshot onto the Velcro on the shotgun's left side.

She nodded, concentrating on her driving. We were tearing through a residential neighborhood, and I did my best to look everywhere at once. School was out for the summer and the last thing we needed was a little kid to step out from between two parked cars in front of us.

"Bloem just pulled a long gun out of the back seat," Grogan said.

"Felony stop. Do it now," Bolle said.

We rounded a corner and there they were. Up ahead was Maddox's black Chevy, followed by Grogan and Byrd in their Charger. Close behind came Bolle in a BMW, one of our low profile cars, and behind him was Eddie in a Toyota.

They all had low profile flashing lights, and now they all lit up in blue and red. Maddox's response was to floor it.

"I'm going to PIT," Bolle said.

"No, no, no," I said, as I held onto the headrest of the front seat with a death grip. Bolle was going to try a Pursuit Intervention Technique, a fancy cop turn for running another car off the road. We didn't want this to end in the middle of a residential neighborhood. Everywhere I looked there were houses and duplexes.

Bolle pulled around Grogan and Byrd, matched speed with the Chevy, and planted the right corner of his front bumper behind driver's side rear wheel of Maddox's Chevy. It should have spun the other car out.

It didn't work. The Chevy was a big sheet metal beast, from back when Detroit Iron wasn't just an expression. The BMW was lighter by hundreds of pounds, and all Bolle managed to do was lock the two bumpers together. The Chevy literally dragged the smaller car down the street, fishtailing, until Byrd floored his Charger and rammed the Chevy from behind.

Maddox lost control of the Chevy and veered off to the right, the car rolled over a sidewalk and came to rest in the parking lot of an apartment complex. It sideswiped one of the parked cars and stopped. Bolle followed it right in, slamming into a small tree and coming to rest with only a foot between the side of his car and Maddox's.

Eddie narrowly avoided rear-ending Bolle, sliding to a stop next to the BMW. Now all three cars were lined up in a row, with barely enough room between them to open a door. Byrd at least managed to stop short of the whole mess, sliding to a stop fifteen yards or so behind the whole mess.

"Stop! Stop! Stop!" I yelled, and Alex obliged by standing on the brakes. I was grateful for the ceramic plates of my vest when I slammed into the back of the front seats. I bit my tongue and wished I'd buckled my seat belt.

We were stopped in the middle of the street, twenty yards or so behind Grogan and Byrd. I pushed my door open. For a second everything was quiet, except for the sound of steam hissing out of the busted radiator of one of the cars. I fought to get out of the back seat.

As soon as my boot soles hit the pavement, the shooting started.

CHAPTER TWO

As usual, it all seemed to happen in slow motion.

Maddox poked the muzzle of an AK-47 out the driver's window and laid on the trigger. It must have been one of his backyard machine gun conversions because a long burst of bullets pulverized all the glass in Bolle's and Eddie's cars. At the same time, Bloem leaned out of the passenger seat window and fired back toward Grogan and Byrd.

Grogan was getting out of the passenger seat when Bloem pulled the trigger. She flinched, dropped her gun, and put her hands to her face before dropping to the ground. I started to bring the Benelli up, with an eye towards putting a round in Bloem, when Maddox turned his attention towards us.

He leaned way out of the driver's side window. I had a fraction of a second to register the muzzle of Maddox's AK swinging towards us when the windshield exploded. A bunch of glass fragments hit me in the face and I was grateful for the safety glasses. I dropped to my knees as the car seemed to fly apart around me. Bits of plastic, stuffing from the seat, and more glass flew through the air and pelted me, as I squatted behind the body of the car. The car wasn't really cover. It just slowed the rifle bullets down a little as they passed through.

I scooted back to the rear bumper, relieved to see Alex squatting there with her pistol in her hand. She looked at me wild-eyed and we both tried to make ourselves small. A bullet passed through the car's trunk between us, leaving a jagged finger of sheet metal sticking out of the trunk. At this range, the rifle was abominably loud.

It seemed like it was taking him entirely too long to run out of ammunition. The AK had a thirty round magazine. Maddox was firing in bursts of four or five rounds, pausing for a fraction of a second to let the gun settle before triggering another one. There was no way to count the individual shots, but I still thought he should have run out by now.

Then the rifle fire stopped. I forced myself to pop up and assess what was going on. Byrd and Grogan were both on the ground. Byrd was curled up in the fetal position, clutching his belly. Grogan was trying to wipe blood out of her eyes. She still had her pistol in her hand. Eddie was crouched by the rear bumper of his car, with empty hands. I had no idea why he wasn't shooting. I couldn't see Bolle, but judging by the number of bullet holes in his car, he wasn't having a good day.

I could see Maddox's silhouette still in the driver's seat. I figured he was reloading. There wasn't enough room for him to open his car door.

Bloem couldn't get his open either, so he was crawling out the car window with a shotgun in one hand. I started running towards Grogan and Byrd's car, hoping to get a little closer. I could easily put a slug through Bloem's chest at this range, but we wanted him alive. In some ways closing the distance didn't seem like a good idea, but I hoped to get to a position where I could put a slug through his lower extremities. If I could get a tourniquet on him quick enough, maybe I could keep him from dying.

Bloem had managed to wiggle out and get his butt on the hood of the car next to him when Grogan rosed shakily to her knees. As I ran up behind her, she raised her pistol with one hand, wiped the blood out of her eyes with the other and squeezed off a single shot at Bloem. He fell off the hood of the car and dropped out of sight. Whether he was hit, or just fell, I didn't know.

The back window of the Chevy exploded as Maddox started firing again. More rounds hit the Charger and the pavement around us. I dropped to my right shoulder behind the back bumper of the car as bullets tore up the bodywork around us. I hoped Alex had the sense to hit the dirt too.

I inched along the pavement to where I had the front corner of the Charger between me and Maddox. I stayed well back from the car. Direct hits from the steel-cored AK-47 rounds would bore right through the sheet metal, but rounds that struck at an angle on the hood might deflect up, and I wanted to be far enough back that they would pass overhead instead of drilling me in the face.

Gritting my teeth, I forced myself up on a knee and leaned out past the front of the car. I imagined a straight line from me to where Maddox was kneeling in the driver's seat, picked a spot on the trunk that lined up and triggered two shots from the shotgun.

Despite the shotgun's gas operated recoil system, the heavy Brenneke slugs had massive recoil. I fired the first and it seemed to take forever before I could drag the red dot down back on target so I could fire the second. I could see two fist-sized dimples in the paint of the Chevy. For a second I thought I'd managed to hit Maddox, but apparently, I'd just attracted his attention. Bullets hit the front of the Charger. A piece of plastic trim flew off and hit me in the helmet.

I turned and ran to the back of the car. I passed Grogan, who had collapsed and was bleeding pretty badly. I wanted to help her, but before I could stop the bleeding, I had to stop the shooting.

Alex had dragged Byrd to the rear bumper and was lying over him, shooting at the Chevy with her pistol. I hadn't even heard the shots until now. Maddox was still firing. I felt like I was in the movies where the guns never run out of ammo. Every time he would pause between bursts, I thought he was out, then another one would come.

Finally, there was a long pause, and I made myself stand up all the way. I could see Maddox still in the car, stuffing a new magazine in his rifle. Out of the corner of my eye, I saw Bolle crawling out of the window of his own BMW, only a car width away from Maddox. If he caught Maddox's eye, he'd be cut to ribbons.

Now I didn't have to guess where to put the slug. I could see the outline of Maddox's body and head, and the only thing between me and him was the seat of the car. I settled the dot and pulled the trigger two more times.

When I recovered from the recoil of the second shot, Maddox was no longer in view. After the deafening roar of the shots, the scene was strangely quiet except for the ringing in my ears.

I reloaded the shotgun by feel. I couldn't recall exactly how many shots I'd fired, but it only held five rounds. I could reload it with my eyes closed, so I let my hands do their work while I scanned the scene.

Bolle had made it over the hood of Eddie's car. They both crouched behind it, and as far as I could tell, neither one of them had a gun in their hands. Alex was kneeling beside Byrd, who was making some very final sounding gurgling noises.

Down the street, I saw our surveillance van moving towards us at a crawl. Holding the shotgun by its pistol grip with my right hand, I keyed my radio microphone with my left.

"Casey. Stop right there and cover the black Chevy with your rifle."

The van jerked to a stop, and Casey hopped out wearing her full kit.

A second later Henry jumped out wearing armor too. Apparently, me, Alex and the computer nerds were the only ones smart enough to show up properly dressed for a gunfight. We'd had trouble finding armor small enough to fit Casey, so she looked like a turtle with the vest up almost to her ears and the helmet almost covering her eyes, but she braced her Heckler and Koch rifle against the door frame with authority. She'd been practicing and I knew if Maddox popped up she'd smoke him.

Alex was cutting away Byrd's clothes with a pair of EMT shears. Grogan was crawling towards the back of the car, mumbling something.

I keyed my radio again. "Casey, I'm moving up. Maddox is in the black car. Bloem fell to the ground in front of it"

"I don't see him from my angle," she said.

I steeled myself, and moved forward, dreading crossing the open ground between me and the Chevy. I had a tattoo on my chest that said "Front Towards Enemy." That had been my general philosophy towards life for a long time, but I wondered how long I could keep rolling the dice before they came up snake-eyes.

I walked forward, shotgun at the ready, my feet crunching on bits of broken glass and plastic. The engine of the Chevy was still running, the burbling sound of the big V-8 engine competing with the sirens of the police cars that were headed towards us. Both the reverse lights were shot out, so I made sure I didn't walk up directly behind it. The last thing I needed was for Maddox to gun the engine in reverse and flatten me like a bug.

I stopped when I could see in. The inside of the car was littered with shell casings and I saw two drum magazines for the AK. That explained the volume of fire. The damn things were heavy and cumbersome but they held fifty rounds.

I took another step and could see Maddox. He was laying across the front seats with his head almost in the passenger side footwell. There was blood and bits of tissue all over the front dash. The AK lay across his legs, a giant hole from a twelve gauge slug blown through the receiver. I realized his chest was rising and falling in quick panting breaths. He shifted his head and looked me in the eye.

"Show me your hands!" I yelled.

He quivered for a second, and I had a half-second to register the big Dan Wesson revolver he was trying to lift in my direction before I put the red dot on the bridge of his nose and pulled the trigger.

There wasn't any need for a second shot.

I hopped up on the trunk of the car to the right. I could see a smear of blood on the hood, courtesy of Grogan's shot into Bloem.

"It's clear!" I yelled. "Bloem ran into the apartment complex."

Everyone converged on me, except Alex, who was still tending to Byrd. Grogan rose to her feet and staggered around with blood pouring out of her face. She held her pistol in her hand still.

Bolle looked ashen. His face was covered in scratches and there were chunks of broken glass in his hair. Blood ran from both nostrils, courtesy of the airbag that had deployed when he crashed the car. Wordlessly, he held up his pistol, an expensive, long slide SIG. I could see a bullet hole in the slide where one of Maddox's rounds had struck it.

"Do you see any bullet holes in me?" he asked. "I feel like there should be some but I can't find any."

I took a minute to look him up and down. It wasn't unheard of for people to get shot and not realize it.

"Looks good to me. Why don't you see if you can help Alex with Grogan and Byrd?"

"Ok," he said, and shambled off. I didn't know if he was concussed from the crash and airbag, or if he was just shell-shocked by having Maddox unload a rifle at him from ten feet away, but he didn't look like he was about to die. I had bigger things on my mind, so I just let him go.

"I put my gun on the seat next to me," Eddie said. "After the crash, I couldn't find it."

Wordlessly, I shucked my Glock out of its holster and handed it to him. Eddie didn't look shell shocked. He looked like somebody who was deeply pissed at himself for losing his pistol before getting in a gunfight.

Henry and Casey trotted up. Henry looked in the car at what was left of Maddox and was noisily sick on the pavement.

Casey looked in the car too, but when she looked back at me her face was dispassionate, like she was watching a tv show or something.

"You good?" I asked her.

"Yep," she said, and I believed her. For a computer nerd and electronic security consultant, Casey had proved herself to have nerves of steel more than once. She'd never been in a gunfight before, but the way things were looking, this might be her chance.

"Ok. Casey and Eddie. You're with me. Henry, go help Alex with the wounded."

He looked like he was going to argue with me, but didn't. Henry pulled his weight on the team, but I wasn't sure now was the right time to have him behind me with a rifle.

I followed the trail of blood at a slow trot. Behind us, the sirens were getting closer. I wanted to find Bloem before the Portland Police arrived. They were a good agency, but coordinating with them was bound to complicate things.

Bloem was leaving a noticeable blood trail on the pavement. The apartments here were in little buildings with four apartments each, two downstairs, two up. On the door of the first building we came to, I saw a big smear of blood on the door handle. Apparently, Bloem was trying doors in the hopes of finding one unlocked.

"Shotgun in the bushes," Casey said.

She had a keen eye. I saw the stock of a long gun sticking out from the bushes by the door. I pulled it out. It was empty and covered in blood. My inner gun nerd noted that it was a Smith and Wesson 3000, kind of an obscure model.

"He's probably still got a pistol," I said. "Stay sharp."

We kept moving, following the blood trail. The drops were getting smaller and farther apart. I doubted the gunshot wound was getting better on its own. Maybe he'd found some way to bandage himself.

We came to an intersection and the blood dried up completely. I looked up and down the streets, which were full of parked cars. The complex was huge. I could see dozens of buildings from where I was standing.

"Can you hear that?" Casey asked. "The woman's voice?"

Truthfully, I couldn't. Between explosions and gunfire, my ears had been taking a pounding lately, and I was living with a constant low hum in my head that drove me crazy at night when I was trying to sleep.

I shook my head, straining to hear.

"That way," Casey said, pointing to our right.

We moved down the street. Up ahead I saw an apartment door that was open.

Now I could clearly hear a man's voice. "Just give me the fucking keys!"

A heard a muffled reply, a woman's voice.

I kept my shotgun trained on the open door as we moved up the sidewalk. It was bright outside, and dark inside, so I couldn't see much. I considered flipping on the powerful light attached but I didn't want to give away my position.

As we got closer to the threshold of the doorway, I could see an empty foyer. A pair of sandals was the only thing inside. There was an opening to the right, and another to the left. Both the voices and the smell of something burning came from the left.

I moved as quietly as I could, careful not to let the bulky vest brush up against the door frame. I slowly peeked around the corner. I saw a stove, with a wok full of what looked like burning stir-fry on top.

"Just take the keys," the woman half said, half sobbed. "It's the green Volvo out front. I don't have any cash."

I remembered passing a green Volvo with a dented fender and a "Visualize World Peace" bumper sticker.

"Put them on the counter." I recognized the man's voice as Bloem's. "Turn around and face away from me."

The alarm bells started ringing. The best way for Bloem to get a head start would be to make sure the woman couldn't call the cops and give a description of her car.

"You don't have to do this," she said. Apparently, she was smart enough to know what was coming.

I took a deep breath. The rounds I'd loaded into the shotgun a couple of minutes ago were buckshot. Each shell held eight lead balls about a third of an inch across. Contrary to popular myth, they wouldn't spread out and spray the entire room. At the ranges in the apartment, the cloud of shot would barely spread out to a pattern bigger than my closed fist, and leave a giant rat hole sized wound.

I'd hoped to take Bloem alive. It looked like that wasn't in the cards for today.

I took a step around the doorway, button-hooking my way into the room. I had a flash of Bloem standing a few feet behind the woman, with his pistol pointed at the back of her head. I settled the red dot on his ear, but at the last second, I changed my mind.

Please don't let me fuck this up, I thought. I wasn't sure who I was asking. I hadn't thought about God in a long time. Maybe it was an appeal to myself, maybe it was to some other power in the universe.

I settled the red dot on Bloem's elbow and gently stroked the trigger. I was so hyper-focused I only heard a muffled pop when the shotgun went off.

When I came down from recoil, I saw the pistol on the floor, and Bloem's forearm dangling from a few strips of flesh. As I watched, they

15

stretched like taffy, then snapped. His arm hit the ground and both he and the woman started screaming.

Bloem clapped his hand over the jet of blood coming from the stump of his arm and started running around the kitchen in circles. Eddie moved from behind me and kicked his legs out from under him, then straddled him and pulled a tourniquet out of his pocket.

Casey slung her rifle over her back and pulled the woman out of the room.

Bolle's voice crackled in my earpiece.

"Dent, what's your status?"

I keyed my microphone. "We got Bloem?"

"Is he alive?"

Eddie cinched the tourniquet tight and the flow of blood decreased dramatically. Alex had drilled us so many times we could all put one on in the dark.

"Yeah," I said. "I disarmed him."

CHAPTER THREE

Later we would figure out that the whole thing took just over five minutes. 145 rounds were fired.

The aftermath and recriminations took the rest of the day. We managed to keep Bloem from bleeding to death, so we could say we got our man, but no sane person could say it was worth it.

Byrd was dead. The soft body armor he'd been wearing didn't even slow down the pair of rifle rounds that scrambled his guts. Alex had done everything she could, but he died before the ambulance even arrived. The paramedics did everything they could to breathe life back into his inert body on the way to the hospital, but the trauma surgeon took a look at the mess inside, shook his head, and pronounced him dead.

Grogan had taken several shotgun pellets in the face. The range had been long enough to slow the pellets down some before they hit her, which was the only reason she was still alive. Still, her cheekbone was cracked, several teeth were blown out, and she was in danger of losing an eye. The fact that she'd managed to put a bullet in Bloem bordered on the superhuman. When she woke up, I was tempted to buy her a beer, but I didn't even know her well enough to know if she drank.

Eddie was fine, but I could tell he was beating himself up for losing his gun at the beginning of the fight. Life and death often hinged on small decisions, and I knew he would spend the rest of his life wondering if he'd kept his pistol in the holster if things would have turned out different.

There was no way we could see this as anything other than an unmitigated disaster, and I could tell Bolle knew it. We had one agent dead, and another permanently injured and all we had to show for it was a guy who we weren't even sure could tell us anything we didn't

17

already know.

As a young Army Ranger in 1993, I'd participated in a raid in Mogadishu, Somalia. By the end of the day, eighteen of us were dead. They were men I'd eaten with, trained with and drank with. Some people tried to focus on the fact that we'd captured our target, a Somali warlord, but I'd found that cold comfort. Today reminded me of that day more than I cared to admit.

Our unit was supposed to be keeping a low profile. A month or so ago, we'd very narrowly foiled a pair of terrorist attacks here in Portland, leaving a trail of dead bodies in our wake. You'd think that would make us heroes, but we'd been operating below the radar of both the Portland Police Bureau and the local field office of the FBI. They wound up with egg on their faces, and no amount of heroics was going to make them forgive us for that.

Bolle was still technically an FBI agent, but our task force was off the books, a secret Justice Department operation. I had a set of credentials in my pocket that deemed me a Special Investigator for the US Government, but the activities of our unit were unmistakably criminal at times. I'd done things I that could put me in prison, and that kept me up at night.

A raging gunfight in a Portland residential neighborhood would have been bad at any time, but the cherry on top of the shit sundae was the fact that we'd just shot a Portland police officer. Even though he was suspended, under investigation and probably on his way to prison himself, he was still a cop, and blowing his arm off hadn't made us any friends with the locals.

So after we got cleaned up, checked ourselves for any wounds we'd missed, and surrendered our weapons into evidence, we spent the next few hours being grilled by the US Attorney for the State of Oregon, Ana Burke. She'd insisted on being kept up to date on our investigation and now that we'd made such a spectacle of ourselves, she was doing the post-shooting interviews herself.

She was pissed, and I didn't blame her. When I'd worked for the Portland Police Bureau, you had the right to cool your jets for twenty-four hours before you had to give a statement about a shooting. I had no idea if I was entitled to that at this job since I'd never even seen so much as a written policy or procedure manual. I decided not to push it with Burke, so I played ball.

She grilled me for over an hour, and I answered honestly, for the most part. I left out the parts about the illegal cell phone hacking. I was pretty sure she already knew about that, but we weren't going to make it part of the official record. I gave honest answers about when I'd fired, and why. She was particularly thorough about having me describe why I'd shot Bloem.

Finally, we wrapped it up. We both stood and walked out in the hallway.

"Ok," she said. "Now let's go off the record."

As far as I knew, there were no recording devices in the hallway. I just stood there and looked at her for a second. I didn't know much about Burke, other than she was in her early fifties, maybe ten years older than me, and had been a well regarded Multnomah County Prosecutor before landing her job with the Feds. I had no idea whether I could trust her or not, or how far she was willing to bend the rules.

"This was a colossal fuck up," Burke said.

I nodded. I couldn't argue with that, but I wasn't about to agree out loud.

"Bolle is in danger of being shut down. He's got enemies you don't even know about. One more fuckup like this and unemployment will be the least of your worries. There are people that want to find a way to put you all in prison."

The truth was, there were plenty of people who would love to see us in the ground.

"We'll be careful," I said.

She stepped closer.

"Any news on Marshall?"

Bolle had been a stepping stone, a way to get to our ultimate quarry: Henderson Marshall. He was the millionaire owner of an aviation company that specialized in moving stuff around the world for the US intelligence community. Along the way his company had been involved in human trafficking, smuggling young homeless women from the United States to different parts of the world. One faction of his company had aided and abetted the two terrorist attacks we'd stopped.

We still weren't sure what he knew. He'd gone into hiding, releasing the occasional video statement to the world. The guy was either off his rocker or a genius. I wasn't sure which. His videos had made him a celebrity among the conspiracy-minded, anti-government groups that flourished on the internet.

I shook my head. "Nothing new."

She stepped closer yet, close enough that I could smell perfume, which was surprisingly flowery.

"He needs to go down. But he needs to be alive. You have a bad habit of putting people on a slab. I'm not sorry to see them go, but I want Henderson Marshall sitting in a room, with some bright lights aimed at him, telling me everything he knows. I won't make any new friends going after him and his cronies, but he's worth a little career suicide."

"Ok," I said. "I want him too."

She slid a Post-it note into my hand.

"It's a secure line. Use it if you need it."

She turned and walked away, leaving me standing there.

I fingered the note on my way down in the elevator. In any normal command structure, any communication I would have with the US attorney would go through Bolle. Jumping my chain of command would be unthinkable.

But this really wasn't a normal command structure.

The surveillance van was the only vehicle we'd been driving that day that hadn't been shot to pieces. I found it idling in the basement garage of the Federal Courthouse, sitting in a puddle of water dripping from the air conditioner. Even down here, it was hot and stuffy.

Henry was behind the wheel. He looked half asleep, but as I walked up the side door slid open. The van was big, but with the racks of electronic gear, it was still cramped inside. Casey was sitting in a swivel chair, wearing a headset and looking at three different computer monitors at once. Eddie was crammed into a fold-down seat between two equipment racks, looking morose. I took a seat across from him and slid the door shut. Henry dropped the van into drive, and we pulled out of the cave-like garage into the blistering sunlight.

"Bolle is at police headquarters, trying to smooth things over with the locals," Casey said. "Jack is going to drive him back to base later. Alex is finishing up at the hospital. Grogan is settled in and doing ok, all things considered."

Jack was our pilot. Our unit had its own helicopter, but it had been grounded today due to some overdue maintenance. I'd asked myself more than once if having an air unit available would have helped with today's debacle, and still hadn't arrived at an answer.

Casey punched a combination into a little safe bolted to the floor of the van, reached in and handed me a bag containing a Glock, spare magazine, a holster, and a magazine carrier. I grunted my thanks and strapped it all on, glad to be armed again.

I settled back into the uncomfortable chair and listened to the hum of the tires on asphalt. It bothered me how normal I felt. I'd been in gunfights before. I'd killed men before. But always before, I'd been wired and anxious afterward. Now I was just hungry and wanted a nap. It seemed like getting in a raging gunfight shouldn't be just another day at the office.

Our little task force had blown its cover last month when we'd foiled a terrorist attack at the Portland Zoo. It hadn't taken any geniuses to figure out the little black helicopter that was seen at the Troutdale Airport, was the same one seen hovering over the Portland Zoo with a sniper strapped to the side. We had a cozy little set up in an abandoned factory out by the airport, and had scrambled to find a replacement site that was both discreet and secure.

In the end, we wound up in jail.

In 2003, Multnomah County Oregon had spent millions to construct a brand new, state of the art, jail. They then promptly refused to provide any funds to operate it, and it sat empty, never housing an inmate for a decade and a half. It had been the focal point of numerous political debate, and no small amount of derision. Rumor had it the county was getting close to a deal to sell it, but for now it still sat empty.

It was perfect for us. It sat on a dead end street in an industrial area and was surrounded by a fence topped by razor wire. It had excellent communications facilities, a surveillance system, a medical facility, and a full commercial kitchen. There was also room to set up a portable shelter under which we could hide our helicopter. We'd thrown some cots and mattresses in some of the empty offices and called it home.

It suited our needs for another reason: it was a bona fide correctional facility. We'd played fast and loose with some laws regarding the housing of prisoners at our old site. We could have been fairly accused of running an off the books, black site prison. Not so in this place. We'd had a cell all picked out for Bloem and a plan on how we could keep him under guard in strict accordance with all the relevant laws.

Instead, he was sitting in a hospital room, doped up on painkillers, with a gunshot wound to the chest and a traumatically amputated arm.

Things had not gone according to plan.

The front gate rattled open, courtesy of Dalton, who was well into a twelve-hour shift as our dispatcher. We were chronically short-handed, and losing two people wasn't going to make that better.

We parked by the sally port where inmates would have been unloaded and buzzed our way in with key cards. Since it had never been used to house inmates, Wapato didn't have the usual jail aroma that consisted of a mix of unwashed ass, body odor, disinfectant, bad food, desperation, and despair. Instead, it just smelled stale and empty. I didn't like living here and took every chance I could to get out on the street. The place was giant, empty and echoing. It gave me the creeps.

Henry and Casey disappeared into their lair, a room they'd crammed full of computers and other gear. Eddie walked off by himself without a word. I was worried about him, but now wasn't the time to deal with that. With Bolle gone, one of us had to try to get a handle on our situation, and as usual, that fell to me.

I followed the smell of coffee to our command center. Originally this room had been the central control facility for the jail. From here we could lock and unlock almost all of the doors and monitor close to a hundred cameras. With the addition of some radios, it was the perfect place to direct our efforts.

Dalton was on the phone when I walked in. He pointed to a corner where the heavenly smell of black coffee was coming from and I filled a mug. Dalton and Henry were both coffee snobs, each hell-bent on besting each other to make the finest brew. I was happy to be caught in the middle.

Dalton hung up the phone and rolled over to me, clutching his own mug. He'd been in a wheelchair since a bullet shattered his femur a few weeks back. Most people would be lying in bed gobbling pain pills, but Dalton put himself to work, pulling long shifts in the command center. He had a complicated metal brace around his leg, and always seemed to have an unhealthy pallor, but he was invaluable to us right now. I admired the former Delta Force operators fortitude, but wondered what it said about us that we depended on a guy recovering from a major injury to keep our operation running.

He held out his mug and I filled it. The brew was excellent, bitter and complex. It tasted the way coffee smelled, maybe even a little better.

"Jack should be pulling in with Bolle and Alex soon," he said. "That was an absolute shitstorm today. How did it happen?"

I walked him through it, step by step. When I got to the part where Bolle had tried to initiate the traffic stop by ramming Maddox's car, Dalton shook his head in disgust.

"That's some crazy Hollywood bullshit right there. What was he thinking?"

I took a drink and let the coffee just sit in my mouth for a minute. It was that good. Lately, I'd been thinking about just going somewhere so I could sit, sip coffee and read a book for a couple of days. If I had a normal life, I'd just take some sort of vacation, but these days I didn't get to do things like that.

"I think it's desperation," I said. "We haven't had a lead on Marshall in weeks. I don't know how that asshole managed to disappear with a business jet, but he did. We've hit every office, business location and home that Marshall owned and we've come up with nothing. I think Bolle is getting desperate. This little flying circus of his can't last forever. It's only a matter of time before somebody shuts him down so he needs to get some results."

Dalton fidgeted in his wheelchair. I noticed his eyes were a little glassy. I knew he was living with a ton of pain, only taking a half, or even a quarter of one of his painkillers when he just couldn't stand it anymore.

"We can't keep making this up as we go along," he said. "There won't be any of us left after a while. I want Marshall as much as anybody, but I'm beginning to wonder if sticking with Bolle is the way to make it happen."

The one thing every member of Bolle's task force had in common was we'd all been wronged by Marshall and his cronies at some point. Bolle had his Army career destroyed. I'd nearly been thrown in prison, framed for a crime because I'd uncovered Cascade Aviation's human smuggling scheme. Alex's father had been killed by a bullet meant for me. Casey had been kidnapped and nearly killed, just because she'd helped me in my investigation.

Eddie and Henry were a little less forthcoming with their histories, but they were clear that it was personal for them as well. Dalton's army career had also been cut short by a run in with Marshall, but he'd never shared the details, and I hadn't pressed.

When Dalton talked about quitting Bolle's task force, he wasn't making plans so he could go sit on the beach and enjoy an idle retirement. We'd dropped plenty of bodies in the last few weeks, but Bolle was committed to the idea of putting Marshall in prison, and holding all his cronies accountable in court. He wanted to blow the lid off the corruption and expose it. What was unspoken between Dalton and me was that if we quit Bolle's team, we'd be diving even deeper into the shadows. We'd keep going until Marshall was dead, or we were. This was a battle you couldn't walk away from. Until Marshall was dead, or in prison, we'd all have to keep looking over our shoulders.

I wondered if it would end, even then.

Over Dalton's shoulder, on one of the surveillance monitors, I saw a car pull up to the gate.

"Looks like they are here," I said and jerked my chin towards the monitor.

Dalton buzzed them in, and that was the end of this conversation, for now. On the camera, I saw one of our black Suburbans pull up to the sally port. Alex got out and stretched, and I felt a physical sense of relief. My life was only further complicated by getting into gunfights with my girlfriend, and even though intellectually I knew she was ok, I hadn't seen her since I'd left her tending to a dying man while huddled behind a shot up car. By the time I'd returned from capturing Bloem, she'd been gone, tending to Grogan in the back of the ambulance.

A minute or so later, Bolle walked into the command center. On the video monitor I saw Alex walking down a hallway towards the office we'd turned into a bedroom, no doubt looking for me.

Bolle looked like he'd aged a decade since I'd last seen him. His suit was torn and dirty, and there were scratches all over his face. He was a big dude, taller than me, but cadaverously lean with an old-fashioned buzz cut. Usually, he looked like he could have played an FBI agent in a movie filmed in the 1950s. Right now he looked like a sack full of whipped dogshit, to borrow a phrase from one of my old drill instructors.

He looked at us with a hundred yard stare.

"They almost shut us down. I got them to agree to a compromise. From now on, the Justice Department wants us only to do investigative work. They're flying in a tactical element from the HRT to handle any apprehensions."

HRT stood for Hostage Rescue Team, the FBI's elite tactical element. Their bread and butter mission was hostage rescue, but they performed all sorts of tactical operations. If we'd had an HRT element with us this morning, Bloem and Maddox would have been face-down in the street wearing handcuffs before they knew what was going on. Even if it had devolved into a shootout, chances were we wouldn't have had over a hundred bullets flying around a residential neighborhood and a dead agent.

"Good," I said. It was out of my mouth before I even realized I was going to say it. Normally, I didn't talk much, and when I did I tried to think about what I said beforehand. But sometimes, my mouth got the better of me.

"Good?" Bolle said. He looked like he'd been slapped. "How can you call this good? I don't trust anybody with this investigation, not even anybody at the Bureau. The whole reason we've been able to come this far is because everyone on this team has some personal reason for being here. Their loyalty is unquestioned."

"If we keep going at this rate, there won't be any of us left," I said. The little voice in the back of my head said I should keep quiet, maybe have this conversation in a better moment, and in a different way. As usual, I disregarded it and steamrolled ahead.

"We've already got two dead," I said. "Streucker last month at the water reservoir, and now Byrd today. Grogan is out. Dalton can't walk. We can't keep taking losses like this. This isn't a tactical team. Today my cover was a pair of computer nerds. They've come a long way but they should have never been in that situation."

He opened his mouth to say something, but I cut him off.

"The biggest problem today is this: you fucked up. You should have never initiated that stop by ramming Maddox's car. That was a crazy ass move and it all went to shit. We've been playing cowboy for too long and our luck caught up with us."

All the color drained from his face and for a second I thought he was going to hit me. I braced myself for a knockdown drag out brawl. In the back of my mind, I wondered if he'd had a chance to replace the pistol that had been shot out of his hand this morning.

He stood there with his teeth and fists clenched, staring at me. Then all the tension seemed to drain out of him. He pivoted and walked out the door without a word.

I looked for my coffee cup and realized I'd set it down on the table next to me, as I unconsciously prepared myself for a fight. I picked it up and took a drink.

"I probably could have handled that better," I said after I swallowed.

Dalton shrugged. "Truths need to be told, man. I agreed with everything you had to say."

He rolled back over to the desk by all our radios and other communication gear.

"Hey," I said. "You want me to take over?"

He shook his head. "Nope. You go see that doc of yours. I'll get Jack to spell me. He's been out playing with the helicopter all day."

At first, Dalton had seemed to not approve of my relationship with Alex. After seeing us work together, and seeing that it didn't impair our effectiveness, he seemed more ok with it. I thanked him for the coffee and left the command center, turning my conversation with Bolle over in my mind. It certainly wasn't the first time I'd told my boss exactly what I thought. It often didn't turn out well.

Fortunately, we didn't have to live in cells. I would have drawn the line at that. Wapato had a huge wing devoted to administrative staff, and we'd set up our sleeping quarters in the warren of offices. Alex and I technically occupied two rooms right next to each other, out of some effort to keep up appearances, but we spent most of our time in her room. It actually had a window that overlooked the razor wire perimeter and Bybee lake beyond.

She'd changed into shorts and a t-shirt and was sitting at a desk with a field stripped pistol in front of her when I walked in.

She rose and gave me a hug. We just held on to each other for a while. Usually my head was very busy. I was constantly thinking about what we were going to do next, thinking about the investigation from different angles, trying to find something we had missed that would lead us to Marshall. But I'd gotten into the habit of making myself think of nothing but her when I held her. It was a welcome break from our day to day existence. I just stood there, enjoying the feel of her pressed against me and the smell of her hair.

Finally, she drew back and sat back down.

"I want to put this back together," she said. "They took my other one as evidence."

"You did good today." Again I blurted something out without really thinking about it. But it was true. I'd seen men who had trained to be soldiers for years freak out and lose their cool when they were on the receiving end of automatic weapon fire, but Alex had kept her act together and functioned effectively.

She didn't answer me for a moment, instead she focused on putting the pistol back together. I sat down on the bed and the weight of the day settled on me. I felt too tired to even move. It was that way pretty often for me anymore. I stayed in constant motion and wasn't aware of how exhausted I was until I stopped. Then it was hard to get moving again.

"Byrd died anyway," she said.

"Not your fault."

Alex finished snapping the pistol together, loaded it and slid it into a holster. Then she pushed me gently on the chest until I fell backward onto the bed and snuggled against me.

"I know it's not my fault, but it was still hard not to save somebody I knew. In the car coming back, I was thinking about how much of my life has been about death. Maybe when all this is over, I'll go do another residency and get a job delivering babies."

We'd been having "when all this is over" conversations lately. We both approached the subject tentatively like we were stepping into a mine field. Alex and I had both dated people before, of course. But for me, this felt different. Before I'd been happy to spend time with somebody and just see what happened. But this felt different. I felt like we were either going to go down in flames or spend the rest of our lives together. I got the feeling she felt the same way.

"Sounds good," I said. "You deliver babies. I'll open a guitar store."

"Mmmm..."

I loved Alex. There was no doubt about that. But sometimes trying to see our future was like a long dark tunnel. Our life right now wasn't normal. I wondered what it would be like to try to settle into some kind of domestic bliss with her when we weren't in constant danger of being shot. That was a new idea to me. Before, I'd been happy that my life had revolved around work.

There was something else though. I couldn't quite articulate it, but there was this feeling that Alex was holding back, that there was a core inside of her that she kept locked up and didn't show to anyone else. I couldn't even put into words what I wished she did differently, but it bugged me sometimes and I kept thinking about it the way a dog worries at a bone.

"What happened with Bolle?" she asked.

I told her about the Justice Department order that we were to hand over all arrests to a tactical element. I also told her about my little confrontation with Bolle.

"I think maybe we should cross international diplomacy off your list of future careers," she said. "God this is such a screwed up situation. Sometimes I wonder if we should just get in a car and drive away."

"Me too," I said.

We snuggled there for a while, not talking, and I realized she was falling asleep. Her breathing slowed down, her legs twitched a couple of times, and I felt her sort of melt into me. She started to snore lightly, courtesy of a broken nose from Judo practice in her teens. I found it kind of endearing.

Sleep wouldn't come for me. For one thing, I still had a gun and a bunch of other equipment strapped to my belt. But I was also in that state of wired exhaustion that I knew wouldn't go away unless I did something different to change the channel.

I hated to move away from Alex, but I slowly extricated myself without waking her. I kissed her on the forehead and put a light blanket on her before turning off the light.

My hand brushed my guitar case. Inside was my old Fender Stratocaster, the only guitar of my former collection that had survived when Marshall's people blew up my house. I'd thought about playing for a little while to take my mind off things, but I needed exercise. I grabbed a gym bag and left the room as quietly as I could.

I changed in a bathroom into my running gear. Even when jogging I kept a pistol on me, in a little chest pack called a Kit Bag made by a company called Hill People Gear.

Jack cocked an eyebrow at me when I told him I was going for a run, but he buzzed me out the gate and promised to keep an eye out for me upon my return.

I needed the exercise, but there was something else I had been meaning to do for a while, and now was the time to do it.

CHAPTER FOUR

As I ran, I found myself getting angry. Alex and I should have been thinking about a real future together, maybe thinking about getting married and buying a house. I'd known Alex for almost twenty years. She was the daughter of my former boss at the Police Bureau. It wasn't quite true to say I'd carried a torch for her for that long. There was a ten-year difference in our ages, and when she'd been a teenager, that would have been weird. But for easily the last ten years, I'd be lying if I said it hadn't been in the back of my mind.

Instead, her dad had been shot down right in front of us, and we were dodging bullets.

I pounded my way down the sidewalk, and a thought that I'd been dwelling on a bunch lately came to mind. I was on the downhill side of my forties, but Alex was not quite thirty-five. If we got our act together soon, we could have a kid, maybe even two. I'd found myself searching the internet for risk factors for women who had babies in their mid-thirties. I hadn't seen that coming.

Marshall had done plenty of things to fuck up my life, but the thing I hated him for the most was complicating my chances with Alex.

The sun had just set, but it was still hot. The heat radiating up at me from the pavement felt like I was running on a griddle. It was mostly warehouses and storage facilities up here. Occasionally a big truck would rumble by, but for the most part, it was quiet at this time of day.

I crossed Marine Drive and found myself running toward where all this had started: Kelly Point Park. Only the city of Portland would put a park out here in the middle of a light industrial area. It was a hundred acres of forested land where the Willamette and Columbia rivers converged, right next to a giant parking lot where ships full of import cars were unloaded.

Last year I'd found a dead teenage girl here. I thought I was investigating another in a long string of tragedies that punctuated my career as a homicide detective, but Heather Swanson's death had been the first link in a chain that had led me to this moment. She'd been picked up by Henderson Marshall's son, Gibson. She thought she was going to do a porn shoot in exchange for a little cash. Gibson's plan was to ship her out of the country on one of his dad's planes and sell her to the highest bidder.

Before it was all over, I was fired from the police bureau and nearly sent to prison. Casey had narrowly escaped being shipped out of the country herself, and my former partner Mandy had been hit in the head so hard she'd never be the same again.

I jogged up to the empty parking lot and stopped. From here you could see the spot where Heather's body had been. I remembered how light she had been as we carried her up to the Medical Examiner's van.

Gibson Marshall was dead. I'd shot him in a highway rest stop that smelled of urine and stale cigarettes. If anybody ever asked, I'd say he tried to attack me with the metal baton he'd been carrying, but the truth was he'd been smarting off to me, taunting me, and I'd shot him in the face.

Ever since, I'd been trying to make myself feel bad about it, with no luck.

Still, I wondered sometimes if my life could be different. If someone else had been on duty the night we found Heather, I wondered if the whole thing would have been swept under the rug. Heather's death would have gone down as another unsolved homicide of an unfortunate runaway teen. Maybe one of my comrades on the detective squad would have suddenly come into some money.

They'd known better than to try that shit with me. They immediately tried to ruin me instead.

I'd lost everything. My job. My pension. My house. My guitars. I'd been dating a woman named Audrey at the time. I couldn't honestly say we would have lasted, but I couldn't say we wouldn't either. When I wound up arrested, framed for beating up my partner, she'd packed her shit and gone home to New Mexico and I hadn't seen her since.

I stood there in the gathering dark, feeling sweat running down my back. The birds in the trees slowly fell silent as the sun set and soon all I could hear was the hiss of traffic out on Marine Drive and the thrum of an engine as a tugboat pushed barges full of Eastern Oregon wheat down the Columbia River.

When I was sixteen, I'd been big for my age, and the kids at my high school in the hills of East Tennessee knew better than to fuck with me. One day I'd seen a handful guys from the football team picking on a little kid, a little freshman that probably wasn't even five feet tall, and I went ballistic. By the time it was over I was sitting in the back of the Sheriff's car, and some of them were on the way to the hospital.

I made quite a few enemies that day, but it was worth it. There was something about protecting someone else that made the world make sense to me.

I felt the same way about Marshall and his crew. I didn't have any regrets. If I'd looked the other way it would eat at me until I died.

It didn't keep me from being angry though.

I looked at the patch of ground that had once held Heather Swanson's body and resolved that one way or another, I was going to get Marshall. I would find out the truth.

But after that, I would walk away. I wanted that quiet life with Alex. Maybe she really could deliver babies while I sold guitars.

Stranger things had happened.

I turned and started running back towards Wapato, letting all the stress I carried in my body burn itself out and fuel my muscles. I'd been working out like crazy lately, using the exercise to beat stress. I'd been a little rough around the edges there for a while. In the last few weeks, I'd been in half a dozen gunfights, killed more men than I cared to count and had damn near died more than once.

Alex and I had a long conversation about my "exaggerated startle response" after I'd pointed a gun at Eddie when I was half awake. I suppose I could have been diagnosed with something, but right now I was content to work out like a madman, stuff my emotions in a box, and deal with all that shit later.

It was full dark now. I managed to cross Marine Drive without getting run over by any of the traffic, then started pounding my way down the sidewalk towards Wapato. Out of my peripheral vision, I saw a pickup truck pass me, then slow. It was a beater Toyota, and in the rear window, right behind the driver, I saw a sticker of a Combat Infantry Badge, an Army award given to infantrymen that saw combat. There was a bumper sticker with the word "Ranger" in a scroll, the symbol of the 75th Ranger Regiment, my old Army outfit.

The driver pulled over to my side of the street and stopped. I came to a stop as alarm bells started going off in my head. I was standing on a sidewalk with an eight-foot chain link fence to my left, and an empty street to my right. I had no cover and no ideas other than to rip my little backup gun out of my kit bag and get ready to take somebody out with me.

I watched the reverse lights flash as the driver shifted into park, then he surprised me by turning on his interior lights and holding up both hands so I could see them. He then looked over his shoulder and cocked an eyebrow at me.

He was a young guy, probably not quite thirty, and had a high and tight haircut that screamed "military" to me. If this was a hit, it was a singularly unusual way to do it. If this guy was here to kill me, he could have just blasted me with a shotgun as he drove by. I looked over my shoulder. There was nobody else on the street.

I pulled a little flashlight out of the kit bag.

"Step on out," I said.

He pushed the door all the way open, then got out, leading with his empty hands. He was a tall rangy kid, and wore a tucked in t-shirt, jeans and a pair of cowboy boots. I lit him up with the flashlight.

"Are you Dent Miller?" he asked. He squinted and raised his hand to shield his eyes. The little light was insanely bright. All he would be able to see was a bright glow coming from my direction.

"Yeah," I said.

"I'm supposed to give you a package. You reckon I could reach in and pull it out of the truck without collecting a bullet?" He had a touch of a Southern drawl.

"Do it," I said.

He pulled out a padded mailer envelope and held it up. My name was written on the outside in big letters in black marker.

"Open it," I said.

He sighed. "It ain't a bomb or nothing."

"Open it."

"Mind if I use my little pocket knife?"

"Go for it," I said, adding *it's your funeral* in my head.

His idea of a "little" pocket knife was a folder with what looked like about a six-inch blade. He cut the envelope open and returned the knife to his pocket.

"Dump it out," I said.

He looked a little irritated but did as I said. A folded piece of paper fluttered out, as well as something small and metal that hit the ground with a *ting*.

"Drop the envelope and get out of here," I asked.

I was tempted to try to hang on to the guy and get him to tell me who sent him, but I had a feeling that might not go well.

"Have a good 'un," he said without a trace of sarcasm and hopped back in the truck. I kept the gun in my hand as he pulled a u-turn and headed off.

I shined my light on the stuff he'd dropped. Next to the folded up piece of paper was a coin. It bore the Ranger scroll and around the border were the words "The Battle of the Black Sea, Mogadishu Somalia."

I picked it up and flipped it over. The back side read "Task Force Ranger October 3-6,1993."

What I was holding was called a challenge coin. Guys in the military carried them, to signify the unit they belonged to or an operation they'd been a part of. Another guy with the same coin could challenge you to produce yours and if you didn't have it, beer was on you. This particular one commemorated the infamous Ranger raid in Mogadishu Somalia that left eighteen US soldiers and hundreds of Somalis dead. The fight had happened in and around the Bakara Market, which we'd dubbed the Black Sea because its twisting warrens of alleyways seemed to just swallow people up.

The coin was scratched and the edges were rounded from being carried in a pocket.

I used to own a coin just like this one until my house was blown up. Presumably, it had melted into an indistinguishable lump of metal along with most of my belongings and had been carted off to the landfill.

I stuck the coin in my kit bag and picked up the letter.

Miller. We have matters of mutual interest. Tomorrow. 2000. Charlie Mikes. Mack.

Mack. Shit. Sergeant Macklin had been my platoon sergeant during those fateful days in Mogadishu. What the hell was he doing mixed up in all this?

I gathered everything up and stuffed it in the kit bag.

I didn't know what the hell was going on, but one thing was clear: our cover was blown. Apparently somebody knew we were at Wapato.

CHAPTER FIVE

The Portland Police Bureau considered me persona non grata before I blew an arm off one of their police officers, so I was surprised when Bolle told me I was going to the hospital to interrogate Bloem. The Bureau was alternating between being livid that we'd moved to arrest him without telling them, and wanting to put as much distance between themselves and Bloem as possible. Apparently the fact that I was the one that had pulled the trigger was lost in the background noise of all the screaming.

Oregon Health Sciences University Hospital held many memories for me. I'd been a patient there once, almost ten years ago, after nearly being beaten to death by a suspect. Last winter I'd actually killed a man in the stairwell because he'd been trying to kill Mandy, my former partner. OHSU was also where Dalton, Eddie, and most of the other shooting victims from the attack at the zoo had been taken. Maybe I should see about getting my own parking place.

I kept stealing glances at Alex as we rode the elevator up with Bolle, wishing in some ways she wasn't here. She was about to do something that flew in the face of medical ethics, and I was surprised she had agreed to it. She didn't look at me, just stood there staring at the reflective surface of the elevator with her face set in a hard thin line.

OHSU had a little corner of one floor with a couple of rooms set aside for special patients. This was where patients that were famous, infamous, or just downright notorious were housed. After a brief stint in the ICU, that's where Bloem was being treated.

There was a uniformed Portland police officer standing outside his room, which I'd expected. What I hadn't expected was the older guy in a suit standing there. It took me a second to recognize him since he'd lost at least twenty pounds since I last saw him. It was Sergeant Dan

Winter, former lackey of my old boss, Steve Lubbock, the guy who had helped frame me last year.

He stepped forward, extended a hand to Bolle.

"Special Agent Bolle, I'm Dan Winter with PPB Internal Affairs. I've been instructed to make Bloem available to you for questioning. I'll be here in the nurse's area if you need anything.

Bolle returned the handshake and did his best to be gracious and play along with the fiction that the Portland Police Bureau could allow us to do anything. Burke had threatened to pull out all the stops and invoke some of the more draconian sections of the Patriot Act if the Bureau hadn't played ball.

Winter had been pretending like I wasn't in the room, so I was surprised when he turned to me and extended a hand.

"Good to see you, Dent. I wonder if I could buy you a cup of coffee when you're done with Bloem."

I would have been less surprised if he'd just punched me in the face.

"Uh, sure, Dan," I said, giving Bolle a sidelong glance.

"See you then." Winter stepped aside and gave the uniform at the door a nod. We walked into Bloem's room and shut the door behind us.

Bloem was a fitness junky, one of those greyhound lean guys that ran marathons and triathlons for fun. Now he looked pale and puffy. Where his right arm ended in a stump, it was wrapped up in bandages. His left arm was bandaged too. He'd been holding the gun out in front of him with both hands when I shot him, and some pellets had passed through his right arm, into his left. They'd plugged the IV lines into his legs because of this.

Bloem blinked at us, his face slack and emotionless. Casey had managed to access his electronic medical records, which showed he was stoned out of his gourd on pain medication. That made what we were about to do both trickier and easier.

"Miller," he said, and a trickle of drool ran out of his mouth.

I wasn't sure if he said it because he remembered me shooting him, or just because he recognized me.

"Mr. Bloem, I'm Special Agent Bolle. I'd like to ask you a few questions."

Bloem looked from me to Bolle, then cleared his throat.

"I'm not saying anything without a lawyer," he said, loud and clear. Apparently, our arrival had spurred him to be a little more lucid.

Bolle sighed and looked at Alex. She took a case out of her shoulder bag, and withdrew a syringe. I noticed her hands were shaking a little when she plugged it into the port in Bloem's IV line. She depressed the plunger.

"What's that?" Bloem asked.

"Something to help you be less of an asshole," Bloem said with a shark's grin.

I couldn't pronounce the name of the drug Alex was giving Bloem. It was supposed to make him talk. It was also safe to give him despite all the pain meds he was on. Probably.

Alex's hand were still shaking a little as she re-capped the needle, something medical people were never supposed to do. Normally it would have gone in the sharps container mounted on the wall, but we couldn't leave evidence behind. She managed to get it re-capped without stabbing herself in the hand and put the needle away.

Bolle put a digital recorder on the tray beside the bed. He identified himself and stated the date and time.

"Mr. Bloem, I'd like to start by asking you why you participated in the attack on Detective Mandy Williams from the Portland Police Bureau."

At first, he said nothing, just sat there swallowing multiple times like he had too much spit in his mouth. Then he smirked.

"Bitch had it coming," he said. "She should have been back in the kitchen where she belonged."

The Bureau had some work to do when it came to its psych evals in its hiring process.

"What exactly were you supposed to do that day?'

Bloem stared up at the corner of the room like there was something up there that captured his attention. Alex was staring intently at his vital signs on the monitors.

"Just what I did," Bloem finally said. "I was supposed to keep a lookout while Todd did his thing. I was supposed to arrest Miller when he came along."

I felt my fingers flex as I remembered that day. I'd actually gone to Mandy's door and turned away, unaware that she lay on the other side with her skull fractured and her brain swelling.

"So Rickson Todd is the person who directed you to do this?"

"Yeah. Todd. Him."

"Why? What did he give you?"

Bloem's eyelids fluttered and for a second I thought he was going to nod off.

"Some money. I wanted a job with him. I was sick of all the touchy-feely, politically correct bullshit at the Bureau. I wanted to kick some ass and take some names."

Before joining the Bureau, Bloem had a lackluster career as a Petroleum Supply Specialist in the Army and had spent a tour in Iraq sitting inside the wire at a Forward Operating Base, although word among his shift partners was he'd tell bullshit stories that made it sound like he'd been GI Joe over there. We'd recruited him during a hiring frenzy six or seven years ago. He wasn't terribly well liked by his peers or his supervisors. He had a reputation for being arrogant way out of proportion to his skill level. He used force more often than the average officer, but nobody could ever say he'd done anything particularly wrong.

I'd worked with guys like him before. I could walk into a disturbance with a bunch of drunk guys being belligerent and usually talk people into handcuffs without having to get rough with them. First, I never talked down to people, and treated them with as much respect as they would let me. Second, I had a pretty good grasp of my abilities and limitations, so guys realized I wasn't afraid of them, I was just coming up with a plan to fuck them up if they got rowdy.

Guys like Bloem always let it be known in subtle ways that they looked down on people on the street, usually in a way that was hard to articulate. Then when a drunk got pissed at that and took a swing, they'd overreact because they weren't confident in their abilities. I hated working with guys like him.

"So Todd offered you a job with Cascade Aviation?"

Bloem didn't look good. He'd gotten even paler and his speech was slurred.

"Yeah. I would have been making twice what I was making at this shitty job."

That was a pipe dream. Cascade Aviation had only employed veterans of elite military units. Bloem's service certainly didn't qualify. Todd had a real talent for stringing people along by telling them what they wanted to hear.

"When?" Bolle asked.

Bloem mumbled something I couldn't quite understand. Alex made a hurry up motion with her hand and pulled a second syringe from her bag.

"Who else did you meet from Cascade Aviation?" Bolle asked.

Bloem shook his head and mumbled.

Alex injected the second syringe into the IV line. Supposedly this would reverse the first drug we'd given him. Now her hands were steady.

"What was that? I didn't hear." Bolle leaned closer.

"No... Nobody, just Todd," Bloem mumbled. His head dipped forward. On the monitor I saw his respiration rate dropping.

"I need to reverse him," Alex said and stood with a Narcan nasal spray in her hand.

Bolle shut off the digital recorder. We'd discussed this possibility earlier. The drug Alex had given Bloem to make him talk wasn't interacting well with the opiates he'd been given for pain. The second injection would counteract the first over the course of a few minutes. But during that time there was a danger Bloem would stop breathing, so now Alex was going to give him Narcan, which would almost instantly reverse the effects of the opiate painkillers in his system.

She squirted the Narcan in his nose and Bloem's eyes went wide.

His eyes went unfocused and he gave a low moan. I saw his respiration rate, heart rate, and oxygen saturation shoot up on the monitors.

"Looks like the party is over," I said.

The downside to giving Bloem the Narcan was that now all those nerve endings in his amputated arm were wide awake and screaming. Bolle and Alex preceded me out of the room. I gave one last look around the room and saw the plastic cap to the Narcan inhaler on the floor. I quickly pocketed it on my way out. Supposedly none of the drugs Alex had given Bloem were detectable, even if somebody thought to look for them. There was no sense giving ourselves away by leaving a piece of physical evidence behind.

Behind us, Bloem gave a louder moan and the nurse at the nurse's station turned around and looked over his shoulder.

"We're done with him," Bolle said. "But it seems like he's in quite a bit of pain."

The nurse closed out the report he was writing and got up to check on Bloem. I guess I should have felt some sympathy for the injured man, but I couldn't muster any.

Winter was looking expectantly at me. I turned to Bolle.

"Can I meet you guys at the car in say, twenty minutes?"

He nodded.

I followed Winter through the bowels of the hospital. He looked like he knew where he was going so I followed, hoping this wasn't some clever way of luring me into an ambush.

"You look well Dan," I said. "I would have thought you would be retired by now."

I didn't mean it as a dig. I was genuinely curious. When I'd still been at the Bureau, Winter had been coasting his way towards retirement and doing as little work as possible. He'd also been carrying a pretty fair sized spare tire that seemed to have been greatly reduced.

"I started working out again," he said.

My fears of an ambush were alleviated when we came around a corner and arrived at a coffee stand. He even paid for me.

We walked over to an out of the way corner.

"Is it true?" he asked. "Did Rickson Todd really beat up Mandy Williams and set you up for it with Bloem's help?"

He watched me intently, waiting for an answer.

"Yep," I said, and took a drink of coffee.

Some of the tension left his body, and I could tell he believed me. It was a big change from a few months ago when he'd sat across an interrogation room from me and accused me of trying to kill Mandy.

"It's hard to believe," he said softly.

"Hell, I was there," I said. "And I hardly believe it myself."

"Lubbock? He was in on it?"

"Yep."

Winter took a sip of his coffee.

"Something changed in him six months or so before it all happened. I thought he was just having an affair. But it was Todd wasn't it?"

"Yep." I didn't see any particular reason to keep all this secret. I was curious why Winter had called me down here.

"I could have retired a month ago," Winter said. "But I fought to get assigned to Internal Affairs instead."

"Why?" During my time as a cop, I would have rather slammed my balls in a car door than work IA. Everybody hated you then.

"When they first accused you of hurting Mandy, I believed them," he said. "Then it all began to unravel, and the truth was nowhere to be found. I was determined to get to the bottom of it, and I was told to shut my hole, mind my own business and collect my pension."

He started walking then, I think as much to burn off nervous energy as anything else. I walked beside him.

"At first I was determined to do exactly that. But I woke up in the middle of the night and realized I didn't want to go out like that. I haven't been a very good cop since the shooting, Dent."

Five or six years ago, Winter had shot a man in a parking lot. He'd pointed a gun at Winter. Winter shot him down, simple as that.

Only it wasn't that simple. The guy had been a vet, struggling with an addiction to pain pills due to an injury from service, and the pistol had been a air gun, and an unloaded one at that. There had never been a chance that Winter would be disciplined or fired. It was one of those things that happened sometimes, but Winter had been dragged through the mud in the media. The Bureau hadn't exactly abandoned him, but it hadn't exactly supported him either. The Bureau only protected itself. It was after that people started counting Winter among the ranks of the "Retired On Active Duty."

I didn't really know what to say to that. The default response among cops about anything emotionally uncomfortable was not to talk about it. Part of me was still shocked Winter was willing to talk to me about this at all.

"So I got a job at IA," he said. "And I'm starting to think like a cop again, instead of like a retiree."

"How's that working out for you?" It came out sounding snarkier than I meant for it to, but he didn't seem to notice.

"Everyone closed ranks," Winter said. "Nobody gave a shit about you or Mandy. Every time I tried to gain some traction into investigating Bloem, I was stonewalled."

I'd busted my ass for the Bureau for most of my adult life, which apparently counted for nothing. I would have been hurt, but I'd had months to get used to the idea. Right now I was trying to decide if Winter was brave or stupid for doing what he was doing.

"So what do you want from me?" I asked.

It took him a little while to answer. He looked out the window stirring the cream in his coffee cup. What was unspoken between us was the last time I'd seen him was the day I'd turned in my badge after being accused of trying to kill my partner.

"I'll take anything you've got, Dent. I don't know if other people in the Bureau knew exactly what Bloem was doing, but I think people had to know he was up to something. They need to pay."

I opened my mouth, then shut it. I could talk for hours about Bloem's connection to Todd, and the whole mess with Cascade Aviation. All of it would be news to Winter. But it didn't sound like Winter had anything for me. He'd never been one of the Bureau's stars. His career had been marked by a willingness to show up on time, keep his mouth shut, and do what he was told. He had been useful to people like Steve Lubbock, my old boss, but he'd never been a skilled investigator or tactician.

The fewer people who knew the details of our investigation the better. I had everything to lose, but nothing to gain by talking to Winter.

I think deep down, he knew it. Asking me for help was an act of desperation.

I took a deep breath and reached in my pocket. I had two sets of business cards. They were both pretty spiffy and said "US Department of Justice Special Investigator Dent Miller." I'd never expected those words to be strung together. The difference between the two sets was one had my personal cell phone number, and the other had the duty phone in our command center. I gave him the duty phone.

"I can't give you the family jewels without talking to my boss," I said. "He's keeping his cards pretty close to the vest. But you can reach me at this number."

He took the card, not meeting my eyes. He fished in a pocket and pulled out one of his own. I took it and we shook hands awkwardly.

"Thanks for talking with me Dent," he said, still not meeting my eyes. He knew I was blowing him off. Investigators shared information under the table all the time. I didn't have to share everything with him, but I wasn't even offering so much as a scrap.

"Thanks for the coffee, Dan."

I turned on my heel and left, chucking my half full cup of coffee in a trash can as I went.

The night before at Kelly Point Park, I'd told myself I didn't have any regrets. Now I was even more sure. Dan could work out all he wanted and convince himself that he was somehow going to redeem himself by exposing the rottenness in the Bureau, but it was too little too late. He didn't have the knowledge, the resources, or the time to make anything happen. They'd force him out soon and he'd find himself retired, sitting home alone at night with a bottle of whiskey and a loaded gun in a desk drawer.

I wasn't sure how my life was going to end, but I had a pretty good idea about Dan's.

My phone buzzed. It was a text from Alex.

U Ok?

I figured I was.

CHAPTER SIX

"I still think this is a bad idea," Alex said.

She'd been quiet since the events at the hospital, with the exception of a vociferous argument in the car on the way back about my meeting with Mack. She didn't think I should go. I was determined to do it. There didn't seem to be any common ground.

"It just seems weird to me that they figured out we were housed out of Wapato, and now they want to get you alone."

I opened my mouth, almost said something snarky and stupid, and for once in my life, bit my tongue before it came out.

I took a deep breath. This relationship stuff was hard, and I was beginning to realize I wasn't very good at it.

We were sitting in the back of the surveillance van. Henry was in the driver's seat, while Alex, Casey and I sat in the back. Casey was holding a cell phone in her hand, looking from Alex to me with an expression on her face that said she'd rather be anywhere than between the two of us at the moment.

"I understand that you don't agree, Alex," I said. We'd rehashed the argument three or four times now, and I didn't feel like either of us had anything new to say. "But I feel like I need to do this. The meeting is supposed to start in a few minutes, and I can't keep doing this. I just need your support. I need to know if I get in a jam, you'll back me up."

She was sitting there in the jump seat sweating in a bulky set of hard body armor under a windbreaker. The a/c couldn't compete with all the heat generated by the electronic gear. Her carbine was slung around her neck and a medical backpack was between her feet. She had her hair pulled back into a severe ponytail, and she looked tired and out of sorts.

She also looked heartbreakingly beautiful to me at that moment, more than she ever had before. I just wanted to hold her and get the hell out of here.

But first, work.

"Back me up, ok?" I asked softly.

She nodded and seemed to relax a little.

Casey glanced at both of us. Then held out the phone.

"Even if you power it down, the microphone will still be hot and broadcasting. If battery is pulled out there's an internal backup that will keep it working for about fifteen minutes, maybe twenty, but I wouldn't count on it for longer than that."

I took it from her and tucked it in the front pocket of my shirt. Unlike everyone else, I wasn't wearing armor, just an untucked button-down shirt with a square hem, perfect for hiding my 10mm that rode in a Milt Sparks Versamax holster on my right hip. I also had my little revolver in my right front pocket, and a couple of knives, my usual outfit for when I was walking around not expecting trouble.

"Ok," I said. "I'm headed out. You guys sit tight."

We were on Foster Road, in far southeast Portland. I'd been to Charlie Mikes a couple of times when I first moved to Portland, but it had been easily fifteen years since my last visit. When most people thought of Portland, they thought of vegans and hipsters. But there was also a thriving population of military vets who settled down here to live out their post-service lives.

Vets who'd spent their time chipping paint in the Navy or driving a truck in the Army could be found down at the local VFW or AMVETS watering hole, drinking cheap beer and lying about their service. Charlie Mikes had a more selective clientele. You couldn't find it written down anywhere, but it was open only to folks who had served in one of the Special Warfare components, Rangers, Army Special Forces, Navy SEALS, Air Force PJs, folks like that. Former CIA spooks were tolerated, although they could expect some ribbing.

Occasionally, wayward Portland hipsters would find their way in the door, and hilarity would ensue. When I'd first discharged from the service and was studying at Portland State, I'd hung out here, but gradually as I de-institutionalized myself from my time in the Army, the appeal wore off.

The vehicles in the parking lot were pretty evenly divided between jacked up trucks, sports cars, and Harley-Davidsons. When I walked in, Johnny Cash was playing on the jukebox. Some guys were playing pool, some were playing darts, and most were sitting around tables talking low. The walls were covered with unit patches and memorabilia. I saw a couple of Iraqi flags, military helmets, a small collection of brassieres dangling from a ceiling fan, and an RPG-7 rocket launcher mounted over the bar. If it was a replica, it was extremely realistic. If it was real, it was a pretty lengthy prison sentence for somebody.

Eyes turned to look at me, but nobody stood up and headed my, way. The bartender was a guy in his sixties without an ounce of body fat on him and faded tattoos on his forearms. He was polishing the already spotless bar when I walked up.

"Getcha?" he asked.

The selection of beers was abysmal.

"Bud Light," I said. If I was going to drink shitty beer, I might as well skip the calories.

He put the beer on the bar. I put down a five spot and the challenge coin. He took the money and pushed the coin back towards me.

"In the back," he said. "The door that's past the shitter."

I picked up my beer and headed towards the back, conscious of eyes following me. Some things hadn't changed. One of the restrooms was labeled "men's restroom." The other was labeled "the other men's restroom." Charlie Mikes wasn't a place you brought a date. There were other bars for that.

Once again I was reminded of some of the reasons I left the Army. There were guys who managed to have a relatively normal life, with a wife and kids, despite the stress of frequent deployments and the risk of getting killed at work. But I'd known plenty of guys like the ones here at Charlie Mikes, dudes in their forties and even fifties that still led an almost adolescent life, with a string of broken marriages and estranged children churning in their wake.

The door past the restroom had gold letters that said "employees only." Below that was neatly stenciled "If you don't work here, stay the fuck out," but I figured I had dispensation.

On the other side of the door was a small office with barely enough room for a desk, a busted pinball machine, and three men.

Two of them I recognized. First was the young guy from the night before, the one who had dropped off the package.

The second was Mack. I hadn't seen him since the mid-nineties, when I'd mustered out, but he didn't look that different. He was tall, powerfully built, with a shaved head. The biggest change was the salt and pepper goatee that hadn't been allowed in the Army.

"Miller," he said, and stuck a hand out.

We shook briefly. The third guy was so bland as to be instantly forgettable. He was medium height, medium build, brown hair, wearing khakis and a polo shirt. He was looking at an electronic tablet.

"I need your phone," he said, without even looking up.

"John here is formerly from the Army of Northern Virginia," Mack said. "He handles all my electronic security needs."

Army of Northern Virginia was slang for the Army's Intelligence Support Activity. Most people have heard of Delta Force and the Navy SEALS. Few of them have heard of the ISA. They were the Joint Special Operations intelligence collections arm.

I handed John my phone. When he saw it was turned off, he popped the back cover off, removed the battery and looked at his tablet again. He gave me a smirk, then pulled a zippered pouch out of his pocket. He put all the parts to my phone inside, then looked at his screen again.

"You're clear," he said. He put the pouch on the desk and walked out of the room.

I recognized the pouch because I owned one just like it. It was designed to block cell phone signals. Apparently, nobody cared that I was carrying a gun, but they didn't want me recording the conversation. Hopefully, the rest of my crew wouldn't freak out when they realized I was off the air.

Mack gestured to the younger guy, who followed John out of the room. He sat down and motioned to a chair.

"You've upset some apple carts here lately, Dent," he said.

"Yep," I said. I wasn't going to make this easy for him. I'd never liked Mack very much. The Ranger Regiment hadn't been full of warm, fuzzy people, but even there, there was a coldness to Mack that made him stick out. People wound up in the service for many different reasons. Some needed a way out of whatever shit hole town they grew up in. Some were motivated by patriotism. Some wanted an adventure. Usually, it was a mix of all three.

With Mack, I'd always gotten the feeling that he would have been just as happy being a Mafia enforcer, or a member of a third world death squad. He got off on feeling powerful, and he was always working an angle.

He waited a few beats, seeing if I would say more. His expression didn't change, but he stiffened a little. Irritated maybe to realize I wasn't the Private First Class he'd browbeat all those years ago.

"Up until about six months ago," he said. "I was making pretty good money working for Cascade Aviation."

"Yeah?" I asked. "Were you in the department that kidnapped women and shipped them overseas, or the department that planned terror attacks on US soil?"

That pissed him off. His forearms flexed like he was going to come over the table at me. I wondered which one of us would wind up dying, but after a second or two, he reined it in.

"That was all Todd and that shitbird Marshall's son. I just had a sweet gig flying around on Cascade planes to various sunny spots and making sure nobody blew us up while we were on the tarmac."

I watched his face closely as he talked. He was lying, but I wasn't sure about what. I wondered if Mack had envisioned me as the young grunt he'd known, and subconsciously failed to take into account the intervening years I'd spent as a homicide detective.

"What do you want, an apology?"

I was intentionally provoking him, not showing him the deference he was used to receiving from guys like John, and whoever the young kid was. Bloem hadn't given us anything, but maybe Mack would be my conduit to the inner workings of Cascade.

"I want to help you," he said through gritted teeth. "I'm done with Cascade. I almost got caught up in their bullshit and wound up having to talk to some Feds. I can write my ticket with any private military company I want."

"How are you going to help me?" I asked. I wasn't surprised to hear that Mack's biggest objection was that Cascade's actions had brought heat down on him. I also wondered which "Feds" had talked to him. It wasn't anyone in our group.

"There's an inner circle at Cascade," Mack said. "The old man, Marshall is at the center of it. Todd was next in line, but word is you put him in the ground a little while back."

The word was right. Todd had been a former Delta guy and Marshall's right-hand man. He'd come close to killing me in the Max train tunnel in Portland, but instead, I'd stabbed the shit out of him, then shot him in the head for good measure. I'd killed more people than I cared to admit. I actually slept better at night knowing Todd was no longer moving air.

"Go on," I said. I wasn't about to confirm out loud whether I'd punched Todd's ticket or not.

"It's a tight crew," Mack said. "They keep their cards pretty close to

47

their vests, but a few days ago one of them reached out to me. He wants out. He's willing to talk in exchange for protection. He wanted my help getting ex-filled out of the country, but this whole thing is just too hot for me."

"Who is it?" I asked.

He shook his head.

"Doesn't work that way, Miller. I'm not even sure who it is. It was an anonymous contact. They provided just enough insider knowledge to establish their bona fides. When I said I couldn't help, they specifically asked that I get them in touch with you."

"Interesting," I said. I tried to maintain a neutral expression, but in my head, my wheels were turning. I forced myself to be cautious. This sounded too good to be true.

"I'm going to reach in the desk and pull out a cell phone," Mack said. "It was couriered to me with instructions to give it to you."

Apparently, he was taking me seriously enough not to reach for something without giving me a heads up. That was progress.

I nodded and he pulled a phone out of the drawer. He slid it across the desk towards me but I didn't take it. Instead, I just stared at him.

"That's it?" I asked.

"What more do you want?"

"You've been wrapped up with an organization that sold American women into slavery and tried to machine-gun kids at the Portland zoo. You're giving me a cell phone and walking away? You think you're done? Don't you want to hurt these fuckers?"

He gave me a twisted little smirk.

"You always were a boy scout Miller. I did my twenty getting paid next to nothing for eating shit food and sleeping in the dirt in one shit hole country after another. The only person I'm looking out for now is me."

Mack was a lost cause. I wasn't going to change his mind tonight, but now that we knew he was a potential source, we could always grab him later. A few days out at Wapato being pumped full of a drug cocktail might change his tune.

I picked up the cell phone. It didn't look remarkable in any way, just a run of the mill Samsung. It was deactivated. I didn't turn it on. Analyzing this thing was a job for Casey and Henry. Instead, I picked up the pouch and took my own phone out. I reassembled it and put the new phone inside.

I pushed my chair back and turned to leave. Mack looked like he was chewing on something that tasted bad, but didn't say anything as I left. The younger guy was standing outside the door when I walked out. I gave him a cold stare, and he gave it right back. I walked across the floor of Charlie Mikes to the tune of that Charlie Daniels song about the devil going down to Georgia as a bunch of eyes followed me.

It smelled like exhaust fumes and ripe garbage as I walked out the door but I was still glad to step out of Charlie Mikes. My phone started buzzing as soon as it powered up.

"Yeah," I said, talking as I walked across the parking lot.

"You good?" Casey asked.

"Easy and breezy," I said. That was our code word that I wasn't under duress. If I'd said "good to go" my crew was supposed to go tactical and rescue me, Justice Department be damned.

"I'm headed to the corner," I said. "Can you get a handle on all the phones in there? We may need to see my contact again."

That was as far as I was willing to go on the phone, supposedly secure line or not. There would be dozens of phones inside Charlie Mikes, but maybe one of them would lead us to Mack and his buddies. Since he had John working for him, maybe not, but it was worth a try.

"Ok," she said. "We're headed your way. Things are complicated right now, but I'll do what I can."

Complicated. Interesting.

I stopped at the corner and a few seconds later the van pulled up with the door sliding open. I'm not sure it even came to a complete stop as I hopped in. Casey was tapping away on two keyboards at once. I shut the door and crammed myself into a seat.

"There was another team surveilling the place," Casey said. "We made them as you went in. Two cars on opposite corners. A man in one, a woman in another."

She was twiddling the joysticks that controlled the video cameras hidden in the equipment rack on top of the van.

"We're about to pass her now," she said.

On the screen, I saw a sedan sitting at the curb. She was sitting in the passenger seat, an old surveillance trick. Somebody sitting in the driver's seat of a parked car for no reason was suspicious. Somebody sitting in the passenger seat was obviously waiting for the driver to come back.

We passed too quick for us to get a look at her, but Casey had been recording as we rolled past. She played it back, found a frame that showed the woman's face, and zoomed in.

"She looked away from the camera as we rolled past," Casey said.

I got the impression of a younger woman, probably in her thirties, with auburn hair. I couldn't tell much else.

"I don't think it's enough for a facial recognition match," Casey said

"I'd know her again if I saw her," I said.

"There's a bunch of phones in there," Casey said. "I'm grabbing all the numbers and we'll sort it all out later. I may need more info to figure out which one belongs to your buddy."

Casey excelled at following trails of digital breadcrumbs. We could easily comb through Mack's credit card records, or airline flight databases, to see where he'd been in the last couple of months. She would then see which of the phones in Charlie Mikes had been in those places at the same time. All that assumed that Mack wasn't just using a phone account in his real name. People could be surprisingly dumb that way.

When I'd been a cop, I'd had a passing familiarity with digital surveillance. Since I'd joined Bolle's crew, it was like I was living in a different world. When all this was over, I was going to go live in a cabin in the woods with no electricity and pay for everything with cash, and maybe wear a hat made of tinfoil all day.

In my head, I was already writing a material witness warrant for Mack. I knew I could get Burke to sign off on it pretty easily. Mack's mistake was thinking I couldn't touch him if he just acted as a middleman.

Maybe we'd put that cell meant for Bloem to good use after all.

CHAPTER SEVEN

"All I'm saying is that Bolle is going to have a fit if he finds out you put a hundred-year-old Mauser pistol on your government credit card," Dalton said.

Even though Wapato was huge, it still felt like we were living in close quarters because we only occupied a small corner of the facility. Due to the reinforced walls, the WiFi signals sucked, so I was sharing space with Dalton and Casey in the operations center, deep diving through Mack's credit card records and drinking coffee. By all rights, I should have been asleep next to Alex, but I knew all I would do was lie next to her and stare at the ceiling.

"Yeah, I guess you're right," Casey said. "Never mind."

One of the side effects of our communal living relationship was I was getting to know everyone's quirks. Big Eddie was a gourmet level cook. Dalton was a voracious reader of anything he could get his hands on. Henry had an annoying propensity to listen to mid-eighties hair metal at a really ridiculous volume.

When Casey got bored, she got into gadgets. Lately, she'd been fascinated by German firearms, and had put her government purchase card to work. She could justify the multiple Heckler and Koch pistols, rifles, and submachine guns, but Dalton had a point. The Broomhandle Mauser was probably pushing it.

"I still think we need a foosball table though," she said.

"Hmmm... Do we have a morale budget?" Dalton started clicking through folders on our shared hard drive.

I was debating whether I should move to a quieter spot with crappier WiFi when the phone rang.

"For you, Dent." Casey handed me the receiver.

It was Dan Winter.

"Dent, about three hours ago you entered an arrest warrant for a guy named Thomas Macklin, right?"

"Yeah," I said, wondering if Dan was actually going to come through for me after all.

"He's dead. He and two other guys were found in a room in the Portland Hilton."

"Dammit," I said. "What happened?"

"Supposedly an overdose."

"All three of them?"

"Yup. Heroin."

That sounded like bullshit to me. Mack was many things, but a junkie wasn't one of them.

"Who caught it?"

"Tanner Reese. You know him."

Reese had been the newest detective in Major Crimes when I'd worked there. I didn't know him well, but he'd always struck me as arrogant, and I didn't think that was just because I was a bitter old fart.

"Have they moved the bodies yet?"

"Not yet. The Medical Examiner should be here within the hour."

"Can you stall them until I get there?"

"I can try."

"Thanks, Dan."

I wasn't sure what Winter could do for me. IA wouldn't have any business interfering in a homicide investigation. I needed Bolle to get Burke out of bed so she could start making noise with the locals.

"Wake everybody up," I said to Casey. "We've got work to do."

Bolle, Alex, and I rode in one car, while Henry, Casey, and Eddie took the van. Bolle spent most of the ride on the phone with either Burke or various lieutenants, captains and assistant chiefs at the Portland Police Bureau. When he hung up from the last call I thought for a second he was going to hurl the phone out his window, but apparently, he thought better of it because he tucked it away in a pocket.

"We're going to be allowed access to the scene," he said. "No photographs and no collecting of evidence."

"Well that's something," I said.

The Portland Hilton wasn't the fanciest hotel in town, but it apparently rated a discreet police response to three dead guys. There were two marked cars, two unmarked and a crime scene van all crammed into the loading dock. We squeezed in behind them while

Casey and the crew in the van kept driving. They were going to circle the area discretely for a while.

A uniform met us and led us up to a suite door guarded by another officer. I didn't recognize either of them, and they didn't seem to recognize me. They both looked too young to buy beer, much less tear around town with a fast car and a gun. It was hell getting old.

They were competent though. They had us sign in and don white Tyvek coveralls, hats, and booties.

It was a nice suite. Mack must have been doing well in his retirement, other than the being dead part. The ambiance was ruined somewhat by the smell of loose bowels. Dead bodies tended to do that after a while, and there were three of them in the space of a modest apartment.

Tanner Reese was over by the mini-bar, typing on a tablet with his hands still in nitrile gloves. Apparently notebooks were a thing of the past. He looked up at me, gave a little smirk, then went back to what he was doing. Punk. I'd been investigating homicides when he was still nervous about asking girls out to the prom.

I saw Mack first, he was sitting up in a chair, staring at a TV with a slack expression on his face. His dead eyes were still open. He looked older in death. The remote control was on the floor in front of him, and he almost looked like he might snap out of it at any moment and bend over and pick it up. Bolle walked over to Reese. I followed Alex over to Mack.

She whipped an old-fashioned magnifying glass out of her shoulder bag, the kind you'd expect to see in a black and white Sherlock Holmes movie. As Tanner typed on his tablet, and the two crime scene techs set up their digital cameras and LED lights, it seemed incongruous.

She bent over and studied Mack's arm.

"Very small puncture wound," she said. "Consistent with a needle."

"Huh," I said.

"The smack is over on the table," Reese said from across the room.

I managed not to say the words "fuck you very much" as he turned back to Bolle.

There was a baggie of crystalline white powder, some syringes, spoons, cotton, a lighter and a bottle of water sitting on a little side table. It was a big baggie. I was guessing there was most of an ounce left. I hadn't been keeping track of the street prices of drugs lately, but I guessed we were looking at a couple grand worth of the drug. Maybe more if it was especially pure, as I was betting this was. I'd pulled my fair share of heroin off suspects in the past, and mostly it ranged from black and tarry looking, to a kind of dirty brown powder. Usually, by the time it was stepped on and diluted down, it looked pretty rough. This stuff looked like it could have come from a laboratory.

"One guy is in the bedroom. The second is in the bathroom," one of the evidence techs said.

I followed Alex into the bedroom. "John," the former ISA guy was laying on the bed, fully clothed except for his shoes. His glasses were folded on his chest and a paperback mystery novel was on the comforter beside him. The only clue that he wasn't asleep was the thin trickle of vomit running out of his mouth.

Alex grabbed his arm and gave it the same treatment with her magnifying glass.

"Same. A small puncture. No needle tracks or marks on his arms. A lot of junkies shoot up between their toes or on their thighs because they want to be discreet though."

I looked over my shoulder out the door of the bedroom and saw Reese had shifted his position so he could still talk to Bolle and watch us. That was a shame because I really wanted to go through "John's" pockets. I would bet a long dollar his name wasn't John. Any documents I would find would likely be a fake as well, but it would be a start.

"Block his view for ten seconds," Alex murmured under her breath. She put the magnifying glass back in her bag and pulled out a mobile biometric scanner. I bent over and pretended to look at something and she swiped John's right index finger across the screen. A green LED lit up and she nodded.

"Good capture," she said.

She slipped the scanner back into her bag like she'd practiced it. Reese was on the phone. I looked around the room, looking for anything else of interest, but I didn't want to push my luck.

Alex walked into the bathroom. The younger guy was fully clothed, but was slumped over soaking wet in the shower. A cell phone sat on the sink.

"The 911 call came from that phone," Reese said from behind us. "The tape has nothing but some mumbles and the sound of water running. We figure they all scored a little horse that was purer than they were used to. This guy tried to wake himself up with a cold shower."

If we'd been looking at typical junkies, I would have accepted that story without a second thought. This stank. Afghanistan was awash in opium and heroin, and the Army had been keeping addiction among soldiers quiet for years. But these guys just didn't seem to fit the mold. I'd been pouring over Mack's financial transactions, and they didn't smell like a junkie's to me. The guy liked to party, but there wasn't the constant drain that I would have expected from somebody with a heroin problem.

"They don't look like junkies," I said.

Reese shrugged. "Not everybody does. We've got upper-class suburban housewives with a smack habit these days. Maybe they aren't regular users and just wanted to have a party."

I could tell he'd already reached a conclusion in his mind, even without the benefit of an autopsy or a review of the crime scene evidence. I'd always thought the best way to get away with murder would be to make everyone think it wasn't a murder in the first place. In Portland, dozens of people died of accidents, suicides, overdoses and sudden health problems every week. Cops were supposed to make a perfunctory investigation of any medically unattended death, and the vast majority of them were not found to be suspicious.

Still, I didn't see a way for someone to overpower the three of them and administer a lethal dose of drugs without signs of a fight. The guy in the shower's t-shirt was hiked up and I could see a holster inside his waistband.

"All three were packing?" I asked.

"Yup," Reese said as he typed on his tablet. "All three had a pistol, an extra magazine, and at least one folding knife on them. The guns had full magazines and a round in the chamber."

So the guns hadn't been fired. There was no sign of a fight. Maybe this really was a giant coincidence.

Alex was examining the dead guy with her magnifying glass. Reese looked at her with an irritated expression.

"The ME is here. He's bringing up his crew right now."

"Well that's that then," I said, and followed Reese out the door, with Alex behind me.

"Whoops, forgot my bag. I set it on the toilet," she turned around and headed back in the bathroom. I figured she was up to something so I tried to distract Reese.

"So what's next?" I asked.

Reese gave me a funny look. That was a stupid question. I'd been investigating homicides back when Reese was still playing with action figures.

"We wait for the ME's report."

He looked back towards the bedroom and frowned just as Alex stepped out. She gave him a high wattage smile and walked past me to Bolle, who was looking at his phone with a nonplussed expression on his face.

"I think I've done everything I can do here," she said.

Bolle nodded and turned to go without a word. We followed him out into the hall, where the deputy ME was pulling his gurney out of the elevator. I didn't recognize her, and Alex apparently didn't either, because she didn't say anything in greeting, and she didn't appear to recognize us.

Alex was silent until the elevator doors shut behind us.

"The guy in the shower has what I believe to be a puncture wound behind his right ear. I took a picture of it, and I'll blow it up when we get back. I really need to access the autopsy to be sure though."

"Behind his ear? Junkies shoot up there?" I asked.

She shook her head. "Dunno. I think I really want to get my hands on those dead guys though."

Those were really weird words to hear come out of the mouth of the woman I loved.

"Dent, you there?" It was Casey's voice in my radio's earpiece.

I keyed the radio attached to my belt.

"Go for Dent."

"Remember the woman who was sitting outside Charlie Mike's? She's outside, across the street from the hotel. Different car, but the same MO. She's sitting in the passenger seat."

"I think we should talk to her," Bolle said. "But we need some kind of PC."

PC stood for "probable cause," the legal standard we would have to meet to arrest somebody for questioning. Sitting around in a car in a public place didn't count.

"I have an idea," I said and explained. Bolle bought off on it, and we climbed into the Charger we'd used to drive over. The others in the surveillance van were still circling downtown. They avoided driving by the hotel too frequently, but they made one more pass to make sure the woman was still there.

I saw her car up ahead, parked on the right side of the one way street. There was a parking space behind her with just barely enough room to squeeze the Charger in with some careful maneuvering.

I didn't maneuver carefully. Instead, I carefully inched forward and tapped her rear bumper with the front end of the Charger. I got out of the car and walked up to her car. It was one of those little low slung, hyper fuel efficient jobs so I had to bend way over to be seen. There was a bar code sticker on the window. A rental.

"M'am, I apologize. I seem to have struck your car. Would you mind stepping out so we can exchange information?"

She had a deer in headlights look. Up close, I could tell she was younger than I thought at first, certainly in her mid-thirties at the oldest, maybe not even that. She had red hair pulled back in a pony tail, wore muted colored clothing, and there was a camera with a long lens on the floorboards between her feet.

"Uhh... I'm sure it's fine, don't worry about it." I could barely hear her through the rolled up window.

I pulled my credentials and slapped them against the window.

"M'am, Oregon law requires that drivers exchange information after an accident. Failing to perform the duties of a driver is a Class A Misdemeanor, and you can be arrested."

All of that was technically true. What I was leaving out was since I only held a Federal commission, I couldn't actually arrest her for breaking an Oregon state law. I figured we'd burn that bridge if we came to it.

She rolled her eyes and got out of the car. She looked at me across the roof.

"This is bullshit, Miller. You can arrest me if you want, but I'm not going to talk to you until you talk to my boss."

CHAPTER EIGHT

Her ID said her name was Diana Hunt, thirty-one years old. She had a valid Oregon Driver's License, a couple of social media accounts with infrequent, innocuous posts and business cards for Hunt Photography, specializing in Wildlife Photography. She even had a valid Oregon Concealed Handgun license for the Glock 19 she'd been carrying in an appendix holster under her sweatshirt.

According to Casey, the camera gear was all top notch. Hunt Photography had a business website and was even registered as a corporation in Wyoming, but there was no mention of it on photography forums or social media. If she was making enough money to afford thirty grand worth of camera gear, she was doing it quietly.

The most unusual thing about her had been the hearing aid in her left ear. We'd removed it, assuming it was some piece of surveillance gear, but according to Henry, it was a real hearing aid and nothing more.

"I don't think she's real," Casey said.

"I don't either," I said as I stared at her on the video screen. We'd stuck her in an interview room at Wapato, where she sat with a preternatural stillness, breathing slowly and staring at the wall. I wondered if she was meditating.

Casey was clicking through screens on the computer so fast I couldn't follow.

"All her Facebook friends have pages just like hers. The pictures could come from a clip art collection. Really bland stuff. I mean, this day and age who doesn't post the occasional political rant on Facebook?"

I didn't, but then again the only social media presence I had was a

MySpace page I'd set up after a couple too many snorts of Johnny Walker and then promptly abandoned.

"You know those pictures they put in a wallet when you buy it? It's almost like she's one of those people come to life," Casey said. "Plus, I can't get into her phone."

That was interesting. Casey had access to dozens of tools she could use to crack just about any cell phone.

The most damning thing of all was when she called me by name. Since then she'd been silent, except for repeated requests to call her boss.

"Well, I guess I'll try again," I said. I picked up the tablet that had been on the desk in front of me and walked into the interrogation room.

I sat down across from her and turned on the tablet. I cued up a picture of a bird I'd downloaded off the internet.

"You're a wildlife photographer, right? What kind of bird is this?"

She cocked her head at me.

"Cedar Waxwing. You really need to let me talk to my boss."

I scrolled to another picture. I really didn't like these tablet things. I preferred the visceral reality of photographs in a manilla folder.

I put a photo of Mack in front of her.

"How about this, recognize him?"

"I really need to talk to my boss."

Next, I flipped to a picture of John, dead on the hotel room bed, and turned the tablet so she could see it.

I had spent many hours sitting across a table from suspects in interrogation rooms. I'd read dozens of books, and attended a handful of courses on how to question people and how to tell when they were lying. There was the Reid Method of Interviewing and Interrogation, which had its uses but had the potential for false confessions. Neuro-Linguistic Programming had been all the rage for the while, but ultimately turned out to be bullshit. Then there was the PEACE method developed by British cops, which I'd begrudgingly accepted as effective, despite its somewhat touchy-feely nature.

The one thing I'd found to be reliable were micro-expressions. Most people thought they had a poker face, and could control their body language and facial expressions through force of will. To a certain extent that was true, but research had shown the amygdala, that primitive, reactionary part of our brain, fed information to our facial muscles faster than our conscious mind could control them.

I'd been watching Diana when I showed her the picture of John, and for a half second, maybe less, a look of fear and sadness went across her face. It was subtle, and if I hadn't been watching for it, I would have missed it. Later, I'd look at a video recording and make sure I hadn't been making it up, but I was pretty sure I'd struck a nerve.

I held the picture up.

"Who was he to you? A friend? Lover? Enemy?"

Her eyes kept going away from the picture, then going back again as if they were pulled there. She had extremely fair skin, and I saw the beginnings of a flush start. Against her now red skin, I could see the faint white lines of a network of fine scars on her temple, cheek, and jawline.

"Gotcha," I said.

She took a deep breath, getting control of herself.

"You should really talk to my boss."

With that, the flush faded, and she started deep, even breathing. Her eyes unfocused. I was tempted to snap my fingers in front of her nose to see if she reacted.

It was kind of spooky.

I left the tablet on the table, with the picture of John still on the screen. There was nothing sensitive on it, so she couldn't cause any mischief with it, although I was halfway hoping she would try to pick it up and send out a message or visit a website or something. Anything would give us some insight. I figured she was too much of a pro for that though.

Bolle was staring at the screen, tapping a finger on the desktop when I walked back into the command center.

"Now what?" I asked.

"She knows John," he said.

"You saw it too."

"Yes. I'm guessing she's a three letter."

"Three letter" was a euphemism for an intelligence officer from one of the big agencies, Central Intelligence Agency, Defense Intelligence Agency, National Security Agency, etc. I had a feeling Bolle was probably right. The question was what to do about it. It wasn't like we could call up the local CIA safe house and ask them to come vouch for their case officer.

"I thought they weren't supposed to operate inside the US," Alex said.

Technically, she was correct, but in reality, it was much murkier than that. I'd just started in Major Crimes after 9/11 and we'd all been going nuts trying to keep track of various extremist groups, along with the FBI and a bunch of other agencies. The CIA had been an acknowledged, and often unseen presence in all of it.

"There's somebody at the front gate," Casey said. She panned a video camera to zoom in on a car sitting at our front gate. The driver shut off the headlights, and we could see a single male occupant. He held a cell phone up where the camera could see it, dialed and held it up to his face.

On the desk, Diana's phone started ringing.

"Let's let her answer it," Bolle said. He was squinting at the grainy picture on the screen.

I carried the ringing phone down the hall and set it down in front of Diana. She was so still I was tempted to check her for a pulse.

"It's for you," I said.

She picked up the phone.

"Hart Wildlife Photography, where we bring the wild to life."

That particular slogan hadn't been on her business cards. I would have bet a truckload of vintage Fender Stratocasters it was her duress code.

She listened for a few seconds, then hung up the phone and locked it.

"My boss is at the front gate. Do you think you could let him in?"

She smirked at me, then went back to staring at the wall.

Even though it was just one guy, we didn't take any chances. We geared up with vests and rifles. Casey opened the outer gate, shut it behind the silver Lexus, and it stopped immediately in front of another gate. Effectively it was penned in until we decided to let it go.

"Driver! Step out of the vehicle!" I yelled from behind a concrete barricade. My rifle was almost, but not quite pointed at the guy.

A silver-haired man stepped out. He wore big round glasses and looked to be not quite sixty. He was wearing a nice suit, even in the heat. His hands were empty.

"Hello Sebastian!" he said. "Is all this really necessary?"

Beside me, Bolle sighed and let his rifle hang on its sling.

"Put the guns away," he said. "I know him."

He stepped out from behind cover.

"Hello, Hubbard."

CHAPTER NINE

I didn't like Hubbard. He exuded a sort of upper class, Ivy league, prep school vibe that made my skin crawl. Part of it was because people like him had always looked down on me, even after I'd managed to learn which fork to use when, and had lost the Tennessee accent. The other reason was people like him always seemed to be wearing a mask. There wasn't a genuine facial expression or word to be found with guys like Hubbard, and I didn't trust that.

Bolle ushered me, Diana and Hubbard into his office. Somehow, I'd fallen into the role of Bolle's second-in-command without it ever being made formal, so I was to be privy to these hush-hush meetings.

Bolle poured tea. I resisted the urge to drink it with my pinky sticking out, just to be ironic.

Hubbard turned to Diana. "It's ok to declare."

She wrinkled up her nose at that and accepted a teacup from Bolle.

"Diana and I both work for CIA," Hubbard said as he accepted a sugar cube from Bolle and dropped it in his tea.

"So Marshall was one of yours," I said. I took a sip of the tea. It tasted like boiled socks.

Hubbard smiled like I was a child that had said something mildly amusing. It made me want to punch him.

"Marshall was an independent contractor. He was very useful to us but it appears his operation was compromised at some point. We're still not sure of his involvement."

"By compromised you mean his men were shipping American women overseas?"

"It's regrettable mistakes were made," Hubbard said, and took a sip of tea.

That just made me want to punch him more.

"Why are you here, Hubbard?" Bolle asked.

Hubbard stirred his tea.

"Marshall has become a major problem. The human trafficking was bad enough. I don't think anyone can argue that the attacks at the reservoir and the zoo were linked to Rickson Todd, Marshall's key associate. It's unfortunate he's no longer around to give an accounting for himself."

He gave me a nod at that. If he wanted me to apologize for killing Todd, he was going to be disappointed.

"Anyway. Now Henderson seems to be having delusions of grandeur and fantasizing that he'll be able to run for political office."

I wanted to ask Hubbard what bothered them the most: the human trafficking, the terror attacks, or the fact that Marshall was making a spectacle of himself in public.

"Where is he?" I asked.

I got that amused smile again. A month ago I probably would have hit him, but I'd had time to catch up on my sleep.

"We don't know. He somehow managed to make a Gulfstream business jet disappear. We've had every technical and human intelligence source available to us looking for that plane and it appears to just be gone."

He turned to Bolle.

"You and I have been at odds in the past, Sebastian, but I think now is a time we should work together."

Bolle seemed to consider that for a while.

"What do you have to offer?" he said finally.

"Information sharing," Hubbard said. "We work together to find Marshall. When he's found, I fade into the woodwork, and you take the credit."

"Ok," Bolle said, tapping his finger on the desk in that habit that annoyed me so much. "Give me some information."

Hubbard had some microexpressions of his own. The flicker of annoyance was brief, but it was real. Hubbard was like a man at a card table that was trying to bluff everyone into believing he had aces when he really didn't.

"Right now, I don't think we know anything you don't," Hubbard said.

"That's not much to go on," Bolle said.

"It's also not true," I said.

Both Hubbard and Bolle looked at me like I'd spoken out of turn while the adults were talking. I gritted my teeth and told myself when this was over, I wouldn't deal with people like this anymore.

I nodded at Diana. "How did you know John?"

Her mouth compressed into a hard, flat line and she looked at her boss. He gave her an almost imperceptible nod.

"We were in the same unit in the Army," she said. Unconsciously, her hand traced the network of scars on her cheek. "When we got out, we went our separate ways. He went to work for private contractors, I went to work for Langley."

That story had the ring of truth. Unlike, Delta and SEAL Team Six, the Intelligence Support Activity was rumored to have a high number of female operators. After just a few years in service, they would be prime targets to be poached by either CIA or a private contractor.

"What did he tell you about Mack and Marshall?" I asked. It was a pretty standard investigators trick, asking a question that assumed part of the answer.

She shook her head, even before I was done asking the question, usually a sign of truthfulness.

"Nothing. I never had a chance to talk to him."

I leaned back in my chair, satisfied that Diana was telling me the truth about that, at least.

"We were certainly curious what Mr. Macklin might have shared with you during your meeting," Hubbard said.

Bolle fielded that one. "He wanted to start a conversation about testifying in return for potential immunity for any wrongdoing he might have committed. We agreed to consider his offer, but learned nothing of any substance before he was killed."

Bolle could tell a bald-faced lie with the best of him. He didn't even blink.

Hubbard put his cup on the desk and stood.

"Well, in that case, it doesn't sound like we have much to offer each other at the moment. I do hope you'll consider my offer of information sharing in the future. I'll give Miss Hunt a ride and we'll get out of your way."

Bolle didn't object. It was curious to watch the two of them. The world of innuendo, double meanings, barbed comments, and outright lies wasn't my natural environment. I'd grown up in a culture where differences between men were frequently solved with a knock down drag out fight. There had certainly been a few off the books boxing matches during my time in the Rangers as well. Cops were known to have the occasional shouting matches. In my early days at the Bureau, fisticuffs had been frowned on, but not unheard of.

Bolle walked with them back to the sally port. Dalton and I watched them shake hands on the video monitor in the command center. As they drove out the gate, Casey stuck her head in the doorway. She was wearing a pair of coveralls, and there was a smudge of grease on her cheek.

"Did you get them placed?" I asked.

"Yep. Both transmitters are installed."

She walked over to a laptop and called up a website.

"Both GPS trackers are broadcasting."

While we'd been drinking tea and sharing lies, Casey and Henry had descended on Hubbard's car like a NASCAR pit crew. The first GPS tracker they'd installed would be moderately difficult to find. It was affixed by zip ties to the undercarriage of the car and broadcast continuously. Experienced spook that he was, Hubbard would probably find it.

The second was more ingenious. Affixed inside the engine compartment with a fast setting epoxy, it would only broadcast while the car was moving. The theory was if Hubbard or his counter-surveillance team used a spectrum analyzer or signal scanner to check for trackers on the car, they would only do it while the car was parked.

"Good work," Bolle said as he walked in the door. He looked over Casey's shoulder at the screen.

"What can you tell us about our new friend?" I asked as I debated getting a cup of coffee. There was a risk it would keep me awake, but I had to do something about the aftertaste of that awful tea.

"He's probably a sociopath," Bolle said. "I ran into him in Iraq. I was never able to determine exactly what he was up to, but he was hip deep in running the Cascade Aviation contract."

Up until now, the phone Mack had given me had been sitting on a desk inside a plastic baggie. We wanted to be able to see the display in case a call came in, but didn't want to let anyone eavesdrop on us in the command center. We experimented in our own phones and determined a regular old sandwich baggie attenuated the audio enough that we could talk freely.

"Hey, look," Casey said and pointed. The phone screen lit up with an incoming message.

Casey put her fingers to her lips and pulled the phone out of the bag. She handed it to me.

I want to talk to Dent Miller. Respond via text.

I looked at Bolle. He shrugged.

"Might as well."

This is Miller, I typed laboriously. The damn keys were never big enough for my fingers.

What year was your Chevy truck made? The reply was almost instant.

It's a Ford, and it's a 1972.

"I'm starting to trace," Casey said from behind her laptop.

There was an almost thirty-second pause before the next message came.

Mascot of the high school you went to?

I felt like I was opening an online banking account.

Lion, I typed. What he was doing made sense. An impostor could figure these answers out, but would likely need at least a few minutes to research them.

Don't have much time. I want out. I want immunity. In return I give you everything you need to nail Marshall.

Bolle was reading over my shoulder.

"Tell him he needs to give us something," he said.

Need something from you, I typed.

"He's in Eastern Oregon," Casey said. "I'm narrowing it down."

We all sat there and stared at the phone as if willing another message to come through. Finally, it buzzed again.

Can't talk any longer. You are already tracing phone. Here's a picture for you. More later. May contact you via other means. Identifier will be CRYPTER.

I opened the picture attached to the message. From the curved ceiling and round windows, I realized it was the interior of a small business jet. Strapped to the deck against the aft bulkhead was a cube-shaped object wrapped in plastic shrink wrap.

I squinted, trying to make it out on the small screen.

"What the hell is that?" I asked.

"Money," Bolle said. "Lots and lots of money."

CHAPTER TEN

"We're guessing it's pretty close to a hundred million dollars," Casey said.

Now that the picture was projected up on the wall in our conference room, it was easy to see it was bundles of shrink-wrapped money.

"That's assuming it's hundred dollar bills," Casey said.

"Oh, I'm sure they are," Bolle said. "Tell me about the plane."

"The interior is consistent with a Gulfstream G100, the same model as the Cascade Aviation jet that departed the Portland airport without authorization right after the reservoir attack. By comparing known measurements of the interior of the plane, we were able to estimate the size of the cubes of money. There are three of them, each about 130 cubic feet and weighing in the neighborhood of 660 pounds."

She paused and blinked. I think we were all trying to wrap our head around that much money. I'd seen some pretty good hauls come out of dope busts, but they had all been orders of magnitude smaller than this.

"Where is it?" Bolle asked.

"Eastern Oregon," Casey said. "Near a town called Lehigh Valley."

"Where the hell is that?" I asked. Sometimes it was easy to forget there was quite a bit of territory on the east side of the Cascade Mountains. It was like a different world over there.

"Mueller County. It's damn near Idaho."

Casey called up a satellite map.

"Specifically we triangulated the signal to a place called Freedom Ranch. It actually has an airstrip and a hangar."

The satellite photo showed plenty of arid, rugged country, with a few scattered buildings and a long ribbon of tarmac that was the airstrip.

"The strip is long enough for that Gulfstream to land, but probably not long enough for it to take off again," Jack said. "Hell of a thing to do with a sixty million dollar aircraft. We've been looking all over the Pacific Rim for that damn plane. Turns out they flew out to sea, did a u-turn and headed back inland. They probably stayed low and weren't even in the air much more than an hour."

"Seems like somebody would have seen a low flying aircraft like that," I wondered aloud.

Jack shook his head. "Not necessarily. There's plenty of places in Oregon where you could stay at about a thousand feet and be off radar as long as your transponder was turned off. My guess is they had a route planned ahead of time that gave them a low probability of observation. Once they made it out over the mountains, their chances of being seen would go way down."

I took Jack's word for it. Sneaking into foreign countries in an aircraft was his forte. It turned out your average third world dictatorship had better radar coverage of its airspace than big swaths of the United States.

"Freedom Ranch is owned by a guy named Owen Webb. He's a big deal in anti-government circles. He always wants to graze his cattle on BLM land but not pay the fees."

Casey clicked her remote again. Now we were looking at a picture of two guys standing under a "Don't Tread On Me!" flag and mugging for the camera.

"The guy on the right is Webb. We all know the guy on the left."

I recognized Henderson Marshall right away. Webb and he looked like two peas in a pod, both were men in their sixties wearing western attire that was way too clean for them to have done any actual work. Marshall was taller. Webb was stockier.

"I wonder if he's still there," Alex said.

"The photo of the money was time-stamped two days ago," Casey said.

"Looks like we need to go to Eastern Oregon," Bolle said.

"Road trip!" Casey said.

"I call shotgun," I said.

CHAPTER ELEVEN

We left at dawn the next morning. Casey, Alex and I rode in a Charger. We were supposed to be an advance party while the rest of the crew frantically packed up the gear we would need to take our show on the road. Alex drove most of the way, while Casey curled up in the back like a cat and took a nap. I sat in the passenger seat with nothing to do but pore over investigative files on my laptop.

In the last few weeks, we'd raided every Cascade Aviation facility we could find, traveling all over the state to hangars, maintenance facilities, and offices. We'd also searched Marshall's private residences, a palatial mansion outside of Salem, a beach house at the coast, and a cabin up in the mountains outside of Welches. We were drowning in information. Most of it was mundane. Even a super secret private military contractor like Cascade Aviation kept invoices and billing records for companies that stocked the vending machines in the employee break room and delivered toilet paper.

We'd even seized the records from Marshall's Political Action Committee. We'd expected a big legal fight over that one, but in the end, his lawyers threw up their hands and walked away. It was tough to bill hours when your client disappeared and all his assets were seized by the government.

We'd been working through it slowly, pulling hours in front of the computer, looking for clues and connections, which often led to more records we seized. If this had been a full-scale FBI investigation, there would have been dozens, maybe a hundred agents and analysts digging through the records. On Bolle's team, loyalty mattered more than ability, so it was just our band of misfits and rogues doing the digging.

Webb had been on the list of leads to check out. He was a major donor to Marshall's PAC, and cell phone records showed the two talked a couple of times a month. Maybe in another week or two, we would have gotten to him and one of us would have had a blinding flash of insight about the rich rancher that happened to own his own air strip.

The trip to Mueller County took just over seven hours, and it was like journeying to a different world. First, we cruised down the scenic Columbia River Gorge, sandwiched between big rigs and commuters. The farther east we moved, the browner and more desolate the country became. At the town of Boardman, the river bent to the north, and the interstate bent to the south. The scenery always reminded me of something out of an old John Wayne or Clint Eastwood western. We left the world of strip malls and chain restaurants behind, trading it for honest to god general stores that sold everything from baby food to shotgun shells, and little mom and pop restaurants that were heavy on beef, potatoes and beer.

We actually swung into Idaho for a little while on the interstate, before bending back into Oregon on Highway 95. We finally stopped at Lehigh Valley, about 30 miles shy of Freedom Ranch. Alex pulled into the parking lot of the KW Cafe. I saw a pair of familiar looking pickup trucks in the parking lot. One of them was hitched up to a big fifth wheel camper.

The inside of the cafe smelled like fried meat and fresh coffee, and my stomach started growling right away. I saw three familiar faces in a booth near the back, where the front door could be easily observed, and the back exit was readily accessible.

Dale Williams stood up as we approached, and shook my hand. I knew the old rancher was on the downhill side of seventy, but you'd never know it by looking at him. He was lean, with forearms like sinewy cables poking out of the sleeves of his rolled up work shirt. His sons were carbon copies. Robert was more muscular. Daniel was taller. But as soon as you walked in the room there was no mistaking that they were father and sons.

"Good to see you, Dent," Dale said. "You all sure are a long way from Portland."

Dale was about three hundred miles from his own ranch outside of Redmond, but Lehigh Valley had much more in common with Redmond than it did with Portland. As the waitress approached, her eyes slid over the Williams clan, in their jeans, work shirts, boots and ball caps, without a second glance, but she looked the rest of us over pretty hard, particularly Casey, who was wearing a black leather jacket and a Fugazi t-shirt. At least her hair was something resembling a natural human color.

After we ordered, I filled Dale in on recent events, using very broad terms and without naming names. The odds were we weren't going to be overheard, but you never knew.

"So we need to get to a place where we can see the property in question, and we need some kind of secure base to operate out of," I said.

Dale started to answer, then paused while our food was delivered, then waited for the waitress to leave.

"I looked at those maps you sent me, and I've got a few ideas for observation posts," he said. "I may have an idea for an operating base as well."

Casey poked her sandwich like she expected it to spring off her plate and take off across the floor. The vegetarian offerings were few and far between out here.

"That would be helpful. We couldn't find anything out here for rent or really even for sale on the Internet."

"It doesn't really work that way out here," Dale said. "I've got a fellow in mind that would have plenty of room on his ranch. His politics are a little on the extreme side, and I doubt he has an internet connection. Hell, he probably won't even answer the phone, so I might have to drive out and go see him."

"We need a secure place with room for seven people, good electrical power, and if possible a place to stash the helicopter," Casey said.

Dale nodded. "The place I have in mind will do, I think. We'll get on it tonight. In the meantime, we took the liberty of researching a route to some possible overlooks."

Robert pulled out a topographical map. We spent the rest of lunch pouring over the map in between bites. Most of the land out here belonged to the Bureau Of Land Management and was leased by various ranchers to run their cattle. The rangeland was crisscrossed with roads in various states of repair. The Williams clan had been busy and had plotted a route that would get us to a ridge overlooking Freedom Ranch. Dale was nicely presenting it to us as if he was asking our opinion, but the truth was, the rest of us had a vague idea at best of the lay of the land. Dale had spent a couple of years in Vietnam as a sniper, and Daniel and Robert had both done tours in Iraq and Afghanistan, so establishing an observation post was second nature to both of them.

Their plan was solid. I wanted to get a lay of the land myself, but we would need to come up with a plan later on how we were going to keep the place manned.

I picked up the check for Dale and his boys on my government credit card and we all stepped outside in the hot sunlight. I felt my nose hairs kind of crisp when I breathed in. As everyone was climbing into vehicles, I drew Dale aside.

"I appreciate the help, Dale."

"Least I can do." He stuck a stick of gum in his mouth and started chewing. He'd been trying to quit smoking of late.

"How's Mandy?"

Mandy was my old partner. She'd once been a promising young detective, now thanks to being beaten and nearly killed, she struggled with the aftereffects of a traumatic brain injury and rarely left the house. Dale was her father.

He looked off in the distance.

"I'm not sure what's worse, watching her think she was going to get better, or watching her realize she isn't. We take it day by day."

I'd visited Mandy pretty frequently in the months right after she'd been hurt, then sort of tapered off. Part of it was Marshall's people had decided to try to kill me, but part of it was it just hurt too bad to watch her struggle.

"We're going to try to take Marshall alive," I said. I didn't know how many people Dale had killed in his life, and I would never be rude enough to ask, but I was pretty sure the number would be staggering. The vast majority of them hadn't had a hand in almost killing his daughter. I was pretty sure he could smoke Marshall and his heart rate wouldn't even go up, but I needed him to be ok with the idea of capturing him instead.

He knew what I was thinking.

"I'm on board, and so are my boys. We rather relish the idea of Marshall having a big, burly amorous roommate, in fact, but the second it looks like he might get away, our plans are going to change."

"Fair enough," I said, and we both headed to our vehicles.

Out of the corner of my eye, I saw the waitress through the tinted windows of the cafe. She jerked her hand down and hid it behind her leg as I turned my head. I was pretty sure I'd seen a cell phone in her hand.

Interesting. She'd either been making a phone call while she watched us, or had been snapping a photo.

I gave her a frank stare and she turned on her heel and walked deeper in the cafe. I was tempted to go badge her, but I wanted to get up on the ridge over the ranch. I put her in my mind as something to deal with later.

Dale took the lead in his truck, followed by Daniel pulling the big trailer, while we brought up the rear. We soon left Highway 95 and started working our way up a network of range roads. I had a handheld GPS and was glad as I was soon disoriented. I did make a mental note that we needed some different vehicles. Everybody out here either drove a truck or a big SUV. The Charger wasn't very low profile even back in Portland, but out here we might as well have been driving a marked car with a light bar and everything.

We pulled off into a primitive campsite, basically a flat spot with room for parking with a fire ring and little else. The Williams busied themselves with unhooking the trailer, and we helped Casey unload some equipment from the trunk of the Charger. She was going to remain here and get the beginnings of a command post set up.

The trailer was designed to accommodate people up front, like a standard camp trailer, and also haul horses in the rear. As much as part of me fancied the idea of roaming the range on a stallion, I was somewhat relieved to see a pair of four-wheeler ATV's in the back instead.

"We've just got the two," Robert said. "We did bring extra helmets though."

I strapped my rifle and backpack to the rack on the back of Dale's ATV, and Alex did the same with hers on the back of Robert's. Dale had a worn old Remington 700 strapped to his rack, while Robert had a more modern, .308 semi-auto very much like mine and Alex's. People driving around on four wheels with rifles strapped to them wouldn't necessarily attract that much attention out here.

I hopped on behind Dale and hung on. The ride wasn't that bad. He was a skilled and conservative driver, but the dust was ever present and insidious. Robert took the lead, following a route on the GPS strapped to his handlebar. Dale stayed well behind and off to the side, but we still were enveloped in a cloud of brown more often than not. I could feel it getting in my mouth, nose, and ears. I made a mental note to clean my guns well.

The road got worse the farther we went, and we gained elevation as we headed for a big rock escarpment. The landscape out here was both foreign and beautiful. It was hard to judge distances accurately. What I thought was a tree several miles away turned out to be a sage bush only a couple hundred yard off, then the exact opposite happened. There was no sign of human beings as far as I could see other than the narrow set of wheel ruts we were following.

Finally, the road petered out. We stashed the ATVs under some camo nets, shouldered our packs and rifles and started climbing. It was a brutal slog. The midday sun bore down on us and I found myself gasping for breath pretty quick. It didn't help that we were almost a mile above sea level. This part of Oregon was on a high desert plateau. I saw a rattlesnake slither off under a rock and added that to my list of things to worry about.

I was tempted to ask and stop for a rest and a drink of water, but two things kept me going. First, I could see the top, so it wouldn't be much longer, and second, Dale was more than twenty-five years older than me and was charging up the hill like a mountain goat, despite the full pack, rifle, and pistol he wore.

The view from the top was incredible. There was also a breeze, which I enjoyed for a few minutes as I huffed and puffed. Dale and Robert didn't seem to mind a little break. I hate to admit it but I was a little pleased to see that Alex was more than a little out of breath as well

After a break, we found a spot to string a camo net between two rocks and all crawled under it. It was like lying on a griddle that was still warm from frying eggs. We set up a pair of spotting scopes and a high tech digital camera. Casey had shown me how to set it up. I anchored its little tripod to the ground and waited for the "link established" LED to light up, then keyed my radio.

"Casey, are you getting the camera feed?" I asked over the radio.

The camera swiveled back and forth on the tripod.

"Got it," she said.

The radio reception was excellent, courtesy of the fact that there was nothing between us but miles of air.

Exactly how to manage surveillance of Freedeom Ranch had occupied my thoughts for most of the drive out here. It had been a couple of decades, but during my military time, I'd spent plenty of time in hide sights just like this one, surveilling airstrips used by drug cartels in Central America, and warlord compounds in Somalia. Ordinarily, you'd keep an observation post like this manned continuously, and swap out crews every couple of days.

We were a little short-handed for that. We'd need at least two people up here at all times, one watching while the other rested. Three would be preferable. The third person would be responsible for the security of the site. When one person was looking through a high powered spotting scope, and the other was trying to catch some sleep, you could find out a bad guy had a gun screwed in your ear before you even knew it. I wasn't sure how much hardball the opposition was going to play, but better safe than sorry.

Dale and his boys were more than up to the task, and I could fake it, even after all this time, but that was about it. Dalton would have been a natural, of course, except for the inconvenient fact that he still needed a cane to get around. Nobody else had the kind of experience we needed for a gig like this, hence the choice to set up cameras. I was much more comfortable with Casey and Henry sitting in front of a monitor drinking Jolt! Cola than I was with the idea of them huddled under a camo net up here on the ridge.

Dale clicked his tongue. "Looks like somebody had some trouble getting their airplane stopped on that runway," he said in an almost whisper. The target location was miles away, but stealth was as much a mindset as anything else, and noise discipline was a part of that.

He scooted to the side so I could take his place in front of the spotting scope. I was pleased that I automatically remembered old habits. I checked the position of the sun, to ensure it wouldn't reflect off the wide lens of the scope. It had an anti-reflective coating, but it wasn't fool proof. Our ridge ran roughly north to south, and we were to the east of the ranch. Right now the sun was off to my left, in the south, and there was no danger of it reflecting off our optics. We'd have to be careful in the evenings though.

I adjusted the focus for my eye. I was looking through a mile of shimmering, hot air at the surface of the runway. The heat mirage made the tarmac look almost like it was a liquid, undulating back and forth, but I could still make out the streaks of rubber on the runway. Down near the end, there were deep gouges in tarmac.

"Huh," I said, wishing Jack was here. We'd have to try to get some pictures to show him.

I panned the scope around carefully. It was a big lens but it was still like looking through a soda straw. At this magnification, even small adjustments shifted the field of view by dozens of yards. There was a small single engine prop plane parked on the apron in front of the hangar. The hangar doors were shut. It looked like an awfully big hangar for a ranch.

"I wonder how big that opening it?" I wondered aloud.

"I already mil'd it," Dale said. "Sixty feet, give or take."

The spotting scope reticle was etched with evenly spaced dots, called "mil-dots." Assuming you knew the range, which we did courtesy of a laser range-finder, you could count the dots and use them to figure out the size of an object. I could count the dots and laboriously do the math with a pencil, paper and preferably a calculator, but Dale could do it without even thinking about it.

"Wide enough," I said. The jet we were looking for had a fifty-five foot wingspan.

"Tall enough too," Dale said, as usual, one step ahead of me. "I find it suggestive that little prop job is parked out in the open instead of in the hangar."

He had a point. Planes were expensive, and there was no reason to have one sitting out, exposed to the elements unless there was no room inside. I panned around the rest of the ranch. There were several sizable outbuildings, garages, shops, that sort of thing. There were a couple bunkhouses, then the main house itself, which was a monster. I saw a half-dozen pickups parked here and there.

"Two guys coming out of the bunkhouse," Alex said. She was lying on her belly looking through binoculars like this was the sort of thing she did all the time.

I panned the scope around just in time to see the bunkhouse door slam shut. Several seconds later the sound carried to us, a reminder of how vast the distances were here. Two men walked across the gravel parking lot in front of the bunkhouse. Through the shimmering air, I could see they were wearing tactical pants, polo shirts, and handguns strapped to their thighs. They each carried a rifle. They got in one of the pickups and drove off on an access road deeper into the ranch.

"That sure looks like a patrol to me," Robert said, from beside me where he was looking through his own scope.

I had to agree. Interesting. Those guys hadn't been dressed like cowboys. They looked like the private military contractors the government paid to do stuff overseas.

We gave it a few more minutes, but nothing else happened. Out over the valley, a vulture drifted lazily around, soaring from thermal to thermal without having to flap its wings.

"Let's get the rest of the gear set up," I said.

We unloaded the backpacks. We set up a second camera. It would be good to have two independent views of the ranch, plus if one of the damn things broke we wouldn't be completely blind. We also set up a couple of antennas and some gear that Casey could use to spy on radio and cell phone communications in and around the ranch. As she confirmed with Casey via radio that it was all working, I took a swallow of flat, plastic tasting water out of my canteen.

The climb down was quicker, but harder on my knees. As I held on to Dale's four-wheeler on the ride back, I had little to do but ruminate. The ranch was a tough nut to crack. If we tried to raid the place, they would see us coming from a long way off. The two armed men we saw were no doubt only the tip of the iceberg. Hell, this was Eastern Oregon, every ranch out here was liable to have a good sized armory, even the ones that didn't have a plane full of a hundred million dollars.

We stopped back at the trailer and I spit dirt as I took off my helmet. Casey stepped out looking the exact opposite of a federal cop wearing cut-off shorts, a tank top, and a big straw hat. I hoped she had some sunscreen somewhere.

From inside I heard the muted sound of radio chatter.

"Is it all working?" I asked.

She nodded. "It sounds like they have two trucks out patrolling. They check in every fifteen minutes."

"That sounds a little extreme to make sure nobody wanders off with their cows," I said.

"Now what?" she asked.

Dale untied a damp bandanna from his face where he'd put it to block the dust, and I wondered why I hadn't thought of that.

"I thought I'd wander up the road a ways, and see if we can't talk to my friend about setting up your headquarters on his land. Robert and Daniel can stay here and help Casey with surveillance."

Unspoken in that was they'd also keep her from being abducted and murdered if Marshall's people figured out we were here. I nodded my thanks.

I looked at my phone and saw I had zero signal.

"We'll head back to town, and get a couple of rooms at that motel we saw," I said. "Even if your friend comes through, it will be good to have a space in town we can use."

The air conditioning was blessedly cool in the car on the way back to town. Alex didn't seem to be in much of a mood to talk, so I was content just to recline my seat back and shut my eyes. I didn't sleep, exactly, just let my brain slip into neutral for a little while. It had been a long day.

At some point I must have fallen asleep, because I jerked awake, realizing that Alex was pulling the car over to the side of the road. Up head I saw Lehigh Junction, a smattering of a dozen or so buildings sitting in the middle of all the brown.

"What's going on?" I said. My tongue felt thick and furry. I needed to drink more water. I realized I could see flashing red and blue lights in my side view mirror.

"We're getting pulled over," Alex said. "Looks like we're about to meet local law enforcement."

CHAPTER TWELVE

My first impression of the Sheriff of Meuller County was that of a large hat, a pair of boots, and not much else in between. He was not a very tall man. When he got closer, I could see the mustache.

Alex had her credentials ready when she stepped up to the window. He put his hand on the butt of his gun.

"Step out of the car please, both of you."

Alex shot me a sidelong look. I shrugged and got out.

I disliked him the second I got a good look at him. He was a sawed-off son of a bitch, with general's stars on his shirt collar, a paunch, and spit-shined cowboy boots. He was wearing a big Smith and Wesson revolver with stag grips in a hand carved leather holster. I couldn't tell if it was a .357 or .44 Magnum from this far away, but my money was on the .44.

"ID," he said, and held out his left hand. The right was still firmly on his gun butt. Unconsciously I started calculating the odds that I could draw and drill him in the face before he could react and get a shot off from that big Magnum. If he missed with the first shot, I figured I could empty half a magazine before he recovered from recoil.

We both plunked our IDs in his hand. Alex was taller than him, and I could tell he didn't like it. She was trying to hide a smile, but alarm bells were ringing in my head. She'd grown up in Portland. The Portland Police Bureau wasn't perfect, but you could expect a certain level of professionalism. I'd grown up in Appalachia, where the local deputies could get away with all sorts of nefarious shit.

He ran his thumb over the surface of our credentials like he didn't believe they were real.

"I'm Sheriff Neal, of Meuller County. Why wasn't I informed that there were two Justice Department Investigators on their way here?"

Even though Alex was standing closer, he directed the question at me. I was tempted to defer to her to answer it, but I didn't want to antagonize him more than our mere presence apparently had.

"We didn't even know we were coming here until this very morning," I said. "Our office values cooperating and liaison with local officials. I'm sorry no one from our office has been in touch with you. It's an extremely fast-moving investigation. I'm sure it's just an oversight."

Alex gave me a raised eyebrow. I'd been working on my diplomacy lately.

He tapped our badge wallets against his ample belly. I could tell he wasn't wearing body armor. In a way I didn't blame him. It was awfully damn hot out here, but I wondered if that was as much a mark of machismo as the hand cannon.

"What's the nature of your investigation in my county?" He had a gruff voice, but it sounded affected, like something he practiced in the car when no one was listening.

"You have to understand, you're putting me in a really delicate situation. I could wind up in hot water with my boss for speaking out of turn. Also, I'm just a little wheel in a big machine. I don't have the big picture."

He scrunched up his face, in a look I suspected was supposed to be intimidating, and didn't say anything.

I took a half step toward him, looked around like I expected somebody to be hiding behind the sagebrush eavesdropping, and lowered my voice.

"All I can say right now Sheriff is that if you happen upon anyone in your county that looks to be of Middle Eastern descent, I'd sure appreciate it if you would call our watch officer."

I pulled a business card out of my pocket with my left hand and we did an awkward little shuffle where he tried to hand me our ID and take the card at the same time. Finally, he remembered to take his hand off the gun and the whole thing got much easier.

"I'll expect a call from your boss no later than tomorrow morning," he all but barked.

I nodded. "Sure thing Sheriff. Now if you'll excuse me, my assistant here is pretty tuckered out from a long day, and we both need to get our beauty rest."

He gave a curt nod at that, spun on his heel and seated himself back in his patrol truck.

We got back in the car and I handed Alex her credentials. She was silent until Sheriff Neal pulled around us in a spray of gravel and drove through town going way too fast, then she punched me on the arm.

"Your assistant? Tuckered out? What the hell was that?"

I rubbed my arm. "Hey, I was just trying to speak the local lingo. I almost called you 'little lady' but I was afraid you'd shoot me right in front of him."

"A strong possibility," she said. "What the hell was that?"

I told her about the waitress at the cafe earlier.

"I bet she dimed the sheriff up the second we left the cafe," I said. "I tried to explain to Bolle that there was no way we were going to keep a low profile out here. The sheriff is probably on the phone with Webb right now."

She drummed her fingers on the steering wheel as she waited for the single stoplight in town to change.

"Seriously? You think he's sold out?"

I snorted. "Rural sheriff with a millionaire living in his county? I'd be surprised if he wasn't."

The light changed and we pulled into the Shepherd's Rest Motel. Judging from the thirty odd rooms, and the fact that there were three cars in the parking lot, it didn't appear that vacancy would be an issue. Alex went into the office while I called Bolle and gave him a synopsis of the day's events. I tried to let him know that my fears that we would be outed almost immediately had been realized without making it sound like I was saying "I told you so."

"Sounds like we're off to a hell of a start," Bolle said. "We're ready to leave whenever you give us the word."

I looked around the motel parking lot. I could see the front door of the cafe from here, and would have bet a long dollar my waitress friend was inside watching me. The lot was visible from the gas station, the general store, and the trailer park across the street. The sun was going down and it was getting dark quick here in the land of very few streetlights. As I watched I saw interior lights come on in the trailers and businesses, but there were plenty of dark windows where somebody could be watching me with a camera, or even a rifle scope and I would never know it.

"Anybody that shows up here is going to stick out," I said. "So unless you fancy camping out on the BLM land, let's wait until Dale talks to his friend. I feel like we've already lost strategic surprise, but maybe we can maintain a tactical advantage if we can slip the rest of you into the county."

"Agreed," Bolle said. "I think we'll split the difference and move to Dale's ranch in Redmond. We can stash all our equipment and the helo there, and be a couple of hours closer to you in case something happens."

I agreed that was a good plan and signed off, just as Alex came out with four keys.

"The clerk was monosyllabic, but managed to get us two pairs of adjoining rooms," she said.

For proprieties sake, we each took a separate room, then opened the connecting doors. I briefed her about my conversation with Bolle as she unbraided her hair.

"I don't think I was prepared for how small this place is," she said. "I've always looked at places like this as a place to stop and get gas, maybe something to eat. I feel like there's no way to be anonymous."

"There isn't," I said. "I grew up in a town not much bigger than this. It's a different world"

She stifled a yawn.

"I feel like I've got dust in places there shouldn't be dust. How about we both shower, then find something to eat."

It was clear from her body language she wasn't inviting me to shower with her. There was a rhythm to the push and pull of our relationship. After we spent hours together, working, it was like she needed some time by herself before she could engage with me again on a personal level. Even though I was a fellow introvert, I'd had to learn not to take it personally.

It only took me a few minutes to shower off the dust, dry off and get dressed, but the water from her bathroom was still running full blast. I found myself antsy and unable to sit still. Television didn't appeal to me so I grabbed the ice bucket and stepped out. The temperature had dropped fifteen degrees since we went inside, and it was hard dark outside. We'd probably need jackets when we went out for dinner.

The ice machine was tucked away in a stairwell. It grunted, wheezed, and finally deposited a half bucket of ice before giving up with a final-sounding thunk, accompanied by a burning electrical smell. I shook my head and grabbed the bucket.

There was a new vehicle in the parking lot, a big pickup with a camper shell, parked right next to our Charger, nose out. The damn thing was huge, with over-sized tires and some kind of suspension lift.

I shook my head. I liked bigger vehicles, but that must have been like driving an aircraft carrier.

I shifted the ice bucket under my left arm and reached in my pocket for my room key.

"Ow!" I slapped my hand on the back of my neck at a sudden pain. It seemed like there shouldn't be mosquitoes out in the high desert.

My lips and fingers suddenly felt numb, and my eyes went unfocused. I swayed back and forth, fighting for balance. I felt hands on my arms and felt myself being lowered to the ground.

I tried to yell but "nnnnn..." was all that came out.

"Grab his legs. Don't forget the ice," I heard a voice say from far away. I tried to look, but couldn't move my head. All I could see was the bright, diamond-like stars in the high desert air. More hands grabbed my legs and I found myself being carried towards my car. A hand dug into my pocket.

"I've got the keys," a different voice said. They were both men's voices, muffled somehow.

I heard the car door click open, and they stuffed me into the passenger seat. My fingers and toes felt like they were on fire like they were waking up from going numb, and I found I could move my head a little bit.

"The paralytic is wearing off. Hurry."

Finally, I saw one of them. His head was wrapped in a shemagh, a traditional middle eastern headscarf. All I could see of his face was two glittering eyes. He was wearing a heavy canvas work coat and gloves. He pushed my head back into the headrest with a pillow covered by a trash bag. Another guy leaned in the driver's door and pinned my arm, while a third grabbed my left arm.

I could move, but I was still weak. I fought the rising panic that came from feeling like I couldn't breathe due to the pillow.

Smart, I thought. The trash bag keeps fiber from being transferred to me, or my DNA from getting on the pillow.

I tried to fight, but couldn't. I felt a sharp prick in my right arm, and a warm, soft glow spread through my body. I felt my muscles go limp again.

"Done," one of them said.

They let go of me, and I felt my head loll to the side. A gloved hand put a baggie, a needle, a spoon, and a lighter on the dash in front of me. The door slammed shut, and I heard an engine start next to me.

"Ahhh," I said.

I felt a wave of euphoria like nothing I'd ever felt before, and utter peace. It was nice to forget about Marshall, Bolle, all of the death and destruction of the last several months, and just lie there, feeling like I was floating on a cloud. I hadn't slept well since last fall, and I finally felt like I could just curl up here in the Charger and nod off for a little while.

I looked at the baggie of white powder on the dash and remembered Mack's hotel room. I realized then that I was dying, but part of me just didn't care.

The other part of me was too stubborn to quit. I found the door handle with my right hand and pulled it. I tumbled out onto the pavement. The impact helped bring me around a little, but I couldn't stand up. I tried to crawl, but that didn't work either. I felt warm wetness as my bladder let go.

Fuck it. Just go to sleep, a voice in my head said.

But I didn't. I saw my keys sitting on the ground next to me, and managed to make my hand work well enough to pinch them between my thumb and forefinger. I mashed down on the panic alarm button.

The honking irritated me. I just wanted to be still and enjoy the feeling of being wrapped up in a warm blanket. I almost pushed the button again to make the noise stop but lacked the energy. Instead, I just looked up a the stars, thinking about how pretty they were.

I decided to just shut my eyes and take that nap after all.

"Dent!"

Alex's wet hair was hanging in my face and she was shaking me. I opened my eyes, but couldn't keep them that way.

"Shit!" I wanted to tell her to calm down and not get so excited, but no words would come out.

I heard her pop the trunk on the car, then come back to me. I had the strangest sensation of floating outside of my body. I couldn't see anything, but my hearing was very acute. I heard a zipper, then the crinkling sound of plastic.

Something was jammed into my nose, and I felt a cold mist that made me feel like I was drowning.

"Gahhh!" I said.

The feeling of dreamy well being was gone instantly. My hip and elbow were sore from hitting the pavement, and I had a massive, crushing headache.

"I'm not really doing heroin." For some reason, it seemed super important that she not think I'd been out here shooting up in secret.

"I know," she said. She held a finger to my neck, taking my pulse. Satisfied by what she found, she grabbed the key fob and turned off the panic alarm.

"Can you stand?"

I was surprised to find that I could. Other than a killer headache, I felt mostly normal, compared to how I'd felt moments ago.

I looked around. The big pickup was gone, of course. Our car's trunk was open and Alex's medical kit was on the ground and unzipped. A used Narcan nasal spray was on the ground.

"You saved me again," I said. I shivered, all of a sudden feeling cold. I wasn't sure if it was just in my head, or the aftereffects of the drug.

"Let's go inside," she said.

A woman was standing in the door of the hotel office, staring at us, and down on the end, a guy poked his head out of a motel room door.

"Sorry folks," I said with a wave. "Got a little dehydrated. Not used to the climate."

The woman rolled her eyes and went back inside, and the guy shook his head but decided to stay outside and smoke a cigarette.

Alex shut the trunk, shouldered her medical kit, and grabbed the stuff off the dashboard. Inside the hotel room, she told me to sit down on the bed, then checked me out by shining a light in my eyes and listening with her stethoscope.

"This thing we keep doing where I have to check you out after you dodge getting killed is getting old," she said. "What happened?"

I explained how I'd been attacked. As I sat there in the bright hotel room, it sounded like I was telling a story that had happened to someone else.

She looked at the back of my head.

"There's a little welt there, just below your hairline."

"One of them said something about a paralytic," I said.

She shook her head. "That's some exotic stuff. Could be synthetic, could be plant or even animal based. I guess the goal is to render you helpless then shoot you up full of opiates and make it look like you overdosed. Just like Mack."

"Just like Mack," I said and shivered again. "Am I gonna be ok?"

"You should. The Narcan reverses the opiates almost instantly. Your heart sounds good, and your breathing is fine. I'm going to keep checking on you through the night. What now?"

As if on cue, my phone rang. It was Dale. I put him on speaker.

"Good news, Dent. I found us a place to hang our hats," his voice boomed from the tinny speaker.

"That's good," I said. "It doesn't sound like we are safe now."

I gave him a brief rundown of what had happened to me. The phones were supposed to be secure, and even if they weren't, the other side knew they had just tried to kill me.

"These are some ornery sons of bitches we're up against here," Dale said. "Let's meet where we dropped the trailer. I'll give Casey and the boys a heads up to be extra careful."

We signed off. It was the work of a few minutes for Alex and me to collect our bags. I felt a tight knot of anticipation in my stomach as I stepped through the doorway. I wondered if someone was going to blow us away.

I still had a screaming headache, was a little uncoordinated, and felt alternately feverish and chilled, so Alex drove. There wasn't much light in town, but once we hit the back roads, it was like we'd been swallowed by darkness, except for the paltry swath lit up by our headlights. Our rifles were on the back seat.

"I'm sorry," I said as we rattled down the washboard road.

"For what?"

"For not being more careful. I just walked past that truck like I was out for an evening stroll."

She was quiet for a while, concentrating on her driving. The rear end had a tendency to swing around on these washboard roads.

"You can't be on high alert all the time, Dent," she said finally. "That's what worries me. You're good at this, but all it takes is one slip. We can't keep getting lucky forever."

Exactly those words had been rattling around in my head for quite a while now. We couldn't keep getting lucky forever.

I jumped as the phone in my breast pocket vibrated. It was the CRYPTER phone, still sealed in its plastic bag.

They know you are here, the message read.

No kidding, I thought. I took the phone out of the baggie, not sure what I was going to say in reply when the phone lost signal completely. I put it back in my pocket and concentrated on hanging on tight and looking out for trouble.

CHAPTER THIRTEEN

It was well past midnight by the time our little caravan arrived at our destination. In the dark, I couldn't tell much about it. We drove through a ranch gate and stopped in front of an old farmhouse with a couple of lights burning. In the darkness, I could see vague outlines of outbuildings and farm machinery. When the breeze blew the right way, I could smell cow manure.

"Might as well go inside and meet Rudder," Dale said. While Casey and Dale's sons busied themselves setting up the trailer and various antennae, Alex and I followed Dale up to the porch. He didn't even bother to knock, just walked right in.

The house smelled old. It wasn't an unpleasant smell, exactly. It reminded me of some of the ancient homes up the hollers in Appalachia where I'd grown up, places that had been in the same family for generations. They were houses where babies had been born, old people had died, and lifetimes of family dramas had played out. The floors were wood, with paths worn in the finish, and plenty of uneven boards. Most of the furniture would qualify as antique, but the living room was lit by the glow of a very modern looking big screen television. The John Wayne classic *Sands of Iwo Jima*, was playing with the sound turned off. An old man was sitting in a recliner snoozing.

"Hey, Rudder!" Dale all but yelled.

Rudder's eyes popped open and he slowly got up from his chair. I couldn't tell how old he was. I would have believed anywhere from sixty to ninety. He was short, probably not even 5'6", and had glasses so thick they made his eyes look unnaturally large. He wore an old patched workshirt that had probably been new when I was in elementary school, jeans and suspenders.

"I'm Rudder. Pleased to meet you," he said sticking out a hand. It felt like a piece of leather, and I got the idea he probably could have broken my hand if he'd wanted.

"Dent Miller," I said.

He then introduced himself to Alex, who he seemed much more interested in. While he was trying to make small talk with her, my eye was drawn to the far wall. There were four pictures and a rifle. Two of the pictures I recognized. One was Franklin Deleano Roosevelt. One was John Wayne, a promotional photo from *Rio Bravo* I wasn't mistaken. The third picture was of a guy holding a guitar. It wasn't Bob Dylan, but I still felt like I should know him. The fourth picture was a faded, sepia-toned snapshot of a young guy holding a rifle in a US Army uniform.

The rifle mounted on the wall was the same kind as the one in the picture. It was an old M1 Garand, the US service weapon from World War 2 and Korea. It was in decent shape, but judging from the scuffs in the wood and the wear on the Parkerized finish, it had seen some use. Someone had engraved the words "This Machine Kills Fascists" on the barrel.

That spurred my memory. The dude with the guitar was Woody Guthrie, the folk singer from the 1930's. He'd had a sticker on his guitar that read "This Machine Kills Fascists."

"That's my old rifle," Rudder said from behind me.

"It's a beaut," I said and meant it. I'd served in an era when rifles were made out of plastic and weighed less than seven pounds.

He pulled it off the wall and handed it to me. Out of habit I pulled back a little on the charging handle and saw the shine of a brass cartridge case in the chamber.

"It's loaded," I said.

"Of course it is," Rudder said. "The damn thing is no more than a club if it isn't loaded. Although it's pretty good at that. If you look down there by the toe of the stock, you'll see teeth marks from some poor German bastard I had to take care of after I ran out of ammo."

I flipped the rifle over in my hands and saw what looked very much like the marks of a pair of front teeth. I'd once carried a shotgun with marks on the stock very much like them.

"You carried this in the war?" Suddenly I realized the photo of the young man with the rifle was Rudder. I was trying to do the math on how old he had to be.

"You betcha. We were separated for damn near twenty years. I had to hand her over at the end of the war. I always remembered the serial number, so when the government started selling them off as surplus, I wrote the Director of the Civillian Marksmanship Program and asked for her by name."

"Wow," I said. The rifle seemed even heavier in my hands now. "What unit were you with?"

"Dog Company, 2nd Ranger Battalion."

"Wow," I said again.

In June of 1944, D company of the 2nd Ranger Battalion had landed at Pointe Du Hoc on the Normandy coast. There they had scaled cliffs under heavy fire, so they could blow up German artillery. They started with just over 250 men, and two days later, only 90 of them could still walk and fight.

Dale ambled over.

"Old Dent here spent some time in 3rd Battalion over there in Somalia."

Rudder's face lit up at that. "I'll be damned," he said and shuffled over to a bookcase on the wall. He didn't have to look for what he wanted. He pulled a DVD off the shelf.

I recognized the movie right away as *Blackhawk Down.*

"This one is a cracker jack," he said. "Did they get it right?"

"Mostly," I said. "Not all the details are perfect, but they nailed how the guys acted."

He slapped me on the back. "Well, I'll be damned. It's nice to have all of you here. We'll have to swap war stories when we get a chance."

Rudder and Dale showed us around the rest of the property. The bunkhouses were clean, but a bit dusty, and we could stash the helicopter in the barn. Casey scampered up an old rusty windmill like a squirrel, trailing a rope behind her, and pulled up some antennas and cables. Within a couple of hours, we had a radio link established to the surveillance cameras on the ridge outside Webb's ranch and a working cell phone repeater.

A couple hours before dawn, we went out in a pasture and dodged cow pies as we put infrared strobes on the ground to mark a landing zone. I stood there shivering in the darkness, wishing I'd brought a heavier coat for about fifteen minutes before I heard the helicopter.

It was on us before I knew it. It was a small helicopter, an MD-500, nicknamed the Little Bird, and our pilot Jack had been flying a computer-generated route that kept the noise signature as low as possible. He brought the little egg-shaped aircraft to a hover. In the greenish tinged display on my night vision goggles, it looked like it was surrounded by a green halo due to the static discharge from the blades, but otherwise it was completely blacked out.

Jack let the Little Bird settle on its skids and shut the engine down. I waited until the rotor blades drooped and stopped before walking under them. When I saw Jack switch on his headlamp, I took off my goggles and turned on my own headlamp and walked up.

Bolle climbed out of the co-pilot's seat, looking more than a little green. I'd taken a quick look at the route they'd flown on a map and gotten nauseous just thinking about all the jinking, turning and nap of earth flying through various valleys to get here unobserved. Dalton was in the backseat, his cane beside him. He looked pale, but that was probably more because of the excruciating pain of sitting on the thinly padded seat for a couple of hours with his busted leg than the in-flight shenanigans.

Dalton handed me the ground wheels that attached to the helicopter's skids and I passed them out to the others. We'd practiced this more than a few times and within a half hour we had the Little Bird's blades folded and rolled it into the barn.

"Eddie and Henry will be here in a couple more hours with the rest of our gear," Bolle said as we walked in the trailer. We'd decided to make it our command center. For one thing, Rudder wouldn't have any reason to go inside, and we could keep our conversations secure. For another, we could pack it up and move it at a moment's notice.

While Casey briefed Dalton on the equipment, I gave Bolle more details about the guys who had tried to kill me at the motel.

"And you're sure you're fine now?" He asked. He sounded genuinely concerned.

Instead of answering, I looked at Alex. I'd been trying to put it behind me all night long, but I was hypersensitive to the slightest hint of trouble with my body. I'd been going non-stop all day long, so it made sense that I felt exhausted, but I kept waiting for my heart to skip a beat, or to get dizzy or something.

"I've been monitoring his vitals ever since," Alex said. "Whatever it was, it was fast acting and his system seems to have flushed it out."

Bolle nodded and looked back and forth between us.

"Good," he said. "We can't afford to lose you."

He pulled a tablet out of his briefcase.

"We've managed to pull a list of employees at Freedom Ranch, using IRS and Social Security records. We're hoping to find someone who we can use as a confidential informant."

I scrolled down the list.

"There are twenty-five people on here. Do ranches normally have this many employees?"

Dale looked over my shoulder.

"Not by a long shot. I run almost twice as many cattle as this Webb fellow, and it's just me, the boys, and Mandy. I hire out work from time to time, but I'd be broke in no time if I kept that many hands on salary."

"Huh," I said. "I wonder if one of them is CRYPTER."

"We had the same question," Bolle said. "We're running checks on all the names right now. It's also possible that CRYPTER is one of Marshall's people, and not on the list."

I heard a buzz from the desk beside Casey.

"Speaking of CRYPTER," she said and handed me the phone in its plastic baggie.

I made sure everyone knew to be quiet and pulled it out of the bag. I showed the latest message to Bolle.

"Not exactly news," I said.

"Tell him we need something actionable," Bolle said.

Before I could type that out, another message came in.

Delivery to ranch scheduled tomorrow via UHL commercial courier. Tracking number attached. Suggest you intercept it. Nothing more tonight. CRYPTER out.

Next came a sixteen-digit string of letters and numbers. Casey typed them in to the UHL website.

"It's a shipment from an outfit in Arizona called AeroCrafters. They sell aircraft parts salvaged from wrecked and crashed aircraft."

Up until now, Jack had been standing silently in a corner, bobbing a tea bag up and down in a cup of hot water.

"I wonder if they bent their plane landing it on that short runway. There sure are some hellacious skid marks in those pictures you showed me."

"I thought they couldn't even take off again from that runway, assuming the plane is there in the first place," I said.

Jack sipped his tea.

"Well, technically, that runway isn't long enough to get that Gulfstream airborne, but that assumes two things. One, that you aren't afraid to over speed the engines on takeoff, and two that the plane is at its normal weight. If you go inside a business jet like that and start stripping stuff out like the wet bar, upholstered seats all that business, you could make that plane much lighter. It might be enough to get her airborne."

"What if it isn't?" Casey asked.

"Then you turn a really expensive airplane into a big pile of smoking parts," he said, sipping his tea.

"You think we can get a warrant in time to intercept that shipment?" I asked Bolle.

"I don't care," Bolle said. "Warrant or no warrant, I want what's in that box."

CHAPTER FOURTEEN

In the end, we didn't get the warrant. Bolle was too paranoid about giving up CRYPTER as a source to even apply for one. We were also afraid that a search warrant based on texts sent from an anonymous source would be too much even for the friendliest of Federal judges. So we winged it.

The next morning, even with the air conditioner running, it was hot sitting in the sun along the highway. Fortunately, we didn't have long to wait before the UHL truck came trundling down the road.

Bolle had surprised me on this one. Since we were breaking all sorts of laws, he took the lead. I sat beside him in the passenger seat of the Charger as he pulled out onto the road, flipped on the red and blue flashing lights, and pulled in behind the delivery truck as it stopped on the side of the road. I covered him as he approached the truck.

"Special Agent Lubbock, FBI," he said, flipping his badge wallet open and shut so fast I was surprised he didn't sprain his wrist. "We have a warrant to search the truck and remove a package."

I stifled a grin. Lubbock was my old boss at the Portland Police Bureau. I wasn't sure where he was these days, but he wasn't a cop anymore, and certainly not an FBI agent.

"Uh... I have to call my boss?" The driver looked at him like we were aliens from another planet.

"Remain in the vehicle with your hands in plain sight," Bolle said.

Dale and Jack pulled in behind us in Dale's pickup as I rolled up the back door of the delivery truck. The package we needed was easy to find. It was a six-foot-long wooden crate in the center of the cargo compartment. I grabbed it and grunted, barely managing to move it a couple of inches. It took all four of us to haul it back to the pickup.

As we pried the lid off with a crowbar, Bolle walked back and handed the driver some paperwork that contained a bunch of legal looking nonsense.

"Don't go to the ranch. Give this paperwork to your boss. If you talk about this to anyone else, I'll put you in federal prison. Now leave."

The delivery truck fishtailed and sprayed gravel.

Dale popped the last nail out of the crate with a grunt. I was no aviation expert, but I was pretty sure what we were looking at was a front landing gear for a medium-sized airplane.

Jack practically crawled into the crate with a penlight, muttering and reading off numbers that Dale jotted down on a pad. Our cell phones didn't work out here, but we could reach the radio repeater Casey set up just fine. Jack read the numbers to her over the encrypted link so she could research them and we high tailed it back to Rudder's ranch. No one had driven down the highway since we stopped the delivery truck and we wanted to make our selves scarce. We particularly wanted to avoid being seen by the sheriff or his deputies.

While we were gone, Eddie and Henry had arrived with the rest of our equipment. Eddie was standing outside the trailer with his hands in his pockets and blinking in the bright sunlight.

"I thought places like this only existed in movies," he said as a cow mooed off in the distance.

"Welcome to the country, city boy," I said and chucked him on the shoulder. He gave me a smile that suggested he was getting over the funk he'd been in since the shooting at the zoo. He'd come very close to dying that day, and sometimes people needed a while to bounce back from that.

Casey was grinning when we walked into the trailer.

"It's from a Gulfstream G100," she said. "The part numbers match."

Bolle nodded his head.

"Now we just need some parallel construction."

The landing gear in the back of Dale's truck was pretty damning evidence that there was a Gulfstream G100 parked in the hangar at Webb's ranch. The problem was, it was illegally obtained evidence. Now we'd have to find some legal means of proving what we already knew: that Marshall, the airplane, and the money were at Webb's ranch.

"Try CRYPTER," Bolle said.

Need to talk, I typed.

He surprised me by answering almost right away.

I have five minutes. Be quick.

Need a picture of Marshall at the ranch, I typed. Might as well go for broke.

Trying to get me killed? No way. They are pissed about the airplane part. Trying to come up with a way to move the money.

Bolle frowned. "Tell him to give us a name."

Over twenty people work at the ranch. Give me a name. Somebody I can use.

The phone was silent for minutes, and we all stared at it as if willing another message to come through.

Most of them are security. Don't even try. The ranch hands go into town to party on Friday night. Try one of them. No more time. CRYPTER out.

"That's tonight," Casey said. "I ran the backgrounds of the people on that list. I think I've sorted out which ones are the ranch hands. They are all local. The rest are all from out of town and have military backgrounds, so they must be the security people he was talking about."

"That's helpful," Bolle said. "But how do we get to them?"

"I have an idea," Casey said. "But I'm going to need some fashion magazines and some new clothes."

She looked at me.

"I'm also going to need to borrow your girlfriend," she said.

CHAPTER FIFTEEN

"I don't think I can do this," Alex said.

"Why not?" Casey asked. "Your ass looks great in those jeans."

I had to admit Casey had a point. The floor of one of the bunkhouses was littered with tags and wrappers from a western wear store in Ontario, Oregon, a town about an hour and a half away. Casey and Alex had taken a quick field trip with a government credit card and returned with a trunk full of Cruel Girl and Ariat clothes, some cowboy boots, and in Casey's case, hair dye. Her hair was now chin-length and platinum blond.

"I just don't think I can pass as a local," Alex said. She looked down at the checked shirt with pearl snap buttons, sequined jeans, and Tony Llama boots she was wearing. "I feel ridiculous."

"We don't have to pass as locals," Casey said as she walked over and put a straw cowboy hat on Alex's head. "We have to pass as girls from the city who are TRYING to pass as locals. Am I right, Robert?"

After she and Alex had changed clothes, Casey had our resident cowboy culture experts, Dale and Robert, come in the bunkhouse. Robert had been sitting quietly on a threadbare couch, surrounded by copies of *Cowgirl Fashion* magazine, and valiantly trying not to stare at Alex's ass, at least not while I was looking.

Robert stared at the floor as he talked. He'd done two tours in Afghanistan and probably had killed more people than the plague, but something about Casey made him get all fumble mouth and embarrassed.

"Well, back home, we often get gals from Portland, and even Seattle that come on vacation and, you know... Dress the part and hit the local bars. I imagine that happens down here too."

"Exactly!" Casey said. "What happens in cowboy country stays in cowboy country. They're all looking to save a horse and ride a cowboy."

Robert turned an even deeper crimson. I suspected that with his good looks, he was likely to have helped save a horse a time or two himself.

"So we will separate our target from his buddies," Casey said. "And then lead him back to the motel in town, where we'll make him an offer he can't refuse."

Our target was Willard Stuckey, thirty-five-year-old ranch hand, high school drop out and twice sentenced for petty theft. He had an outstanding warrant for non-payment of child support from the state of Idaho. We had exactly zero jurisdiction over that, but Willard didn't need to know that.

"Won't this guy be a little suspicious when you pick him out of the crowd for your attentions?" Alex asked. "He's no prize."

Judging from his picture, Willard may have been gifted in some way, but good looks wasn't it. He was a homely, paunchy guy with somewhat vacant-looking eyes.

"I suspect there won't be enough blood flow to his brain to allow for too much analysis of the situation," Dale said from over in his corner. He seemed somewhat amused by the whole thing.

"But I can't just walk in there and… seduce him," Alex said.

Alex was tall, good-looking, highly intelligent, and in some ways extremely shy. When it came to her work she could be outgoing and confident, but she'd more than once described her dating life as a disaster. She intimidated many men, and it seemed like sometimes she had no idea how attractive she was. It was hard to say which of us was the most introverted, but it was probably a safe bet that after all this was over we would be spending lots of quiet evenings at home.

"Not your job," Casey said. "I'll hook old Willard. I just need you to be my wingman. Or wingwoman. Or wing… person. Or whatever. I'm not walking in there alone like chum in a swimming pool full of sharks."

Alex still looked doubtful.

"Look," Casey said. "I'll be the fun, risk-taking sister, and you can be the older, sensible one who comes along to keep an eye on me."

Alex blew a strand of hair out of her eye.

"Ok. I can do that."

"Let's remember that this is plan B," I said. "If we can get this guy alone and stop him on the road, that's our first choice."

Dale shook his head. "If I know ranch hands, they are all gonna pile in one truck to go spend their payday. Less money spent on gas that way. You'll have to cut this feller out of the herd just like Casey said."

I suspected he was right, but I still didn't like this plan very much.

Dale stood up and stretched. I heard a couple of joints pop and he grimaced.

"I propose a little alteration to the plan," Dale said. "Robert and I can travel to whatever bar the ranch hands, Casey and Alex wind up in. We can slip in all unobtrusive like and keep an eye on things without attracting attention."

I instantly felt better. Casey and Alex were capable, but Dale and Robert's ability to perform acts of mayhem was an order of magnitude higher.

I realized everybody was looking at me as if I had the final say in how this little charade was supposed to happen.

"Ok," I said. "Let's do it."

Two hours later, I was fidgeting in one of the motel rooms back in Lehigh Valley, listening to Alex's body microphone in my earpiece. She was wearing the wire, and two guns. One for her and one for Casey. Casey had weighed the odds of wearing a wire and a gun and judged the chances of discovery were too great. She'd settled for the tracking app on her cell phone, and a microphone installed in the car we were using.

Via our video link, we'd watched a bunch of Webb's ranch hands head into town. Just as Dale had predicted, they'd all piled into one crew cab pickup. They'd wasted no time heading into Lehigh Valley and pulling into the parking lot of The Oasis, the local watering hole, meat market, and fight club.

Rudder had loaned us a little hatchback he used to get groceries in town. Casey and Alex drove over to The Oasis in their cowgirl getups so Casey could peel Stuckey away from his buddies. The plan was under no circumstances was she to get in any other vehicle with Stuckey. If he insisted she was supposed to abort, and if Stuckey wouldn't take no for an answer, Daniel, Dale's other son would be sitting out in the parking lot in case Stuckey wanted to be a kinesthetic learner.

The music in my earpiece was modern, slickly produced faux country music that I hated. I could hear a general mishmash of voices, only rarely could I make out what exactly was being said. Alex's voice was loud when she talked, and picked up the resonance in her chest, but she was being pretty quiet.

I hated this. I'd never worked narcotics, so I'd rarely had a reason to back up an officer who was going in undercover, but our vice and dope guys did it all the time, and every one of them said it was harder to be on the back up team than it was to be the officer that was going in disguised. Things could go to shit in a matter of seconds, and no matter how fast you tried to respond, your officer could be dead before you got there.

It was even worse when it was your girlfriend.

Bolle, Eddie and I sat in the dark motel room listening. I recognized Casey's voice, but couldn't hear what she was saying.

"Nice to meet you, Stuckey," Alex said. That was for our benefit. They'd made contact.

I sat there and listened to Alex give monosyllabic answers to a drunk guy who mumbled when he talked and tried not to squeeze the arm of the couch so hard it would break. I could hear Casey laughing and chatting in the background. Before our lives all went to shit, she'd studied method acting and joined an improv group to help her deal with her own social awkwardness, and it had paid off in spades.

After what seemed like forever, but was only twenty minutes, Alex said, "I'm going to head off to the ladies."

Casey had given her the sign that she was going to try to reel Stuckey in and get him to leave with her. Casey was supposed to take her opportunity when her sourpuss older sister got up to go to the bathroom.

"Casey is headed to the door with Stuckey," Dale said. I wondered how he was managing to murmur into his microphone without attracting attention, but I figured Dale knew what he was doing.

"They're coming out the door," Daniel said. I relaxed a little. It sounded like the plan was working. So far Casey had been under our observation the whole time. The biggest risk was that we would lose sight of her.

"What the fuck?" Alex said over the radio. Her voice sort of echoed, and there was less background noise.

There was a thump and a crash. I thought I heard a woman's voice say "bitch." I was out of my seat and halfway to the front door when Alex's voice came over the radio.

"Dale. I need you in the women's restroom." She sounded calm, but she was breathing a little hard.

"Wait," Bolle said. "Don't blow it."

I walked back to the couch and sat down. It was one of the hardest things I'd ever done.

"Casey is getting in the car with the target," Daniel said. "Do you all need me inside the bar?"

"Nope," Dale said. His voice had the same echo now. "We're good. Pull around the back. We'll be going out the service entrance with Alex and the other woman."

Other woman? What the hell was going on? I reached up to key my microphone when Casey's voice cut into my earpiece.

"Move your hand, baby. We'll be at my motel room soon enough," she said. She was in the car with Stuckey now and had activated the microphone. I heard the little subcompacts engine whine as she worked through the gears.

Even though I was desperate to know what was going on I kept quiet. We had way too much going for it all to be on one radio net, but it was too late to change it now. Both the microphone in the car, and Alex's bodymic were constantly transmitting. It was like trying to listen to two radio stations at once.

I heard a muffled woman's voice, then Alex said: "Shut up or I'll shoot you in the back of the head." After that, her microphone abruptly cut off.

Bolle, Eddie and I all exchanged glances and raised eyebrows.

"Dent, we're a few minutes behind Casey," Dale said. "I need you to unlock the front door to the other motel room, the adjacent one and meet us there."

I had a million questions, but I did as he asked. I walked through the doors to the adjoining room and propped open the front door. I saw the battered little subcompact pulling into the lot. The passenger looked like he was practically sitting in Casey's lap.

I hurried back into the other room. We had the lights off except for the one in the bathroom. Eddie and I took up positions on either side of the door. I heard the car doors slam outside, then Casey stepped through the door. As we'd arranged, she immediately sprinted to the back of the room.

"What are you doing?" Stuckey asked as he stepped through the door. Eddie and I each grabbed an arm and pushed him face down into the bed. Bolle shoved a set of credentials in his face.

"We're Federal Agents Willard," Bolle said. "Do you want to cooperate, or should my colleagues break some of your bones first?"

"I ain't done nothing," Stuckey said. His voice was kind of muffled from his face being shoved in the comforter.

Bolle gave him a shark's grin.

"On the contrary, my friend. There is a warrant for your arrest. Unpaid child support I believe?"

He leaned over and whispered theatrically into Stuckey's ear.

"But it isn't what you've done that's important. It's what you are going to do for us that matters."

"Ok. Let me up. I'll do whatever you want."

We lifted him up and frogmarched him over to a chair. Bolle sat down on the bed facing him and picked a tablet up off the desk.

"Now Willard, I'm going to show you some pictures and I want you to tell me if you've seen this man at the ranch."

"Pulling into the motel," Dale's voice said in my ear.

I walked into the next room. Dale came in first, followed by Alex who had another woman in a hammerlock. She was almost a foot shorter than Alex, and I wasn't sure her feet were touching the ground all the time. She had long dark hair that hung in her face. She was wearing western jeans, a halter top and cowboy boots."

"Who's that?" I said.

The woman twisted to get free and Alex swept her feet and face-planted her onto the floor. She landed with a thud and gave a moan as Alex came down and shoved her knee between the woman's shoulder blades.

"Don't recognize her?" Alex asked. She looked agnrier than I'd ever seen her before. She reached down, grabbed a handful of hair and yanked. For one queasy second, I thought she'd scalped the woman, then realized it was a wig. Underneath was a tight braid of red hair and a face I recognized.

"Diana," I said.

"I ran into her in the ladies' room," Alex said.

Diana had a fat lip with some dried blood in the corner of her mouth, and as I looked at her, a big red mark started to swell on her forehead from being slammed on the floor.

"Well, this is interesting," I said. I glanced at the connecting door. I could hear Bolle's voice from the next room, but couldn't tell what he was saying.

Daniel and Robert walked in. Robert was holding a little clutch purse in his hands.

"Show them what was in the purse, Robert?"

Gingerly, Robert pulled a small handgun, of a type I didn't

recognize.

"She pulled that on me in the bathroom when I recognized her. She almost shot me with it before I dumped her. Give it to me."

She held out her hand and Robert put the gun in it. She shoved the barrel under Diana's jaw.

"Is this what I think it is?"

"Calm down. You need to talk to my boss. Again."

"How about if I just pull the trigger?"

"Don't do that!" Diana said.

"Whoa," Dale and I both said at the same time. We each reached for Alex, then pulled back. Her finger was on the trigger. She jerked the muzzle aside, then pulled the trigger. Instead of the loud bang I expected, there was a soft *pfft* barely louder than a cough, and a dart stuck in the carpet next to Diana's face.

Alex put the gun back under Diana's jaw.

"I want to know what it is. Either you can tell me, or I pull the trigger and we find out the hard way."

"It's a paralytic," Diana said. "Some kind of synthetic drug. It isn't lethal, but if you pull the trigger with it pressed against my skin you could tear the artery in my neck."

"Huh," I said, feeling like events were moving faster than I could keep up.

"Maybe we could let her up," Dale said. "I think the five of us could keep her from escaping."

I didn't know if Dale was motivated from some innate chivalry, or if he didn't want to be a witness to Alex committing murder on a helpless prisoner, but fortunately, she listened to him. She handed me the pistol and picked Diana up, then deposited her on the bed.

"There's a safety catch on the right side of the grip, but to make it safe you have to unscrew the CO_2 cartridge," Diana said.

I nodded and rendered the little gun safe. I plucked the dart out of the carpet and put them both in the bathroom, well out of range of a desperate grab by Diana.

When I stepped back out, I rocked back on my heels. Alex had her hand down the front of Diana's shirt. All three of the Williams men's eyes were sort of bugging out of their heads. Before I could say anything, Alex pulled her hand out with a ripping sound. Diana gave a yelp and Alex held up a microphone with tape wrapped around it.

"Well, apparently someone has been listening," she said. She looked at Daniel "You should have searched her better."

He blushed.

"Ok," I said. "Everybody just sit tight for a second."

I walked over to the adjoining room and stepped in the next door. Stuckey and Bolle were in deep conversation, their knees almost touching, while Eddie and Casey looked on.

"Mr. Stuckey is cooperating fully," Bolle said and raised his eyebrows. I didn't need to be telepathic to know he wanted me to get the hell out of the room and make sure nothing happened to screw up the deal.

"What's going on over there?" Stuckey asked.

"Uhhh… Somebody else isn't being smart and cooperating," I said.

Bolle rolled his eyes and I walked back next door again. Casey followed me and picked up the dart pistol from the bathroom counter.

"Huh," she said. "This looks like a cut down Teledart 206. Cool. You can put a rhino to sleep with one of these."

Every head in the room swiveled in her direction.

"How do you know stuff like that?" Robert asked.

"I watch lots of *Animal Planet*," she said with a shrug.

I turned back to Diana.

"So are you the one that shot me with a dart last night, or was it Hubbard, your boss?"

I was watching her face closely, and the little jolt of eyes widening made me pretty sure that question came as a surprise to her.

"I don't know what you're talking about," she said.

"She's lying," Alex said. "Fuck her. Where's the pistol that has the suppressor on it?"

"It's out in the truck," Dale said. "We need to get her in the shower though, so we can wash all that DNA evidence down the drain instead of getting it all over the bed and carpet and such."

I was pretty sure Dale was acting. I wasn't so sure about Alex. She'd always had a bit of temper. Once, she'd even slugged her step-mother in the face, but I'd never seen her like this. I was not entirely convinced that she wouldn't put a round in Diana's head in that particular moment. The stress had been building in all of us. I'd made a few bad decisions myself a few weeks back, so I could empathize, but I couldn't let her just shoot Diana in the head. She'd regret it. Maybe.

"Sounds like you need to do some more convincing," I said to Diana.

"I don't know anything about Miller being shot with a dart," she said. "The pistols are Agency issue. There are dozens of them in the field. You people know about the money on the plane."

She looked around the room. Nobody nodded or said anything, but nobody denied it either.

"There's a bunch of moving parts to this. There are more players on the chess board than any of us know about I think. I don't know who tried to dart you, but it wasn't me."

I was inclined to believe her. Essentially Alex and the Williams crew had just kidnapped her, and now she was in a hotel room with no backup and at least one person that seemed cheerfully willing to put a bullet in her head. I'd seen big, trained men break in less stressful circumstances than this, but she was remarkably calm. The tells were there though if you knew what to look for. She was digging both hands into the comforter of the bed she was sitting on, probably to keep them from shaking. She couldn't keep her left leg from quivering though.

As I watched, she reached up, wiped blood from the corner of her mouth, and smeared it on the comforter. Apparently, Dale's comment about DNA had got some gears turning in her head. She wanted to leave some evidence of her presence behind in the room.

It was the act of someone who was afraid she was about to die. I realized I needed to defuse the situation before her fight or flight response kicked in full force and she did something stupid.

"Look," I said. "Nobody is going to shoot you in the head tonight. We're not going to kill you. You have to understand how this looks though. Alex found you in the same bar where we were operating, and you've got a dart gun on you. What were you doing there?"

"Same thing as you. Trying to catch a cowboy."

She looked at Alex. "You weren't very convincing by the way. You looked like a mortified nun dressed up in cowgirl clothes."

"I guess pretending to be a slut comes a little more naturally to some than others," Alex said through clenched teeth. Casey cocked her head at that.

I stepped between them and held up both hands.

"Ok. It sounds like we were all after the same thing," I said.

"Car just pulled into the lot," Daniel said from over by the window, where he'd been standing and keeping an eye out. At least one of us hadn't been hijacked by the situation.

"Older dude is getting out and walking towards our door."

"Hubbard," I said.

Dale shucked his worn old Colt Combat Commander out from under his jeans jacket, where it usually rode in a Milt Sparks holster.

Alex pulled one pistol out of her belly band and handed it to Casey. Then she pulled the second one out of her boot and aimed it pointedly at Diana.

There was a knock at the door. I nodded at Daniel and he opened it. Hubbard stood framed in the doorway wearing jeans and a tan windbreaker. He looked like a grandfather on vacation. His hands were pointedly in view.

"Hello Hubbard," I said.

He ignored me and looked at Diana.

"Let's go, my dear."

I put my hand on Diana's shoulder.

"Not so fast. Why don't you come in and talk Hubbard?"

He shook his head and gave me a tight grin.

"I don't believe I will. I think I'll collect my employee, and we'll be on our way."

I looked around the room.

"I think we're holding all the cards here," I said.

"I don't think you are. It's true that there's just me, standing here empty-handed. It's true that there are six of you holding guns in that tiny little hotel room. But if you use them, what's left of your flimsy cover will be erased. It would be horrible if someone were to make a scene."

With those last few words, he raised his voice to a near shout.

I took my hand of Diana's shoulder.

"Get up and walk out," I said.

She stood, and I thought for a second her legs were going to give out from under her, but she got her balance. She glanced at the dart gun on the desk.

"Touch it and I'll shoot you in the ass," Alex said.

Diana threw her head back and walked out with as much pride as she could muster. Daniel shut the door behind them and I let out a breath I hadn't realized I'd been holding.

"Well," I said. "That went well."

CHAPTER SIXTEEN

I walked back next door and Stuckey was signing a statement that Bolle had prepared for him. Whether he understood any of it was an open question, but that was Stuckey's problem, not mine.

"How are things next door?" Bolle asked.

"Not as bad as they could have been," I said.

He seemed to accept that, for the moment, although I knew I'd have quite a bit of explaining to do later.

"Mr. Stuckey is signing an affidavit that he has seen the subject of our investigation on the grounds of Freedom Ranch as recently as this very morning," Bolle said. He was practically vibrating with suppressed energy. I wouldn't have been completely surprised if he had jumped up and started capering around the room.

"Outstanding," I said. Maybe all this craziness hadn't been for nothing after all.

Stuckey was one of those people that poked his tongue out of the corner of his mouth when he wrote. Finally, he was done and set the pen down.

"Now what?" he asked.

"Now you go back to your friends with exaggerated tales of your sexual prowess and don't breathe a word about what really happened to anyone, or I will make your life miserable," Bolle said with a smile.

"Uh. Ok. Can I get a ride back to the Oasis? Maybe with Candy?"

It took me a minute to remember that Candy was the alias Casey had been using.

"No." Casey's voice came through the connecting door.

I pulled my keys out of my pocket.

"I'll give you a ride," I said. "I'll drop you off around the corner so nobody will see you're with me."

When I came back from depositing Stuckey, Bolle and Eddie were already gone. He'd apparently been on his phone, talking ninety miles a minute with Burke, arranging the search warrant.

Casey rode back with Dale, while Alex and I got in the Charger. She asked me to drive, uncharacteristic of her. As we drove down the dark desert highway, she sat silently curled up in her seat.

"You were pretty convincing back there with Diana," I said after a while.

"It wasn't an act," she said. "I really was pretty close to killing her. I was so angry."

"Why?" I asked.

We pulled off the pavement and onto the long gravel road that led to Rudder's ranch. I slowed down, partly to save my kidneys from the rough ride, partly because of the deer and elk that liked to cross here at night, and partly because I wanted to hear what she had to say, and I felt like if we got out of the car she'd clam up and not want to talk.

"People keep getting taken from me," she said. "First my mom. Then my dad. Now everything has been taken from me. My job is gone. My house is gone. You're the only thing I have left, and when I saw that dart gun I just snapped. I keep waiting for you to go too. I feel like one way or another it's inevitable. In some ways, I wish we could just get it over with so I could stop dreading it."

I pulled the car to a stop outside of the bunkhouse and we sat there for a second, listening to the engine tick as it cooled. Later, I'd realize that I should have said something comforting, or maybe just said nothing at all. But because I'm me, of course I said something stupid.

"That's kind of messed up, Alex."

She opened her door. "Yeah. That's me. Messed up Alex."

She got out of the car and stalked off, her footsteps crunching in the gravel. I almost followed her, almost called out after her, but instead, I just stood there. I think at the time I told myself I was too tired to deal with her moody bullshit, but the truth was I was growing increasingly resentful of how much she controlled our relationship. When she wanted to be close, we were close. When she withdrew, chasing after her made her withdraw more. I didn't feel like she was being intentionally malicious, but I was getting tired of wondering which Alex I was going to wake up to in the morning.

We'd staked out a room at the end of one of the bunkhouses, formerly where one of the chief hands would have made his abode, and thrown down an air mattress, but I didn't want to join her just yet.

I felt like there was a pretty good likelihood one or both of us would say something stupid, with the added bonus of everybody else being able to overhear. Besides, I was hungry.

I could see the flickering of Rudder's giant TV so I walked on in. *Sands of Iwo Jima* was just ending. I stood in the doorway to the living room and watched as the members of Sergeant Stryker's squad read his final letter, and watched the flag raised. When the credits rolled, Rudder turned to me.

"Sandwich fixins are in the kitchen. *Fighting Seebees* is up next."

By the time I was done making myself a plate, Rudder had the movie cued up. He motioned to the easy chair next to him and I had a seat. I hadn't seen a John Wayne movie in ages, since before I'd been to war myself, and part of me wanted to laugh at the simplistic plot and wooden characters. But part of me wanted the real world to be like that, instead of the morass I was in right now. I just decided to stop being so damn introspective, turn my brain off, and enjoy the movie.

Just like in *Sands of Iwo Jima,* John Wayne's character died in the end. As the credits rolled, I saw Rudder had fallen asleep. I shut down the home entertainment system and crept out of the house. It was cold outside, and there were a million stars. I stood for a minute to look at them, wishing Alex was out here to enjoy them with me. Over the last couple of months, I'd developed a habit of appreciating small things: sunsets, stars, a good meal. I'd come close to dying so many times lately I didn't want to take anything for granted.

One of the surveillance cameras we'd mounted on top of the trailer swiveled in my direction and I gave it a wave. I was tempted to go inside and talk to whoever was on duty, but it was already late, so I headed in the bunkhouse instead. When I climbed into bed, Alex scooted over as close to the wall as she could get. The foot of distance between us felt like a mile. I was still trying to think of something to say to her when I fell asleep.

When I woke up the next morning, she was already gone. I pulled some fresh, but rumpled clothes out of a duffel and followed the smell of coffee into the trailer. Bolle was hanging up a satellite phone when I walked in.

"Burke's coming with a search warrant," he said by way of greeting. "And she's bringing HRT with her."

Alex was seated at the trailer's little dinette table with a laptop open in front of her. She looked up at me briefly, then looked away. I shoved all that firmly out of my mind. Business first. I reached for a cup of coffee and sent some caffeine towards my brain before I responded to Bolle.

"How many HRT people are they sending?"

"Half the team."

"Holy shit," I said. Last time I heard, the FBI's elite Hostage Rescue unit had just over a hundred operators. Even sending half of them, with all their support staff and equipment, was a major undertaking.

"There goes the element of surprise," Dalton said from over by the radio console. "They won't be here and ready to go for two days at least. Maybe three."

"Yeah," I said. "Has anybody left since last night?"

Dalton pointed at the monitors.

"No vehicle traffic in or out of the main gate of the ranch since the cowboys went home late last night. We've seen the usual vehicle patrols around the ranch, but nothing out of the ordinary. We don't have complete coverage of the ranch though. There are all sorts of unimproved roads and what not."

I took another drink of coffee.

"They could load Marshall and the money into a pickup and be gone," I said. "We don't have enough bodies to prevent it."

"I have some ideas," Dalton said.

He pulled up a topographical map on the big screen in front of him. He'd marked it up with all sorts of symbols and lines.

"The ranch essentially runs up this valley," he said, tracing a line that ran more or less north and south. "We've got our observation post on the ridge to the east. There's a network of roads up here, but they're rough, and there aren't THAT many. I've identified a half a dozen or so possible routes besides the main road that could be used to sneak out of the ranch in a truck."

Now it was Casey's turn to speak up. "We can't get live video coverage of all of them. The terrain is too rugged to get a line of sight. But there's a couple of places where we can set up a live feed."

Dale helped himself to another cup of coffee. "And for the rest, we've got some of those motion activated cameras we use during elk season. Strap 'em to a tree near the road and they'll take a picture of anyone who happens to drive past. We'll have to go out and check them every now and again, so if somebody sneaks out that way, they'll have a few hours head start, but it's better than nothing."

"We were hoping you, Dale, and his sons could go place the remote cameras," Bolle said. "Eddie and I will stay near the ranch entrance to follow any traffic that leaves. We'll have Jack standing by here to get in the air to follow anyone that gets away."

I wasn't looking forward to another day riding on the back of Dale's ATV, but at least I wouldn't have to spend it in awkward silence with Alex.

"Let's hit it," I said.

It took us an hour to eat, pack our gear, and load the ATVs into the backs of two pickups. Dale and I rode in one truck, Robert and Daniel in the other. We split the sites between us and soon Dale and I were jouncing down a rutted pair of wheel tracks that could only charitably be called a road. Branches scraped either side of the truck. After one particularly bone-jarring thud, Dale saw a spot between two trees and parked the truck.

"Reckon we better take the four-wheeler from here. Last thing I want to do is blow a ball joint out here in Hell's half acre."

While Dale readied the four-wheeler, I tried my radio. When I keyed the microphone, I was greeted with the harsh buzz that meant I wasn't connecting to our repeater. I had a satellite phone stashed in my pack, so that was our only form of communication.

I held on for dear life for a couple of miles on the four-wheeler, then Dale brought us to a stop, cut the engine and removed his helmet.

"Reckon we're about a mile from the junction," he said, pointing to the GPS unit strapped to his wrist.

After we dismounted, I donned my rucksack full of cameras and grabbed my rifle. I mounted a suppressor on the barrel. It wasn't as quiet as the movies would have you believe, but it would keep the report of the .308 rounds from echoing through the canyons. I made sure the variable power scope was dialed down to its lowest setting, optimal for close range engagements.

We kept a slow pace, moving for ten minutes then stopping to listen for five. The woods were mostly lodgepole pine, big tall trees with straight trunks and no branches low to the ground. The undergrowth wasn't very tall, so we could actually see quite a way through the forest, but there was still a myriad of places behind tree trunks and fallen logs where somebody could be hiding.

When we came to the road junction, we stopped and observed for several minutes. The road that led into the ranch was recently graded and graveled, and the BLM road that continued past the junction was in much better shape than the stretch we'd been traveling.

"Looks like we found their escape route," Dale whispered in my ear.

I suspected he was right. There was a whole lot of nothing up here. If a person knew what they were doing, they could work their way through the maze of BLM and private ranch roads, and eventually emerge out on one of the sparse two lane highways. It would be a long, slow, journey, hard on vehicles and it would be easy to get lost, but it was almost guaranteed that it would be unobserved.

"Cover me, and I'll place the cameras," Dale said.

I nodded. He unzipped the bag and pulled out a pair of motion-activated cameras. I tried to look everywhere at once as he walked out into the open.

Dale slung his rifle and started strapping the camera to a tree when the first shot came. I wasn't the only one with a suppressor on his rifle. Dale dropped the little memory card for the camera, bent to retrieve it, and there was the *hiss-crack* of a silenced rifle shot. The report of the rifle was muffled, but the supersonic bullet made a sound like a whip cracking and a sheet ripping at the same time. A big sliver of bark blew off the tree right where Dale's head had been.

Dale rolled on the ground, going for a section of downed log not even a foot high.

"Federal agents! Stop shooting!" I yelled. The only response was a pair of rifle rounds that cracked overhead.

I looked around, desperate to find the shooter. More shots came. The other guys suppressor didn't make his shots silent, it just made it hard to track down where they were coming from. Finally, I saw some vegetation waving. I cranked up the magnification on my scope and suddenly the image resolved of a guy in a camo face mask with a rifle. I put the crosshairs between the two eye holes of the mask and stroked the trigger.

When I came down from recoil, he wasn't there anymore. I couldn't even tell how many people were shooting. I'd think the firing was coming from my left, then the next volley of shots would seem to come from my right. I heard a thud from overhead, and splinters of bark hit the back of my neck.

"Pop smoke Dent," Dale said. He sounded like he was asking me to pass the creamer for his coffee. He triggered a couple of shots. His rifle wasn't suppressed and they echoed off the hills.

I cursed myself for forgetting the smoke grenade hanging off my backpack harness. Another round hit the tree behind me and I dropped, and rolled. Once I was a dozen or so feet away, I snatched the grenade out of its pouch, pulled the pin and flung it into the middle of the crossroads. Purple smoke filled the air.

"Break contact," Dale said. "Cover me."

I started dumping rounds into the trees, shooting blindly through the smoke. Dale stood, ran about fifty yards down the road and then took a knee and started shooting right about the time I ran out of ammo.

I took a deep breath and ran as fast as I could down the road. I heard a round snap past my ear. I changed magazines as I ran, found a spot, and dropped to one knee. Now it was my turn to dump rounds down range, careful not to hit Dale as he charged down the road.

We repeated this a couple times, then Dale stopped beside me. The firing behind us had stopped. We could barely see the purple cloud down the road. There was no wind and it was lingering.

"I think that did it," Dale said. "I'm fifty percent on ammo."

I realized I'd burned through four of the six rifle magazines I'd been carrying. Rounds went quickly at times like these.

"Less than that," I said.

"Ok. I'm going to pop another smoke and then let's run for it."

He dropped another smoke grenade, yellow this time, then we took off at a run. Dale easily kept pace with me and didn't even seem all that winded as we mounted up. I managed to hang on to the wheeler and keep hold of my rifle as we blasted over the ruts and bumps.

When we arrived at the truck, there were no signs of pursuit. I covered while he loaded the wheeler. As we drove out in the pickup, I tried the satellite phone, but it wouldn't lock on while the truck was moving.

An hour or so later, we stopped on an open ridgeline, miles from the ambush site and in a spot where we could easily see someone in rifle range. The satellite phone locked on. I dialed our operations number and Dalton answered.

"We got ambushed," I said. "No casualties."

"I know," Dalton said. "You're already on YouTube."

"What?"

"It's complicated. You might want to get back here as fast as you can."

CHAPTER SEVENTEEN

The video had been hastily edited, but they'd managed to make it look like we started shooting first. Henderson Marshall's voice over lacked audio quality, but he made up for it with hyperbole and inflammatory rhetoric.

"Here you can see the death squad sent to my friend's ranch using military tactics," Marshall narrated as the video showed Dale and me shooting and throwing the smoke grenade. "I ask you, is this Iraq or the United States, a land of free people?"

The video cut to a picture of Stuckey's corpse laying on the ground with a gaping wound in his forehead.

"This is our innocent ranch hand, cut down by the jackbooted thugs the government sent to harass us."

"I can't believe you shot Stuckey," Casey said.

"He didn't," Dale said. "That's an exit wound. Also the guy Dent shot was wearing camo. Stuckey is wearing work clothes, and there are blood stains on them, so he was wearing them when he was shot."

"He must have told them about us, and they executed him," I said.

"Yup," Dale said.

On screen, the picture cut away to Henderson Marshall standing in front of the flagpole at Freedom Ranch.

"This is the time for patriots to unite!" Marshall said, holding a rifle over his head. "I'm asking all free men of good character to report for duty. It's time to stand up to the beast that our government has become and strike a blow for freedom!"

"What the hell?" I said.

"The video has received over a thousand views in the last hour," Henry said. "I've been monitoring the comments section."

"I'm sorry," Casey said.

"Yeah. I feel like my IQ is lower. Anyway, over a dozen groups have responded and pledged help. The Sons of Freedom. Some white supremacists from Idaho. A Ku Klux Klan chapter from Northern California. A bunch of individuals."

"What's his angle?" I asked.

"Our psych profile suggests that Marshall has started to see himself in an almost messianic light since his son was killed," Bolle said. Eyes shifted uncomfortably around the room. I was the one responsible for Marshall's son's death.

"He genuinely believes he's going to ignite a political movement that is going to take the country by storm and change things to look the way he wants," Bolle continued. "He may be intent on going out in a blaze of glory, with the whole world watching."

"What about all the other people? Webb? All those security people" Alex asked from over in the corner. She'd barely greeted me when I came in.

Bolle shrugged. "We don't have a handle on them. Some of them may be motivated by similar ideology, some of them may be motivated by the millions of dollars in cash sitting in that airplane."

"What a shit sandwich," I said. I replayed the ambush in the woods in my mind. There was nothing we could have done differently.

"Yes," Bolle said. "The FBI will be here tonight to assume on-scene command."

"I'm not sure if that makes me feel better," I said.

Nobody seemed inclined to argue with that.

For the rest of the day, we watched a caravan of pickup trucks, RV's, motorcycles and even one guy on horseback show up at Freedom Ranch. People started live streaming video from the ranch, showing lots of overweight dudes wearing cheap camo clothes and carrying rifles walking around and setting up defensive positions. From our surveillance cameras, we saw Webb reposition his security people in a ring around the airplane hangar, while the newcomers spread out all over the ranch.

The main thing we watched for was a vehicle departing the ranch via the newly graded road. We were dead certain that somebody would try to make their escape with at least part of the money, either by the road, or via the light aircraft parked outside the hangar. We rolled the Little Bird out of the barn, unfolded the blades, and attached the bench seats to the sides, intending to intercept any escape attempts by air, Burke's orders to not apprehend anyone be damned. I sat in the air-conditioned trailer with all my gear on and tried to nap, standing by in case somebody made a run for it with some portion of the hundred million dollars hidden in the plane or truck.

But all the traffic was into the ranch, none of it went out.

After dark, I took off all my commando gear and drove into Lehigh Valley with Bolle. The town middle school had been designated as the command post, and it was a madhouse. The parking lot was full of unmarked government sedans and SUVs. A pair of Lenco Bearcat armored cars sat on trailers, guarded by a couple of guys in FBI windbreakers toting assault rifles. Everywhere I looked, I saw lean, fit people wearing tactical pants and polo shirts that did a poor job of covering pistols on their belts.

"I don't see any nuclear weapons, so they must be keeping a low profile," I said.

Bolle just shook his head. The guard at the door scrutinized our credentials, made a couple of phone calls and finally, we were led inside the gymnasium, where dozens of tables holding communications gear, computers, and whiteboards had been set up.

The HRT commander was a guy named Roger Laughlin, and he looked at Bolle and me like we smelled bad

"We're serving the warrant tomorrow at 0800. I understand your people have an observation post set up on a ridge?"

"We do," Bolle said. "I..."

Laughlin cut him off. "You can put some of your people up there if you want. If you see anything of interest, report it on the secondary radio net. Stay off the primary."

With that he turned on his heel and walked off, leaving me and Bolle standing there like two dismissed schoolboys. When I looked at Bolle out of the corner of my eye, I could see he was white. He had his fists clenched at his sides and they were trembling.

Without a word to me, he walked out of the room and marched back to the car, back ramrod straight, head straight ahead. I had to almost jog to keep up with him. He sat in the passenger seat and folded his arms across his chest. Wordlessly, I started the car and headed for the exit.

Across the street from the school, a TV news truck pulled up and the hydraulic mast for a satellite antenna started going up. Apparently, we were all about to be famous.

As we pulled out of the lot, another car pulled in. I recognized the driver as Diana. Her face was still bruised and puffy. I was pretty sure the silhouette beside her was Hubbard. I glanced over at Bolle to see if he'd noticed.

"All the pieces are on the board," he said.

I wasn't quite sure what to make of that comment, so I let it be. We rode in silence for a few miles as I turned the situation over in my head. Finally, I spoke.

"I think some people are going to die tomorrow," I said.

He nodded. "I want you and Dale up on the ridge tomorrow with the fifty. At least we can make sure it's the right people."

Our little arsenal included a massive Barret fifty caliber rifle. Dale could do frightening things with it, even from a couple of miles away.

I almost asked him why we were taking an active role in the raid, when we'd been clearly ordered not to. I wondered what the repercussions would be if we wound up shooting people, but at this point, I was past the point of caring. We'd done so much sketchy stuff already, what was one more thing?

I found myself just wanting the whole thing to be over. Hopefully tomorrow Marshall would be either in custody or dead, and I could concentrate on having some kind of life again.

Everyone was waiting for us in the trailer when we pulled up. Bolle briefed everyone about the plan. There was silence all around for a while.

"That's it?" Casey said. "We're just going to watch?"

"That may not be a bad thing," Dale said. "I think those FBI boys are expecting to roll in there, wave some machine guns around and just take the place over. I'm not sure it's going to go that way."

That was part of what was bothering me. It was almost like somebody wanted a confrontation.

"Have we heard from CRYPTER?" I asked.

Casey craned her neck over to look at the phone in its plastic bag.

"Nope. Nothing."

"Should we tell him?" I asked Bolle.

He took a deep breath and looked out the window for a minute.

"No. I can't be responsible for tipping off the people at the ranch to raid."

I almost pointed out that since there were a hundred or so federal agents and two armored cars sitting at the local middle school, any chance of surprise was lost already, but I held my tongue. Bolle was still tense and agitated. He'd worked hard on this investigation for years, and now it was being jerked out of his hands right at the end. It occurred to me, not for the first time, that I knew nothing about Bolle personally. I didn't know if he had a wife, kids, a lover, a boyfriend, anything. We'd never talked about what would happen after we finally had Marshall in custody if he had an expectation that we were going to keep working together.

The meeting broke up and Alex walked out of the trailer without a word. I waited for a while before leaving myself. I watched the video monitors. There were a couple of bonfires on the property and dozens of people standing around them. I couldn't count the number of pickup trucks, camper vans and recreational vehicles that had been parked all over the grass between the ranch gate and the main house. Clearly more people had arrived while Bolle and I were in town.

"It's sort of like an anti-Woodstock," Casey said as she panned the camera around.

"Yeah. Well, hopefully, they will all eat the brown acid and will be feeling groovy when the Feds show up," I said. I was exhausted, but still feeling restless and edgy, courtesy of unburned adrenaline left over from the fight earlier in the day. I walked outside into the fresh air and saw Rudder silhouetted in the glow of his TV. I really needed to go to bed, but I walked into the living room instead.

There was something about Rudder I really liked. When I'd been in the Army, the D-Day Rangers had been venerated, part of the pantheon of heroes we all worshiped. I also just genuinely enjoyed being around the old fart.

He waved at me and pointed to the extra recliner when I came into the room. Instead of the John Wayne movie I'd been hoping for, he was watching the news out of Portland. A perfectly coiffed reporter I vaguely recognized was doing a stand up in front of the Lehigh Valley Middle School.

"Tonight the sleepy community of Lehigh valley looks like something from a war zone, with heavily armed federal agents assembling at the local middle school, and armed militants congregating at the Freedom Ranch. Earlier today, we got impressions from local residents."

The screen cut to footage shot earlier in the day of the reporter holding the microphone in the face of a woman in her sixties. Her hair was pulled back in a bun and she wore a work shirt and jeans.

"Those people out at that ranch don't represent the people of Lehigh Valley or Mueller County. They're a bunch of radicals. We don't need them, or a bunch of Federal Agents waving guns around either.

Hopefully, all of you will just go away."

The reporter opened his mouth to ask a question, but she turned and walked away. The feed cut back to the live shot in front of the middle school.

"Strong words from a local resident in this small community that is overwhelmed with tension. We'll keep you updated as events unfold. Back to you Tom."

Rudder killed the sound.

"She's goddamn right we don't need all this here. No offense but hope all of you will just go home soon."

He glanced over at me and I nodded.

"None taken. I don't blame you."

"Those people out at that ranch are a bunch of wingnuts. They bought the land cheap because old Henry Patton went bankrupt, like far too many ranchers these last few years. They thought they'd roll in here, buy a bunch of jeans, boots and cowboy hats and we'd just lap up their bullshit like a cat taking to cream. Most of us don't have much use for you Portland people, but that doesn't mean we are going to go marching along with this Marshall fellow either."

I wasn't sure how I felt about being lumped in with the "Portland people," but I could see what Rudder meant. In many ways, this place reminded me of where I grew up in Appalachia. The land was vastly different, the accents were different, and the ways people made their living were different, but what they had in common was a desire to just make a living, raise their kids, and generally be left alone. I realized I'd missed places like this. I'd never go back to Tennessee, but there was quite a bit of this country that wasn't Tennessee but wasn't Portland either.

"Well, hopefully, you'll be shut of him soon," I said.

Rudder gave me a knowing look. "Got the jitters about tomorrow morning do you?"

It was stupid to deny it. Any idiot could see that now that any hope of surprise was lost. The raid would have to happen soon, so I wasn't going to insult his intelligence by playing dumb.

"I don't think it's going to go well," I said.

"I don't either," Rudder said. "Those dumb sonsabitches at the middle school might as well have sent flowers in ahead of time. You boys have a piece of work cut out for you, that's for sure. Hell, if I was ten years younger, I might sign up and join you. I'd love to help clean those miscreants out of my county."

He started thumbing through the channels with his remote.

"Hundred and thirty-two channels and not a fit thing for a man to watch. I've got *The Searchers* cued up in the DVD. You want to watch?"

I stood.

"I'd love to, but I've got to get some sleep."

"Enjoy it while you can. I don't get more than three or four hours at a stretch anymore. It's hell getting old."

I left him to the sweeping vistas of John Ford's masterpiece. Alex was asleep or pretending to be, so I stared into the darkness until sleep finally came.

CHAPTER EIGHTEEN

"I'm getting too old for this shit," Dale said as he took a drink from his canteen.

Even though it was early, and we were under a camouflage net, it was already getting hot. Below us, Freedom Ranch was a beehive of activity. We'd systematically divided the area around the house into a grid, and counted fifty-three people around the various campsites. Most of them were carrying visible firearms, usually rifles, but thankfully all of them seemed to be adults. My biggest fear was that some of these nut cases were going to turn this into a family affair. Hopefully, the FBI would have had the good sense to change plans if that was the case.

What worried me the most was the roadblock. Overnight two full-size pickup trucks had been parked nose to nose across the ranch gates. The beds were full of dirt and crushed concrete. I wasn't sure how much they weighed, but I was sure it was several tons. We'd let the FBI command post know, and sent digital pictures, and received a curt acknowledgment.

I wiped sweat out of my eyes and checked my watch. The FBI was two hours late. If they'd changed plans, they weren't telling us. The last we'd heard, they'd blocked the highway on either side of the ranch entrance, and a huge convoy of vehicles was staged a couple of miles away.

"There's the drone again," Robert said. About thirty seconds later, I heard the high pitched whine of the drone's engines. We'd figured out that he could hear it long before Dale or I could. I wondered at what point I'd just have to go get hearing aids. I wasn't that old, but the mixture of gunfire, flash-bang grenades, explosions, and too much loud electric guitar was taking its toll.

It was devilishly difficult to see. I figured it was about six feet long or so, with a wingspan of maybe a little more. If it had been painted a shade that was a little less gray, and a little more blue, we would have never seen it against the cloudless sky. It settled into an orbit maybe a thousand feet above the ranch. That was new. It had done several flyovers this morning, usually doing a grid pattern of the ranch for a half hour or so, then leaving.

For the first couple of hours after sunrise, we'd been busy. First, we'd tried to get a good count of all the people milling around. Then I'd worked a camera with a ridiculously long lens, trying to get facial shots of everyone down there, while Robert and Dale meticulously created a sketch of the compound, then used our tripod-mounted laser range finder to create a range card. At this distance, if Dale had to put the big .50 caliber rifle to work, he'd have to make precise adjustments for range. If he miscalculated by even a few percent, the bullet could hit the ground well short of its target. He also would have to account for the wind. The problem was, the wind wasn't blowing the same way across the whole mile plus trajectory the bullet would have to follow. In our immediate vicinity, the sun was warming the air in the valley below us, creating a gentle breeze that was blowing into our faces. Down below in the valley, gusts would kick up blowing generally from our left to right.

I'd listen for a while as Dale and Robert discussed the wind values, then just tuned them out. I understood at a high level what they were talking about, but after awhile they left me in the weeds.

I was using a high powered spotting scope to keep an eye on the hangar, and the little single-engine aircraft parked out front. As I watched a jeep drove up. A guy in his mid-30's got out. He was dressed in khaki pants, a polo shirt and was wearing aviator shades. He started walking around the airplane.

"See that?" I said.

"Yup," Dale said. "That sure looks like a pre-flight inspection to me."

I snapped a couple of pictures of the guy, then slid the camera's memory card into a little gadget hooked up to my satellite phone. It transmitted the pictures back to our trailer. Beside me, Robert worked the joystick to center the video camera on the airplane. The guy in the shades moved the rudder of the plane back and forth, then stuck his head in the cockpit.

"Hypothetically speaking, this here fifty cal would make pretty short work of that little airplane's engine," Dale said conversationally.

A black SUV pulled up next to the jeep, and three men got out. I recognized two of them: Webb and Marshall. They walked into the hangar, carrying duffel bags, while the third stood by the doorway with a rifle slung across his chest.

I took my eyes away from the scope for a second. It was fatiguing to look through it for too long, and I was constantly on the verge of a killer migraine. The crowd down below had been milling around aimlessly, but now they were gathered into a big circle, listening to somebody I didn't recognize.

I started to key my microphone to report into Bolle, when his voice came over the radio.

"We just got word the convoy is moving," Bolle said.

"Apparently, the folks down there knew it before we did," I said, but didn't transmit it over the air.

I put my eye back to the scope just in time to see Webb and Marshall walk out of the hangar. The duffel bags were now quite a bit heavier.

"Looks like those boys are carrying quite a few mortgage payments," Dale said from behind his rifle scope.

Another SUV drove up to the tarmac. This time two women got out and pulled a couple of suitcases from the back.

"Well I do believe that's Mrs. Webb, and Mrs. Marshall," Dale said. "That plane is a six-seater, if I'm not mistaken."

"Yup," I said. "Cessna 206."

"Looks like Marshall and Webb are taking off with their wives, a pilot and a hired gun, and leaving the faithful to deal with the FBI," Dale said. "Maybe Marshall does really have leadership potential. He'd fit right into congress."

"That's a shit load of money in those bags too," Robert chimed in.

"Yup," Dale said. "Let's confirm our range to that airplane."

While Dale and Robert worked the rangefinder and talked sniper speak to each other, I clicked my microphone.

"You getting this?" I asked. "It looks like Webb and Marshall are fixing to fly away."

There was silence for a few seconds. Way out by the ranch gates, I saw a sea of blue and red flashing lights.

"Dale, can you confirm that you have a can mounted on the fifty?"

We'd hauled the Barret M82 rifle up here in pieces, and assembled it. The damn thing weighed almost thirty pounds and was four feet long, to which Dale had added another foot of QDL suppressor.

"I can," he said. "It isn't exactly silent, but it shouldn't raise too many eyebrows."

This was horrible timing. The armed protesters were about to come face to face with a gaggle of even more heavily armed Federal agents. With that many itchy trigger fingers, the boom of heavy rifle fire echoing off the mountains might be just enough to ignite the whole powder keg.

"Can you disable that plane without hurting anybody?"

"I can as long as I do it before they all get inside. After that no guarantees. That little tin can won't even slow these rounds down very much."

"Do it," Bolle said. "I'm directing you to disable that aircraft with gunfire, as long as you can do it without seriously injuring anyone."

To his credit, Bolle was standing up and taking responsibility. We were recording our radio net, and now there was a record of him ordering Dale to shoot the plane.

"My pleasure," Dale said. "Robert, spot my rounds. Dent, I need you to keep a wide view to make sure nobody wanders into the line of fire."

I lowered the magnification on my spotting scope. Webb, Marshall, their wives, and the guard were standing by the vehicles, safely out of harm's way. The pilot was another matter. He had the engine cowling up and his head was stuck underneath. I wasn't sure how Dale was going to deal with that.

"Gonna send a round over that fellow's head, see if he takes the hint. On the way."

He squeezed the trigger. With the suppressor, it didn't sound like a gunshot, more like some kind of giant piece of machinery. There was a sharp crack and the clank of the action cycling. It took the bullet a few seconds to travel the distance. The sun was just right, and I actually saw the wake of disturbed air in its wake. The shot passed over the head of the pilot and dug up a huge geyser of dirt a hundred yards or so behind him.

The pilot was apparently smart enough to recognize it for what it was. He took off running from the plane and dove into the ditch beside the runway.

"Perfect," Dale said, and squeezed the trigger again.

I watched that round sail into the engine compartment of the airplane. The giant slug was as long as my thumb and weighed almost an ounce. Metal parts flew a dozen feet in the air.

"I believe you've got the range," Robert said from behind his scope.

"Yup," Dale said, and squeezed the trigger eight more times. Glass shattered, aluminum flew, and the plane's front landing gear collapsed, bending the prop. We heard the sounds of the impact a few seconds later. It sounded like somebody banging on a metal drum with a giant hammer.

"Not fixing that with duct tape," Robert said.

"Nope," Dale said. "Feed me."

The ten round magazines for the giant rifle were the size of a book. Robert had hauled a backpack full of them up the mountain. He handed one to his dad while I checked out the crowd. A few heads had turned towards the airstrip, but nobody seemed excited, and most importantly, nobody was shooting.

It was somewhat comical to watch Marshall, Webb, their wives, the pilot and the guard all try to pile into a single SUV at the same time. They took off in a cloud of dust back towards the ranch house.

"Not leaving that way," Dale said as he slid the new magazine home.

"No sir," Robert said. "Looks like the cops are at the gate."

I focused my scope on the front gate. There was a sea of official vehicles out there. There were black unmarked SUVs, Oregon State Police, and Department of Homeland Security vehicles. The local sheriff's office was conspicuously absent. Leading the way were the two Lenco Bearcat armored cars. They stopped by the roadblock, and a pair of figures dressed in body armor and helmets hopped out, while riflemen in the turrets covered them.

There was a tow strap already coiled on the hoods of Bearcats, and hooked to the front chassis. Each officer grabbed the hook on the end of a tow strap, attached it to one of the trucks blocking the road and ran back to the safety of the armored vehicles. The drivers backed up and jerked the front ends of the heavy trucks around, opening a narrow passage just wide enough for a single vehicle.

The Bearcats led the way through the gap, followed by a van with a dozen tactical officers hanging off of running boards, then a dozen SUVs and cars. They raced down the half mile road towards the ranch house in a single file, bumper to bumper, scattering cows as they went.

People would argue for years about who fired first. Ultimately it was unknowable. I thought for a moment that the direct assault was going to work. Some folks in the crowd had their hands up, others were shifting from foot to foot with rifles slung over their backs. My first clue that something was wrong was when an officer fell off the side of the van, his arms pinwheeling like a rag doll. A couple of seconds later, the flat crack of a shot echoed through the air.

"Oh shit," Dale said.

The driver of the van slammed on the brakes and was promptly rear-ended by the SUV behind him. The Bearcats kept going, while behind the van, vehicles slid to a halt. Some of them pulled off the road and tried to go around, but the dry ground was deceptively rough, and the sage brush higher than it looked. Several officers jumped off the van and ran for their wounded comrade.

Then everyone started shooting at once. Dozens, then hundreds of gunshots filled the air. It was impossible to follow it all at once, even from our perfect vantage point. Both Bearcats stopped. The rifle men in the armored turrets were shooting in different directions. The crowd scattered. Some people ran. Some dove to the ground. Some started shooting.

The convoy of police vehicles was hard to see through the billowing dust. I realized trying to see everything at once was futile. Instead I focused the scope and started methodically scanning the crowd.

One guy was hiding behind a pickup with his rifle held over his head, firing blindly. Before I could say anything, he stood and scampered into the crowd and I lost him because of the narrow field of view of the scope.

A man on the roof of the ranch house caught my eye. He was balancing a long barreled precision rifle on the peak of the roof and firing slow, measured shots.

"Dale, guy on the roof with a scoped long gun," I said.

"I see him," Dale said. There was a second or two pause while the fire control computer in Dale's head calculated range, wind and a million other factors that influenced a shot at this range, then he said: "On the way."

The big fifty coughed and a second or two later, the guy on the roof vanished in a cloud of pink mist. I saw an arm pinwheel through the air and his rifle slid down the roof.

"Dent, you give me targets west of the ranch road. Robert, you focus to the east," Dale said.

That made sense. The scene below us was mass chaos. There were police vehicles parked on and around the ranch road with cops hunkered behind them. I saw several bodies in black tactical gear lying in the dirt, being tended to by their teammates. Some of the vehicles were shot full of holes and looked un-drivable. One of the Bearcats was parked straddling the road and had been turned into a de facto bunker, with some officers firing from the inside through the gunports, while others took cover behind the armored car and popped out for the occasional shot.

The other Bearcat was plodding through the sagebrush with officers taking cover beside it. It was headed for a gaggle of cops surrounding the first officer who had been shot off the van.

The advance was stalled out. Some police vehicles were trying to move forward and maneuver around stalled and shot up cars. Others were trying to back down the road. It looked like nobody was in charge. I flipped my radio over to the main tactical channel and was rewarded with a dozen voices all trying to talk at once, and issuing contradictory orders.

On the other side, a bunch of the protesters were on the ground, some of them because they'd been shot, some of them because they clearly wanted no part of the gunfight. A dozen or so were shooting. A few of them looked like they knew what they were doing.

I didn't designate them as targets. We had one rifle to contribute to this fight, and we needed to maximize our efforts. I had a feeling some of Marshall's people were seeded into the protesters, and I wanted to pick them out.

I focused on a pickup parked on a slight rise a few hundred yards east of the ranch road. The long bed was covered by a canopy. The tailgate was down and the inside of the bed was hidden in shadow, but as I focused the scope I saw a brief flash from inside, followed a couple of seconds later by another.

"Dale, see that truck on that rise about four hundred meters west of the ranch house? I think there is a guy in the bed shooting."

Dale was quiet, but out of my peripheral vision, I saw him shift the rifle.

"Yep," he said finally. "Sneaky fucker. On the way."

The fifty barked and the truck rocked on its suspension. I saw a plume of dust on the other side where the round hit the ground after passing all the way through the canopy and side of the bed. The truck started to roll forward slowly and Dale triggered another round. That one missed, but Dale saw the bullet hit the ground in his scope and used it to correct his aim. Dinner plate sized dents appeared in the sheet metal, and big splinters of fiberglass flew off the canopy as Dale unloaded the rifle. The truck stopped on a flat tire and didn't move for several seconds. No more flashes came from the bed.

"Reckon that ought to do it." I heard the clunk of an empty magazine hitting the ground and the snick of another one being rammed home as I scanned through my scope. I looked away from my scope for a second, both to give my eye a break, and to take in the larger scene.

On the radio, some of the chaos had been tamed. Laughlin sounded pretty calm, considering his career was likely about to end. He was organizing a withdrawal, and it was starting to work. The vehicles closest to the highway were backing down on to the blacktop. Officers with disabled vehicles were dashing to vehicles that were still running and either diving in or jumping on to running boards and bumpers. I saw one limp form being carried by four others stuffed into the back of an SUV and evacuated. The Bearcats were backing down towards the highway.

The pace of firing had slackened, although there were still plenty of bullets flying through the air. I got back on the scope and started looking for targets for Dale to destroy.

"I think I've got muzzle flashes coming out of the upstairs of the house," Robert said. "One side. Third floor. Fourth window."

The "one" side of the building was the side with the front door. I aimed the scope at the third floor, and counted four windows over from the left. The window was open, but all I saw inside was darkness. If there was a shooter inside, he was well trained enough to stay deep in the room and not stick his barrel out the window like in the movies.

As I focused the scope, I saw a flash from inside. It was hard to pick out the sound of a corresponding shot, especially with the delay. The window was also at a slight angle to us, so we weren't looking directly in. I watched for a few more seconds and thought I saw a second flash.

"I believe you're right," Dale said. "Thing is, there's no telling who else is in that house. These rounds will go through one side of that house and out the other."

He had a point. We were reasonably sure there were no children on the ranch, but there were all sorts of ranch hands, cooks, maids and other employees we'd watched come and go through the cameras. They were just innocent bystanders. Even a hit to the extremities from the big fifty was liable to be lethal. Dale could kill a combatant without his heart rate even going up, but he didn't want to shoot an uninvolved party, and I didn't blame him.

"Now what?" Dale said.

Over the radio, I heard Laughlin yelling at everyone to hold their fire. I pulled away from the scope and saw something that made me do a double take. A man on a Harley Davidson motorcycle was driving up the ranch road, weaving among the police vehicles that were backing up. I managed to find him in the scope,and saw it was Sheriff Neal, dressed in his uniform and wearing a Stetson.

The firing slackened even more as he stopped the bike halfway between the two parties and hopped off. He pulled a bullhorn out of a saddlebag.

"He's got balls. I'll give him that," Dale said.

We saw him raise the bullhorn to his lips, and a few seconds later the words echoed around us.

"All of you stop shooting! You goddamn federals get out of here. The rest of you at the ranch lower your rifles. We need to talk about this."

Somehow it worked. There were a few more odd shots, from both sides, but eventually, the silence stretched to a few seconds, then a minute, then longer. The police continued backing down the driveway, while the people around the ranch house started to get off the ground, collect themselves and tend to their wounded.

We kept scanning, looking for threats, but there was no more shooting. Finally, the cops stopped at the main road.

Dale clicked on the Barret's safety, stood and stretched his back.

"Well, that was a shit sandwich. Now we've got ourselves a good old-fashioned siege."

CHAPTER NINETEEN

By the time I made it to the Lehigh Valley Middle School, helicopters
were landing in the parking lot every few minutes, carrying wounded
to Bend and Boise. Bolle and I pulled into the lot just in time to see
Alex and a couple of volunteer firemen pushing a wounded officer on
an office chair. He had bandages wrapped around his head and face.
They ducked under the blades of the Little Bird, strapped him in, and
Jack took off, pushed the nose of the helicopter down and poured on
the power.

A stunned-looking guy in an FBI windbreaker was mopping blood
off the floor of the school lobby when we walked in. Our ID had been
checked three times, but people still looked at us like they expected us
to open fire at any minute. I made a mental note for Dale and his boys
to stay the hell away from this place. They looked just like the folks
who had just shot up the convoy, and that might not end well for
anyone.

Everyone had a spooked, haunted look that I knew all too well.
When I'd been in the Rangers, we were used to dominating every
situation we were involved in. Casualties were always a possibility, but
they were rare. We were used to stepping over the bodies of our
enemies, not our friends. That day in Mogadishu, eighteen of us had
been killed, and just about everyone else had been wounded to one
degree or another. Days like that changed the way you looked at the
world.

After showing our credentials a fourth time, we managed to get in
the command center. It was bedlam, with phones ringing and people
talking. Burke was standing in a corner, her arms folded over her chest
and her mouth a flat line. She saw us and cocked her head towards a
door. We went through and the noise level dropped when it shut

129

behind us, leaving only the sound of her heels echoing off the rows of lockers as we followed her down an empty hall.

We wound up in a science classroom full of Bunson burners and glassware.

"Four dead and sixteen wounded," she said by way of greeting. "Most of them are FBI, although I think some State Police guys got hit too."

"What a mess," I said.

"Webb and Marshall were supposed to surrender," she said. "They were supposed to tell their people to comply and not shoot. Rumor has it the guy who feel off the van had a gunshot wound in the foot, delivered from very close range."

"He shot himself in the foot, and every body started pulling triggers," Bolle said, shaking his head.

"Webb and Marshall were trying to leave," I said. "They were loading the plane."

"Part of the deal was their wives were supposed to fly away, and Marshall and Webb were going to surrender, but somebody shot up their airplane."

She looked from me to Bolle.

"We didn't know about the deal," he said. "Nobody put us in the loop."

"They could have easily gotten in that plane and flew away," I said. "And you would have had nothing but a bunch of malcontents in custody."

"Well, I guess we'll never know will we?"

Bolle bristled and started to speak, but she cut him off.

"We all bear some of the blame in this," she said. "Right now what you have going for you is almost nobody knows you are here. The FBI is taking the heat for this. It's a shit storm like nothing I've ever seen before. The drone shows almost twenty bodies on the ranch grounds. Most of them have a weapon next to them, but plenty of them don't. We're negotiating right now to get wounded, and people who want to surrender out of the compound."

"They're willing to negotiate?" Bolle asked.

"Webb is being fairly reasonable. He knows he can't escape, and he can't hold out forever. He's just trying to cut the best deal for himself. Marshall is ranting and raving about a revolution and refusing to talk to anybody but the local sheriff. The shrinks think there is a good chance he'll try to go out in a blaze of glory."

"And take plenty of people with him," I said.

"That's exactly what we don't want," Burke said. "He keeps making hints that he's got information that could put a bunch of people in prison. I want that guy sitting in an interview room spilling his guts."

"What are we offering him?" Bolle asked. His eyes didn't quite slide over to look at me, but I could tell he was fighting the urge.

"It depends on what he has," Burke said. Then she did look at me. "And everybody needs to be ok with that."

I wanted Marshall dead or in prison. From moment to moment, that preference could change. The thought of him walking away in some kind of immunity deal stuck in my throat. His people had almost killed Mandy, killed my best friend, taken my job, and burned my damn house down.

But then again, if he was out walking around, I would be able to find him eventually.

"I'll play ball with whatever happens," I said. It sounded hesitant even to my own ears.

Burke didn't look like she believed me but she let it go for now.

"What now?" Bolle asked.

"Right now you're going to report directly to me. I'm guessing Laughlin will be relieved of command, but I'm not sure who his replacement will be. I don't think anybody sees this shit sandwich as a career enhancer. I need you to stay flexible. Your people don't have the firepower to storm that place, and I wouldn't want you to even if you did. But right now I need information more than I need trigger pullers."

That was the first sensible thing I had heard in a while. If this was Iraq, we could have just carpet bombed the ranch and used a vacuum to suck up what was left for DNA analysis, but this was the United States, where we weren't supposed to wantonly kill our own citizens. I was guessing heads would roll over today's shootout, and I was glad. They deserved to.

"Our equipment on the ridge line is still functioning," Bolle said. "We can continue to man the observation post"

Burke nodded. "Do that. The main thing I want your crew to do is just fade into the woodwork. There's going to be a giant investigation into all this eventually, and you're going to have to account for the rounds you fired from that ridiculous gun you have, but I can hold that off for a while. Right now everyone just wants the siege over before it turns into some kind of mass suicide or something."

We made sure we all had up to date cell phone numbers and Bolle and I slipped out without attracting any more attention.

Alex was waiting for us by the car when we came out. There was blood on her shirt and she looked tired. She looked at Bolle rather than me.

"I've done all I can do here. We flew the last casualty out a few minutes ago."

Bolle surprised me by sitting in the back and letting Alex stretch out up front. We had barely left the city limits when I realized she was asleep with her head against the window. Nobody said a word during the whole drive. I was alone with my own thoughts, Bolle was alone with his.

I brought the car to a halt outside of the trailer. Bolle got out without a word, leaving me with Alex.

I shook her awake. She jumped and her arms flailed, not quite punching me in the face. I pulled back and put my hands in front of my face.

"Hey. It's me."

She was breathing fast, not quite hyperventilating, but close. Her hands clutched the dash and she stared down at her feet.

"Deep breaths," I said. "Breathe in for a four count, hold it for a four count, then let it out for a four count."

She did it, and I could see her start to calm.

"Don't they tell women who are giving birth to do this?" she asked after a while.

"Yeah. But we have to call it combat breathing when we teach it to cops," I said.

I didn't know if she wanted me to hug her or touch her or what, so I didn't.

"I'm tired of this," she said. "I want my old life back."

"Me too," I said. I wanted it for her and I wanted it for me.

She slammed her hand on the dash. Once, twice, then a third time. I heard plastic crack the last time.

"You're going to break your hand," I said.

She was breathing hard again. I opened my mouth to suggest she try the deep breathing again, but she started doing it on her own, so I didn't say anything.

"How did you do this for so long?"

I opened my mouth to say something, then shut it, surprised by the question.

"People thought it was bad that I had to deal with dead bodies all the time," she said. "But at least I wasn't there when they actually got shot or stabbed, and I wasn't too worried about somebody trying to kill me. You've been doing this since you were in the army. How do you do it?"

"I guess I just don't think about it too much," I said. That sounded pretty lame the second it was out of my mouth.

"I guess that's my problem. I think too much," she said and got out of the car. She stalked across the gravel and into the bunkhouse.

With a sigh, I pulled myself out of the car. I was sore and tired from humping up and down the ridge, on top of everything else that had happened. I was tempted to go after Alex and ask her to get in the car with me so we could just get the hell out of here, but once again my rational mind reminded me that I had to see this through. I let her go, figuring we'd sort it all out later.

Everyone else was in the trailer, which was crowded and smelled of stale coffee. Bolle shot me an irritated look. Apparently, he'd been waiting for me.

I grabbed a cup of coffee and listened while he briefed everyone. There was silence all around for a few minutes as everyone digested what had happened.

"What now?" Eddie asked.

"We need a lever," Bolle said. "The first one that comes to mind is the sheriff. It sounds like he has quite the relationship with Marshall and Webb."

I nodded my head. It made sense.

"I bet he's dirty," I said. "These guys spoil everything they touch. There's a local guy I've been meaning to get in touch with. He used to work for the Portland Police Bureau before he came out here and went to work for the sheriff's office. Apparently when the new guy got elected, he fired a bunch of the old deputies and hired his own crew."

"I can start digging into him," Casey said. "Phone records. Social media. That sort of thing."

"What if we can't find anything?" Dalton asked.

Casey shrugged. "We can plant it. Suspicious financial transactions. Stuff like that. I could even drop kiddie porn on his county work computer, but I really don't want to deal with stuff like that."

"You scare the shit out of me sometimes, girl," Dale said. Dalton and I were both nodding our heads. Between the three of us Dale, Dalton and I had probably killed enough people to populate a small town, but sometimes I thought Casey was the most dangerous member of our little group.

I heard a buzz from the desk. Casey grabbed the phone in the plastic bag and held it out to me.

"CRYPTER," she said.

WTF? I almost got killed.

Not our call, I typed back. **That was the FBI.**

I need an out. Marshall is a lunatic and is going to get us all killed. Get me out of here.

I looked at Bolle.

"I want to know who he is," Bolle said.

We want your name.

The phone was quiet for a while, and I was convinced he'd broken it off when a reply finally came.

You can know who I am when I'm standing in front of you. If I find a way to break out, can you protect me? I'm afraid if the FBI takes me I'll be disappeared.

"Tell him if he can make it out of the perimeter, I can guarantee his safety. He'll be in our custody and not the FBI."

I had no idea how we were going to keep that promise, but I typed it out anyway.

There was another long pause.

I'm working on a plan. I'll let you know. CRYPTER out.

"Who is he?" I said it out loud without meaning to.

"We don't even have a good guess," Bolle said. "That's what worries me."

CHAPTER TWENTY

The next day things became truly bizarre.

With four federal agents dead, and over a dozen more wounded, Mueller County was now on the map. Previously unknown to damn near everybody, it was now the subject of laser like focus of the federal government, the news media, and extremist crackpots from all over the political spectrum.

Through the night, there were a couple of brief skirmishes and firefights, as the cops struggled to set up a perimeter around the ranch house, and a couple of groups inside tried to escape on foot. Nobody was killed, but it emphasized how difficult it was to secure an area as big as Freedom Ranch. There were a couple hundred cops on the scene now, but even if only half of them were resting at a given time, it was still quite a bit of ground to cover.

That all changed in the morning. Someone had done a momentous job of cutting through red tape, because not even twenty four hours after the initial shoot out, six US Army Stryker vehicles showed up. They weren't quite full fledged tanks, but they dwarfed the Lenco Bearcats the FBI had brought along. The eight wheeled behemoths were armored to withstand up to a .50 caliber machine gun, had a variety of sensors that let them see in the dark, and most importantly they were air conditioned.

The task force set four of them in a circle around the ranch buildings, as sort of mobile bunkers. The other two were held in reserve and used to swap out crews every few hours.

Overnight, the crazies had descended on Lehigh Valley, and the Strykers didn't help to calm anyone's nerves. A bunch of guys on one side of the street were waving upside down American flags and screaming about Posse Commitatus and how taxation was illegal, while on the other side the beads and braids contingent was having a sit in and trying to send everybody calming, non-violent vibes by drumming and chanting. The media, gleefully grateful for a change from the usual political debates, was covering all of it with the rapt attention of a ten-year-old country kid going to the state fair for the first time.

Over the next few days, we fell into a routine. Robert, Dale and I climbed the ridge at first light, spent a mind numbing day in the heat maintaining over watch on the compound, and climbed down the ridge in the late evening to go back to Rudder's and repeat the whole thing again. We radioed intelligence back to the FBI command post in Lehigh, which was received with a curt "copy."

The siege settled into a routine. The negotiators spent hours on the phone with Marshall, listening to long rants and unrealistic demands. At first, the occupiers were live streaming internet videos from inside the ranch, but the FBI figured out a way to jam local cell phone transmissions. Electricity to the compound was cut off, and a FBI sniper disabled the backup generator. They also shot out the tires on all the vehicles. Several people were caught trying to sneak through the lines with food and supplies.

The hope was with no air conditioning, and no way to pump water from the well, the occupants would give up quickly. During the first 36 hours, several folks walked out with their hands up. Apparently this whole thing hadn't turned out to be as much fun as they'd hoped. None of them were Marshall's people, or Webb's security staff. They were all folks from various fringe groups that had descended on the ranch after the initial shootout. The FBI debriefed them for intelligence about conditions inside the house, but didn't share the results with us.

After a while hope of a quick resolution faded. Webb had fancied himself a survivalist, and the house was stocked with food, and a giant cistern of water. The people left were apparently content to sit in the 100 degree heat and sweat.

One evening we arrived back at Rudder's to find Casey waiting for us outside the trailer.

"I've got something you need to see," she said.

My hopes of dinner, a shower, and maybe a little time with Alex vanished as she led me in a big arc around one of Rudder's pastures.

"What are we doing?" I asked.

"You'll see," she said. "Try to act casual."

Finally we entered a little stand of woods from the side opposite the ranch house and trailer. I started to ask her why she hadn't led me there in a straight line when she handed me a pair of binoculars she'd brought with her.

"See the big dead tree? Look about a third of the way down."

I focused the binoculars, hoping she hadn't led me up here to see a cool birds nest or something. I almost missed the camera attached to the tree because it was painted a dull gray with brown stripes. Apparently we weren't the only ones who liked to do remote surveillance.

"It looks like a bump on the tree," I said. "How the hell did you find it?"

"It was tricky," Casey said. "Henry and I were doing a signals sweep when we noticed the transmissions we couldn't account for. We almost missed it. That gave us a general direction. Then I flew around with Jack, triangulating the signal, but you know, without LOOKING like we were triangulating the signal. That gave me a circle about a hundred yards or so around. Then I hiked up here and started looking at trees."

"Do you think they saw you?" I only had a vague understanding of what Henry and Casey had done to find the camera overlooking the ranch, but I knew if whoever was watching us had seen her looking for it, the jig was up.

"I don't think so," she said. "I crept in the back way. The same way I led you in."

"Shit," I said. "Who does it belong to?"

If it was the FBI keeping track of us, I wasn't too worried. But if it was Marshall's people, that was different. We'd been sweeping the cars for tracking devices and bugs. It had pained me to do it, but we'd even been monitoring Rudder's phone calls. The old guy didn't seem to communicate with anyone. He didn't even own a computer or a cell phone, and there had been no activity on the ranch's single land line telephone.

"It's possible somebody tracked us via the CRYPTER phone."

"Which means we aren't the only ones that know about CRYPTER," I said.

"Right."

I scratched the stubble of my beard and wished I hadn't skipped lunch.

"So I guess the question is, do we take it down, or leave it up," I said. I had my .308 with me and was tempted to put a 168-grain hollow point through the camera lens just because it irritated me.

"I have an idea," she said. "Let's go back to the ranch and I'll show everybody at once."

She seemed to enjoy piloting the four-wheeler, so I let her drive and hung on for dear life. Of all of us, Casey seemed to be genuinely enjoying herself at times. We managed to make it back to Rudder's without acquiring any new broken bones. Once we had a chance to shake off the dust, we gathered everyone together in the trailer.

Casey put her helmet down and started typing on one of the computers.

"Remember the tracker I put in Hubbard's car? We've been getting good data from it," she said. She showed us a map on the screen.

"If I overlay the data from the last few days, it shows me the car has mostly been sitting still, either at the middle school the feds are using as a command post, or at the motel in town."

I looked at the red lines on the map. They mostly followed the route from the motel to the school, like Casey said. But there were a couple trips outside of town. Hubbard looked like he was randomly driving back roads, going around in circles.

"That's a surveillance detection route," I said.

"Yep," Casey said. "Out here it's pretty easy to see if someone is following you. It looks like he's done a perfunctory SDR a couple of times before going here."

She zoomed in on a spot on the map. "After he does his surveillance detection route, he always winds up here."

"What's there?" Bolle asked.

Casey flipped over to a satellite view.

"It's a twelve-acre parcel of land at the end of a dirt road. There's a manufactured home on it and it's been in foreclosure for a couple of years due to unpaid property taxes."

"A perfect place to hide out," Bolle said. "What's he doing out there?"

"Only one way to find out," I said.

"I reckon we're going on a nature hike," Dale said.

A few hours later I found myself hiding in the woods, looking at a familiar pickup. It was the monster truck that had been parked outside the motel where I'd been darted and almost kidnapped. I felt a surprising surge of anger when I saw it. Bolle, Eddie, Dale and I had carefully moved on foot from a road about a mile away, bushwhacking through the woods with the aid of a handheld GPS unit.

The house was ramshackle, with one window boarded up. It was surrounded by knee-high weeds and there was trash all over the place. A late model SUV was parked next to the truck. We could hear the hum of a generator from behind the house.

The most interesting thing was the round satellite dish screwed to the roof. A cable ran from the dish and into a window. It was exactly the kind of dish Casey had told us to look out for.

Bolle gave me a nod and I pulled out the satellite phone.

Casey answered on the first ring.

"Do it," I said.

"Five minutes," she said and hung up.

With Robert's help, she'd sneaked back up to the tree watching Rudder's ranch. Now with the aid of a climbing belt and some improvised spikes, she'd climb the tree, and disconnect the camera from its antenna that was aimed at the sky.

Right on schedule, a guy wearing jeans, a t-shirt and sandals came outside. He was carrying a coffee cup and looked up at the antenna on the roof. After shaking his head, he went back in and we heard voices coming from inside.

Another guy came out. He was tall and fit, probably in his late thirties or early forties, and wore tactical pants with a holstered pistol. He unfolded the antenna of a satellite phone almost identical to my own and had a brief conversation. We were too far away to tell what he was saying but the conversation was short, and mostly one-sided. He did more talking than listening.

He went back inside and after a few minutes emerged with two other men. There were all virtual clones: all white, same age, almost the same clothes. They were either military, former military or cops, and didn't even bother trying to hide it. They carried backpacks and rifles and piled into the truck. We listened to the fading sound of the truck's engine for a few minutes, then huddled up.

"Let's go in," Bolle said.

I nodded. We'd formulated a plan earlier and now we executed it. Eddie and I circled to the back of the house. It took us almost half an hour to do it, but we figured we had plenty of time. The guys in the truck would have to drive to the back side of Rudder's ranch and walk at least a couple of miles to the camera so they could fix it.

Eddie was surprisingly quiet for such a big guy, but you could tell the woods weren't his natural environment. He was getting better at moving through the brush without making noise, and how to pick the most efficient route.

We paused right at the tree line. There were about twenty yards of open space between us and the back door of the house. I keyed my radio microphone twice and was rewarded with two answering clicks in my earpiece. Bolle and Dale were in position as well.

I dashed across the open ground to the wall of the house while Eddie covered, then he followed. He covered the back door while I crept from window to window. The place was mostly empty. There were sleeping bags and duffel bags in the bedrooms. The living room was full of plastic equipment cases. A folding table was covered with monitors and electronic gear that looked almost identical to the stuff we had in our trailer back at Rudder's.

The guy in the t-shirt was sitting with his back to me, watching a pornographic movie on his laptop. I didn't see anyone else inside.

I gave Eddie a thumbs up. He pointed his rifle at the back door while I went over to the generator. I found the kill switch and pressed it.

The sudden silence was broken by a "shit" from inside and the guy stepped out the back door, to find the fat suppressor on the end of Eddie's rifle pointed right at his face.

"Whoa," he said, and put his hands up.

"We're Federal Agents," I said. "Who else is inside?"

"Nobody," he said.

"What's your name?" I asked.

He took a long time to answer and looked like he was thinking way too hard.

"John," he said.

"John what?"

"John Smith. I want to talk to an attorney."

I slung my rifle so it was hanging across my back, took two steps forward and round kicked him in the leg just above his left kneecap. His leg buckled and he dropped like a sack of shit.

He gave a moan and grabbed his thigh. I'd blasted the kick right into his common peroneal nerve, and right now his leg probably felt like it was on fire.

I leaned over and grabbed a handful of lank hair in my gloved hand.

"That's funny," I said. "My name is John Smith too. The other funny thing is, your three buddies that just left in that truck bear a striking resemblance to the guys that drugged me and tried to kill me a few nights ago, so I'm taking this kind of personally. I don't think there are really any lawyers available in this neck of the woods, but I do see a rusty ass shovel leaning against the wall over there, and quite a few places I could dig a hole to bury you in. So you want to try this again?"

"Fuck! You can't do this dude."

"You know, my moral compass has been pretty defective lately, so if you want to try me, I'm more than willing to show you what I can do."

I picked him up by the hair and was contemplating whether to slam his head into the side of the house or throw him across the yard.

"Ok! Ok! My name is Walter. I'm just a technician. I swear! I'm here on a contract."

I stifled the rage I hadn't even been aware I'd been carrying with me and set him down.

"Excellent choice Walt."

I prodded him inside. I pulled the chair into the center of the room, away from any place he could grab a weapon and sat him down. Dale and Bolle came in the front door.

Bolle gave Walter a salesman's grin and sat on a folding camp chair. We'd agreed ahead of time that I would be the bad cop and Bolle would be the good cop.

"Walter, pleased to meet you. Why don't you tell me all about how you came to be in this godforsaken place."

"I told that guy I wanted a lawyer. If you guys are really cops you should get me one."

"Walter, have you ever really read The Patriot Act?" Bolle asked. "It's actually quite fascinating to read the thousands of pages, but in the interests of time, I'll paraphrase for you."

He leaned in close.

"Basically, it says I can do whatever the fuck I want with you. I can keep you locked in a windowless cell until I get tired of hearing you scream. I can even lock you in a room with my friend over there. Do you know that I once saw him beat a man so bad he lost the vision in one eye?"

Apparently we'd gone from "good cop/bad cop" to "bad cop/ worse cop."

Walter swallowed hard.

"I'm just a contractor," he said. "I flew in two nights ago. I'm here to babysit some camera equipment watching some ranch. I got it all up and running and I'm supposed to fly out tonight."

"You're making much better choices Walter. Tell me about the three men who just left in the pickup truck."

Walter shrugged. "They're door kickers. I guess former military, but they don't tell me anything. They call each other Mr. Black, Mr. White, and Mr. Green."

"Obviously Tarantino film buffs. Who else Walter? Who else have you seen here?"

"An old guy. And a woman."

Bolle pulled out his phone and scrolled through pictures.

"This man?" He showed him a picture of Hubbard from our security cameras back at Wapato.

Walter nodded. Bolle scrolled some more.

"And her?" He showed her a picture of Diana.

Walter nodded again.

"Excellent."

As they talked, Eddie and I had been searching the house while Dale kept watch for traffic coming up the road. The equipment cases I opened had foam cutouts for rifles and pistols that were empty. There was quite a bit of ammo still in boxes, food, cooking gear, radio equipment, and some medical gear. It all looked pretty familiar from my own deployments in the Army, although this was better, lighter, and more expensive stuff.

I opened one last case and paused. Inside was one of the dart guns like we'd taken off Diana. There were cutouts in the foam for two guns. One was missing, along with a container of darts.

I showed it to Bolle.

"Fascinating," he said with a lifted eyebrow. "We'll be taking that with us."

Eddie walked back into the living room.

"Nothing back there but bedrolls and dirty underwear," he said.

He leaned back in towards Walter.

"Now Walter, you're a bright boy. I assume you were recruited because of your military background. I'm guessing you were in signals intelligence, something like that?"

Walter nodded. His eyes danced from me to Bolle.

"Now, I'm guessing there are some things you haven't told me," Bolle said. He held his thumb and forefinger about an inch apart. "We are this close to me letting you get in that SUV parked outside and drive away, but you could still fuck it up and wind up locked in a room with my associate over there, so it's important that you be honest. Do you understand?"

Beads of sweat were popping out on Walter's face. He gave an almost imperceptible nod.

"Tell me about the cell phone you've been monitoring for your client."

Walter blew out a breath. "I localized the two ends of the conversation. One is at that ranch the cops have surrounded. The other is there."

He jerked his chin at the now blank monitor.

"Excellent. Were you able to read the messages?"

"We could. Somebody named CRYPTER."

I tried to keep my face impassive. Hubbard knew about CRYPTER.

I'm not going to lie. I took a great deal of pleasure in smashing all the equipment in the house. We'd considered just burning the damn thing down, but we didn't need the attention. We relieved Walter of his cell phone and searched the SUV for any other means of communication before sending him on his way. We had little doubt he would contact Hubbard eventually, but it would take a while.

We discussed ambushing the three contractors when they came back, but didn't want to risk a gunfight, for very little gain. The three were most likely contractors just like Walter. Granted, what they were doing was illegal, but I'd been around the block enough times to know people like them were useful to people like Hubbard. The only difference between using their skill sets in places like Afghanistan, Iraq and Pakistan and using them in the US was the price.

So we left all the electronic gear in pieces, cut up the sleeping bags out of spite, and pitched all the food into the backyard before we hiked back to our vehicle. I put the case holding the dart gun behind the seat of Dale's truck and climbed in.

We were all silent for a while as we jounced down the bad road. I enjoyed the scenery out here, but I was starting to miss smooth pavement.

"Hubbard knows about the money," Eddie said.

"I suspect Hubbard has always known about the money," Bolle said. "And very soon he will know that we know. It will be interesting to see how this changes things."

"I get tired of all this spook shit," Dale said as he navigated around a particularly deep rut. "Can we arrest the son of a bitch?"

"With our unlawfully obtained evidence?" Bolle asked. "No. But Mr. Hubbard may still get his comeuppance yet."

"You think he's working with Marshall?" I asked.

"I think it's more likely that Marshall is Hubbard's tool. Nothing ever points directly at Hubbard, but he's always around, on the periphery. I think many people dismiss him as a mid-level functionary at CIA, but I'm beginning to suspect that there's more to him than that."

I mulled that over for a while. One question I'd been chewing on for quite a while was exactly how far this investigation should go. How many people would we have to pick off before we got to the top? It seemed like this could go on forever, and Bolle, in his messianic zeal, would probably keep on trucking until he either died or he was convinced he'd rooted out every last participant in the conspiracy.

I wasn't so sure I was on board with that. I wasn't quite sure when I would be done, but I hoped I'd know it when I saw it.

"Now what?" I asked.

Bolle looked at his watch. "I would imagine Walter will have found a way to contact his boss by now. I'd like to see how Hubbard reacts. He doesn't take setbacks well."

I wanted to ask Bolle how he knew Hubbard, but I knew I'd likely get some kind of bullshit, evasive answer. I was so sick of these people.

Instead, I just leaned my head back against the seat and tried to relax, thinking about a day when I would be in the driver's seat of my own life again.

CHAPTER TWENTY-ONE

Alex was petting a horse when we pulled in. It stuck it's head out over the split rail fence so she could scratch it between the eyes. While the others went in the trailer and the bunkhouse, I just stood there and watched her for a minute in the fading light of sundown. She was wearing jeans and an unbuttoned plaid shirt over a tank top. Her hair blew in the evening wind and I realized anew how much I loved her. I felt a lump in my throat, and the distance between us hurt so bad it was almost a physical ache. I felt a moment of panic and just wanted to run, try to get to a place where she wasn't. I'd been shot at, nearly strangled, and blown up in the last few months, but what I was afraid of more than anything was her turning around and telling me she didn't want to see me again.

For some reason, I was oddly reminiscent of the first time I'd stood in the door of an airplane and prepared to fling myself out. I swallowed hard and made myself walk up to her.

"How'd it go?" she asked, without turning around.

"Ok," I said. I stood there with my hands in my pockets, feeling like I was back in middle school again, all tongue-tied and awkward.

"Didn't shoot anybody?" she asked.

I didn't say anything for a minute, trying to keep myself from getting pissed.

She turned around and put her hands on her hips.

"I'm sorry. That came out snarkier than I meant. I was joking."

"Ok," I said. Part of me wanted to step closer to her, maybe take her in my arms, but I stubbornly refused to make the first move.

"Besides," she said, softly. "I was sitting there in the radio room with my medical kit, in case somebody really did get shot."

She crossed her arms over her chest. "In case you got shot."

I blinked, realized my eyes were wet.

"Thanks," I said around the lump in my throat. "Good to know you've got my back."

She took a step towards me, and I finally gave. I pulled her to me and hugged her close. I realized that one of the reasons she was wearing the un-tucked shirt was to hide the gun she had on her hip. Part of me was glad she was armed, even in our supposedly safe little compound. Part of me was still able to realize how messed up it was that we were constantly armed.

"I don't want it to be this way," she said. "In some ways, I wish we'd never gotten together. I just don't want to lose anybody else. But I can't imagine things without you either, because you're all I have left."

I just stood there and held her as the sun went down. The horse, bored with our human drama apparently, wandered off and started chomping at grass.

"Let's pretend we're normal," I said.

"What the hell does that mean?"

"Let's go get in the car, go have dinner, and talk about something normal."

She pulled back and looked me in the eye.

"I'm not even sure how to do that anymore."

"See? When we're together, what do we spend most of our time talking about?"

"All of this," she said, waving her hand to take in the trailer and everything around us.

"Ok," I said. "I won't talk about it if you won't."

"Promise?"

"Pinky swear." I held up a pinky and tried to look solemn. She giggled, and put a hand over her mouth, a gesture that I remembered from when she was much younger, and much more self-conscious. We touched pinkies and walked toward our car, holding hands.

"What are we going to eat?" she asked.

"No idea. But around here I'm guessing it will involve beef and potatoes."

There was little point in trying to talk on the rough gravel road that led from Rudder's place, but once we hit the blacktop it was quieter. I tried to think of something to say, thought of several things only to reject them, and wound up sitting there in silence, waiting for her to say something. It reminded me again so much of high school I didn't know whether to laugh or scream.

She gave that laugh again, and I had a flashback to the first time I'd seen her, all those years ago. I'd been sitting on her dad's back porch, nursing a beer and icing some bruised knuckles as I debriefed with her dad a fight that had happened the night before.

"I don't know what to say," she said. "We can't talk about work, so what should we talk about? I think that's kind of sad."

I nodded.

"And a little scary," she said more quietly.

I felt like it wouldn't take much for the mood of the evening to flip and go straight to hell. Things felt so tenuous that I was afraid one wrong word would be the undoing of us. Usually, at times like this, I got quiet and refused to talk. That had cost me more relationships than I could count, so I resolved to do something different this time. If I was going to go down in flames, at least it wouldn't be because I repeated the same old mistakes.

"I don't want to talk about work," I said, holding up the pinkie I used to swear with. "We could talk about after, though."

"After?"

"After all this is over, and I hand Bolle these credentials I've got in my pocket and walk away."

"You really think you'll do that?" she asked.

I held up my pinkie. "I'll swear to it if you want."

She looked out the window. I was headed towards Lehigh Valley. A plan was forming in my head. It wasn't the best plan, but maybe it would work.

"I don't want to go back to Portland," she said. "I want to go somewhere else. Somewhere small, maybe with mountains."

She spoke slowly, haltingly, like each word cost her a drop of blood. I found myself nodding.

"Me too," I said. "I was maybe thinking of traveling around for a while, seeing the country and finding a place that felt like a good fit."

"That sounds fun," she said. "I don't want to deal with dead people anymore."

"Me neither," I said. I rolled that idea around in my head for a minute. What if there would be a time when I would see my last dead body, and I wouldn't have to see any more after that. It sounded nice.

"I'd probably have to take some continuing education, but I'm still a doctor. I bet I could find a job in some rural clinic, or maybe a small hospital."

"That sounds good," I said as the lights of Lehigh Valley came into view. "You could help people."

"What about you?"

I thought about it, not for the first time, as I slowed for the town's lone traffic light.

"I don't know," I said. "Maybe I'll go back to school and learn a trade. Auto mechanic. Electrician. Something like that."

We couldn't escape our reality in town. There were satellite news trucks parked everywhere and people stood on the streets waving signs and banners. Alex sighed.

We decided to go through the drive-through at the local burger joint. We figured if we sat down in a restaurant dining room it would be a matter of time before somebody hassled us for being out of town Feds, or a reporter shoved a microphone into our faces. The girl in the window handed us a bag of food that smelled like meat, potatoes and grease and I drove to the boat ramp on the outskirts of town where I'd met with Stonebrook. Luckily it was deserted. We rolled down the windows and let the sound of the river fill the car as we pulled out our food.

"This is actually pretty good," she said around mouthfuls of burger. "But I bet I'm still going to feel like crap after I eat it."

Alex could be a bit of a health nut. I was used to grabbing food wherever I found it, although I was more careful in my forties, as the pounds tended to accumulate a little easier

Somehow, over food, the conversation flowed more easily. We both reiterated that we wanted to live out in the country somewhere, maybe with some land, although that might be more than we wanted to maintain. We both wanted to stay somewhere in the Western US. She wanted to travel overseas. I was open to the idea but didn't want to go anywhere vulnerable to terrorist attacks. I wanted to visit Graceland. She thought I was joking at first but agreed to go when she realized I wasn't.

The ideas flowed back and forth, and I think we were both relieved to find out we agreed much more than we didn't. At first it was like we were probing each other, neither willing to tip their hand too much, but gradually we grew more comfortable, and the conversation became more animated and spontaneous.

The issue neither of us broached was children. I almost brought it up a couple of times, and I figured she had to be thinking about it too, but ultimately I didn't say anything. Alex's confidence seemed to be razor thin tonight. She'd express some preference for the future and then give me an expectant look, like she thought I'd get pissed and declare it the deal breaker right there. She was normally so self-assured it was hard for me to know what to do. I realized then that she was just as worried this wouldn't work out as I was, and in a weird sort of way, that made me feel better.

She finished her burger and slurped the last of her soda. I'd long finished eating, a habit born of years of gulping down lunch in between radio calls.

"I'm glad we did this," she said. "It was like a real date."

I laughed. "We've been through a lot together, but we've never really been on a date."

She put her hands on the side of my face and kissed me, light at first, then deeper. She drew back for a second and laughed.

"You taste like cheeseburger."

I pulled her back to me and kissed her and she pressed herself against me as much as the cramped front seat of the Charger would allow. Feeling like a high school kid, I slid my hands under her tank top and bra and cupped her breasts. She made a noise in the back of her throat and started tugging at the buttons of my jeans.

"Here?" I asked.

"Why not?" she asked. "If we're going to act like high school kids on a date, we might as well go all the way. We just have to get these guns off without shooting each other."

I kissed her neck and tried to decide if the front seat or back seat would be easier. I tried to remember if there was a blanket in the trunk, but my higher cognitive skills were a little impaired.

My phone rang.

"Oh no," she moaned.

"Leave it," I said. "I'll call them back in a few minutes."

"It better be longer than a few minutes," she said as she pulled my shirt tail out of my pants.

My phone quit ringing but hers started.

"Shit," she said and grabbed the phone. She tried to throw it out the window but it bounced off the B-piller and fell into the back seat.

"I'm going to find it and smash it," she said, pulling away from me.

My phone started again.

"I'm going to get it," I said.

"I know you are," she said. "That's why I'm going to smash my phone. It'll make me feel better."

It was Casey.

"Where are you?"

"Town," I said, fighting the urge to let my irritation show.

"You need to get back here. Bolle is doing something stupid."

CHAPTER TWENTY-TWO

"I can't believe he's doing this," Alex said.

I grunted in reply. I'd kept a low profile driving back through town, but once on the other side, I'd turned on the Charger's red and blue lights and floored it. The road was straight and empty, but I was still worried about wildlife and wayward livestock. At this speed, I risked what was called "overdriving my headlights." By the time an obstacle showed up in my lights, I would be going too fast to stop the vehicle before I hit it. I would only be able to swerve.

It didn't help that the blue and red flashers caused the shadows to constantly shift. I felt a knot of tension in the base of my neck. I'd once come to the realization that if I died in a car crash while running lights and siren, I'd be just as dead as if somebody shot me. I needed to concentrate on the road ahead of me, but I couldn't get Casey's message entirely out of my mind.

"He's desperate to get his hands on Marshall," I said. "CRYPTER might be a key to doing that."

"Yeah, but to bring him to Rudder's?"

Earlier, a single pickup truck had left Freedom Ranch, busted past one of the Strykers and vanished into the network of logging roads behind the ranch. It sounded like the Feds had been expecting another boring night of armed standoff and had been caught by surprise. They were trying to coordinate a passel of FBI agents bouncing around in rented SUVs and getting lost on the unmarked roads, with a couple of unmanned drones and a helicopter.

"Hopefully, Dalton will talk some sense into him," I said.

We had to stop talking as I bounced us down Rudder's ranch road. I pushed the Charger as fast as I dared. I didn't want to risk popping a tire or blowing a ball joint. Several people were milling around outside the trailer. As I brought the car to a halt I saw Dale, Robert and Jack head towards the barn where we had the helicopter stashed.

I stepped out of the car and Casey walked up.

"The plan is CRYPTER is going to drive here, and we're going to fly him somewhere safe in the Little Bird before the FBI shows up," she said.

"Wonderful," I said as I walked around to the trunk of the car. "Do we know it's actually CRYPTER that's coming?"

"That's kind of what the argument is about."

Bolle was trying to talk on a satellite phone and argue with Dalton at the same time, while Eddie stood by, looking back and forth at them.

"CRYPTER is on a satellite phone," Casey said. "Bolle is actually talking to him. He won't tell us who he really is though."

"Huh," I said, and unlocked the trunk. I was having trouble switching gears. Twenty minutes ago I'd been making out with my girlfriend, now we had an informant headed our way with the FBI in hot pursuit. I pulled my shotgun out of its case. I had no idea what was about to happen but figured I'd rather have a long gun in my hands than not.

"He's turning onto the ranch road," Bolle said.

Off in the distance, I heard the growl of an engine and the sound of a truck bottoming out on a particularly bad pothole in Rudder's ranch road. I figured we had maybe two minutes before he got here.

"Fuck this," Dalton said. "I'm blocking the gate.

Bolle grabbed his arm but he broke free. Dalton hobbled over to one of our SUVs and started it. He pulled forward and blocked the gate of the ranch. It was largely symbolic, as it would be simple enough to just drive off the road and go around the gate in grass but that would give us some information about CRYPTERs intentions.

"Goddammit! Don't spook him off!" Bolle said.

I didn't say anything but I approved of what Dalton had done. Stopping the truck at the gate would give us some standoff distance, to see what we were really dealing with. I handed Alex her rifle. She took it wordlessly and I turned to Casey.

"Hey," I said quietly. "You want to grab your long gun and get on top of the trailer?"

She nodded and took off at a run. Dalton was pulling himself out of the SUV. I could see the glow of headlights as the truck bounced down the ranch road.

"We need to come up with a plan here," I said to Bole.

"The plan is to get him out of that truck and put his ass on a helicopter before the FBI grabs him," Bolle snapped at me. He was pissed at what he no doubt perceived as a near mutiny from his people. If I had the time, I could probably talk some sense into him.

"Come on," he said to Eddie, and they started walking towards the gate.

I abandoned all hope of reasoning with Bolle. I looked around the big gravel lot that sat between Rudder's house, barn, bunkhouse and equipment sheds. There was a big piece of farm equipment parked on one edge.

"Let's go," I said to Alex, and trotted across the gravel. The combine, or whatever the hell it was, looked solid enough to stop bullets.

Dalton saw us and changed course towards us, limping across the gravel as fast as his bum leg and cane could carry him.

The truck drifted over towards the side of the ranch road, and for a second I thought it was going to drive onto the grass and around our makeshift roadblock. I started to raise my shotgun so I could put some slugs through the windshield, Bolle's wishes be damned, when the truck stopped.

I couldn't see inside the truck. Bolle raised his hand.

"Go ahead and get out," he said.

The door to the truck opened slowly. There was a powerful light attached to the handguard of my shotgun. I hit the switch and in the harsh glare, I recognized Marshall's pilot, the guy who had been on the runway a few days back when we shot up the plane.

It was a warm night. I was perfectly comfortable in a short sleeve shirt. The pilot was wearing a heavy, bulky coat. There was something in his left hand about the size of an apple.

Dalton saw it the same time I did. In my peripheral vision, I saw him drop to the gravel and cover his head with his hands.

The pilot looked at Bolle.

"I'm sorry," he said. "They have my family."

I debated shooting the pilot in the head, but instead, I turned, bear hugged Alex, and drove her to the ground, where I covered her with my body.

I never actually heard the explosion. There was a bright, white light and a sound like the ocean in my ears. The next thing I knew I was on my back, looking at the stars. At first, I thought it was raining, then I realized it was gravel hitting me, blown up into the sky and now falling back to earth. I felt really far away from my body like I was watching all this happen to somebody else.

Beside me, Alex pushed herself up on all fours. She pulled a headlamp out of the cargo pocket of her khakis, switched it on, and ran her hands all over my body. At first, it seemed like a strange thing to do, then I realized she was checking me for wounds.

I realized she was talking to me. It sounded like she was miles away, and underwater.

"I'm ok," I said or at least tried to. I sat up and everything spun for a minute.

She said something. I was pretty sure it was "I'm going to get my medical kit," then she was gone.

I sat there, blinked a couple of times, and decided to stand up. I grabbed the side of the combine and pulled myself up. I held on until everything quit spinning.

The scene was lit by the two burning vehicles. The SUV Dalton had set as a roadblock was on fire. Its tires and interior were burning. The pilot's truck was unrecognizable, just a twisted heap of burning metal. The gravel was blown out of the lot in a circle around the two rigs. The force of the explosion had scoured it away down to the bare earth.

Dalton sat up. He had blood running from his hairline but all his parts seemed to be there.

There were random pieces of the two vehicles scattered in the parking lot, some of them on fire. I coughed from the dense black smoke billowing from the burning tires, then the wind shifted and blew it away from me. In the red glow of the flames, I saw Eddie lying on his back, spreadeagled.

I walked up to him, taking it slow because everything around me seemed to spin a little bit every time my foot hit the ground. At first, I thought he was going to be ok. He looked peaceful laying there, the right side of his body untouched, but as I got closer I could see the other side of him, and I knew he was gone. I figured he must have turned away from the blast.

Knowing it was hopeless, I bent over to check him for a pulse anyway. There wasn't one. I wanted to shut the one good eye he had left, rather than leave him there staring up at the night sky, but I knew from experience the eyelid would just open again.

I stood, and almost fell over. There was a voice in the back of my head saying I was probably hurt, and should probably take it easy, but I ignored it. Everything had a slow motion, dreamlike quality. I saw red and blue lights down at the end of Rudder's ranch road, then something else caught my eye.

It was Bolle. He was on his side, doubled up clutching his belly. The legs of his suit pants were on fire. I stumbled over and did the only thing I could think of. I pulled off my own shirt and used it to smother the flames on his legs. I burned my own hands a little in the process, but I finally got the fire out. His legs were a mess. I choked on the smell of burnt hair and charred meat and swallowed a little vomit.

I realized why Bolle was doubled over. There was a jagged point of metal sticking out of his back, between his shoulder blades. His hands were grasping the other side, which was sticking out of his chest. His hands were slick with blood, and every time he tried to pull it out, they slipped.

"Don't pull on it," I said, and knelt down beside him.

He looked at me, but I wasn't sure he recognized me. His mouth was puckering like a fish out of water and blood ran out of his mouth and nose. All I saw in his eyes was panic.

He grabbed my wrist, spasmed once, and died. His body went from rigid and clenched to relaxed in the span of a few seconds, and I knew the life had gone out of him. I couldn't see any sign of the pilot. There was a crater where he'd been standing, and I realized some of the parts I saw on the ground weren't car parts.

Fire was licking along the bottom of Dalton's SUV. A hand grabbed my arm and Alex dragged me away from the gate. I heard her say something about a gas tank, right before the SUV blew up.

It wasn't a big Hollywood explosion, just a giant *whumpf* and a fireball that went up into the sky. I still felt my nose hairs crisp a little bit as the wave of hot air washed over us. Alex pulled me along, and I suddenly didn't feel very well at all. I felt like my legs were rubber, and things around me would first spin one way, then another.

She walked me over to the trailer and helped me up the steps. All the windows were blown in, and both Henry and Daniel had blood on their faces. They were being tended to by Casey, who had blood running out of her own nose. Alex sat me down at the little dinette and shined a flashlight in my eyes.

The roaring in my ears was changing to a high pitched whine that was downright painful. Alex ran her hands over my head and neck, and down my bare chest. I tried to make a crack about continuing our activities from earlier, but she didn't seem to hear me. I realized I couldn't tell how loud I was talking. I could have been whispering or yelling. I wasn't sure. Mostly I just heard the reverberations in my head.

She said something, and I concentrated on her lips, but I couldn't make it out. I shrugged.

"I said I think you have a little bit of concussion." I realized she was yelling.

"Why aren't you hurt?" I asked. I hoped I wasn't yelling too loud.

"You pushed me down behind the tire."

I realized she had fine little scratches on her face, and one palm and knee were skinned. For some reason, that made me incredibly angry. The fact that Bolle and Eddie were dead hadn't really registered yet but seeing Alex hurt made me realize how bad things really were.

I faintly heard people yelling outside, and Alex disappeared out the door for a minute.

"FBI," she said. "And ambulances."

She pulled me out of the chair and I followed her like a puppy on a leash.

Outside the trailer, things were bedlam. A bunch of FBI agents in tactical gear were milling around. A guy with an EMT patch on his body armor came and grabbed my other arm. He and Alex walked me around the burning vehicles as a volunteer fire department crew rolled up and started spraying foam. I saw Dalton arguing with a pair of FBI suits with Eddie and Bolle's bodies in the background.

I looked over my shoulder and saw Henry, Casey, and Robert following us, being helped by more agents and firefighters.

The inside of the ambulance was bright and smelled like antiseptic. I recognized one of the rescue squad members as the young woman who had handed us our food at the drive through not an hour before. She still smelled like French fries. They packed all of us into the one ambulance: me, Henry, and Robert. We all expected Casey to climb in as well but she shook her head, and darted back towards the ranch.

It was a tight fit with all of us in the back, but we made it work as we bounced down the ranch road. I squeezed into a corner and tried not to get in the way as Alex and the EMT worked. Henry's wounds didn't look that bad. I guessed he'd probably need some stitches. Daniel had nearly been scalped. Alex wrapped bandage after bandage around his head, but they soaked through. He was getting pale and clammy looking. Alex started an IV and kept bandaging. Finally, the pace of the bleeding slowed.

There were wheelchairs lined up waiting for us at the emergency room entrance. Part of me wanted to John Wayne it and try to walk in under my own power. I could tell Alex knew what I was thinking. She shot me a look that said she'd pull an Aikido move on me if I didn't go with the program, so I acquiesced to being wheeled shirtless and singed into the ER.

There was a minor kerfuffle when the triage nurse discovered I still had a pistol strapped to my belt. Alex solved the problem by taking it off me and threading the holster onto her belt on her left side, cross-draw style. She looked a little funny walking around with two guns like that, but nobody seemed to be in a mood to argue with her. When the nurse turned her head, I surreptitiously slipped Alex the little .38 out of my pocket and a knife or two.

"You're gonna clank when you walk," I said.

"That's ok. One of us needs to be armed. I'm sticking close to you."

Up until now, my usual paranoia had taken a back seat to other events. I was in a wheelchair in the hallway shirtless, unarmed and concussed. If somebody wanted to make a play for me, now would be the time to do it.

I was glad Alex was there.

Over the next couple of hours, I was poked, prodded, and had my head stuck in some kind of scanner. I never could keep CAT scans and MRI machines straight. Finally, a fresh-faced young doctor who was probably hoping to get his student loan debt forgiven by working in a rural area, told me I had a mild concussion and I should take it easy for a few days. I managed not to laugh at him.

By then Dale had shown up, looking pissed. He tossed a fresh shirt at me.

"How's Robert?" I said as I pulled the shirt over my head.

"He'll live. Boy's face ain't ever gonna be the same again though."

"What's going on back at the ranch?" I asked, then tried standing up. The room wobbled a little bit, but I was ok. I was trying very hard to ignore the ice pick headache. Everything still sounded muffled and I was nauseous.

Fuck it. Drive on.

"It's a madhouse," Dale said. "The FBI, ATF, DHS, hell a bunch of agencies I've never heard of are crawling all over the place. They all but kicked us out, so we hopped in the truck and came over here."

"Is Rudder ok?" The doctor had left the room, so Alex un-threaded my holster from her belt and handed it to me. It felt good to be armed again.

"Yup," Dale said. "He's trying to round up some of his stock that got scared off by the explosion. I figure we'll help him with that when we get back. The question I have for you all is, where's Casey? We ain't seen her here in the hospital."

I shook my head, then regretted it. I held on to the edge of a counter and eyed the trash can, calculating whether I could get to it in case I threw up.

"She stayed at the ranch," Alex said.

"Huh," Dale said. "We didn't see her."

I felt a twinge of worry, but my thinking was fuzzy and I was having trouble processing all of it. Alex pulled out her phone.

"I'll text her," she said.

The door to my room banged open and Henry walked in. He had bandages all over his face but looked otherwise ok. Burke walked in right behind him, followed by two guys in suits that looked so much alike they could be twins. One scanned us, the other turned so he could see the door. It was getting awfully crowded in here.

"You're shut down," she said without preamble. "I don't know what you were thinking, or what Bolle was thinking, trying to get Lyle to come to that ranch. Even if he hadn't been wired with explosives, that was a dumb move."

She looked pale, and to be honest, frightened.

"I'm supposed to take everyone's credentials," she said. "As of right now you're all suspended with pay pending an investigation."

Wordlessly, I pulled my leather credential holder out of my pocket and flipped it onto the bed. Everybody else followed. She hadn't asked for my gun, so I left it where it was.

"There's a block of hotel rooms in Ontario. You're authorized to stay there tonight, then leave Eastern Oregon immediately. Go home to Portland and be available for questioning."

"My boy's in the hospital here, and we ain't from Portland," Dale said.

"We're arranging for his transfer to a hospital in Portland," Burke said.

Dale crossed his arms across his chest and gave her a flat stare, but didn't object.

"What's going to happen with Marshall?" I asked.

Burke gave me a haunted look that I didn't quite know how to read. Her eyes jerked toward one of the suits, and I started wondering if they were here to protect her or watch her.

"The justice department is going to appoint a special prosecutor from DC to take over the case," she said.

"Who?" Dale asked.

"I don't know yet. I suspect the announcement is going to be made in the next few hours," she said.

I felt that old familiar feeling of the rug being pulled out from under my feet. Burke had been our ace in the hole. She wanted Marshall in prison, and more. She was willing to keep climbing the ladder as high as it went beyond Marshall, and she had the guts and brains to make it stick. But right now she looked defeated and scared.

"I'm supposed to order you to stay away from Freedom Ranch, the Rudder Ranch, the command post here in town, and any other location associated with the ongoing investigation. Since all of you are here at the hospital, I'd suggest you just get in your vehicles and drive to the hotel we have booked for you in Ontario right now."

Again, that twitching of the eye toward the guy standing in the doorway. I didn't recognize him, which didn't mean anything. He was so blandly generic that it was almost comical. Light 30's, short hair, blue eyes, average height, athletic build. He wore a sports coat, jeans, and button-down shirt. He wasn't displaying any credentials, but I could have picked him out of a crowd as a cop or military guy in a heartbeat.

Out of the corner of my eye, I saw Alex open her mouth to say something, then shut it. Good. Either Burke hadn't noticed or had pretended not to notice that Casey wasn't there. Nobody else in the room seemed inclined to bring her up.

"Well, that's it then," I said. "You can't win them all. Let's get out of town. I could use a shower and a decent night's sleep."

Henry looked at me like I'd suggested something obscene and rude, but everybody else stayed impassive. The two suits turned towards the door and Burke followed. As they crossed the threshold of the door, one suit looked right, the other one followed and looked left. It was clear they'd done this before.

Burke suddenly turned towards me and reached for Alex's shoulder. I had to take an awkward little step to avoid her and bumped into one of her handlers.

"Oh Alex," Burke said. "I wanted to thank you for the consulting work on that case last month. I don't think we've ever gotten your fees straightened out."

"Uh. You're welcome?"

I turned and saw Burke brush Alex's chest as she pulled her hand away, almost like she was groping her. Alex had a horrible poker face, which I normally found endearing. Now, I gritted my teeth and willed her to play along.

The guard in the doorway looked over his shoulder with his eyes narrowed. Burke squeezed past me.

"Let's go," Burke said to the guard. "I need to get back to the command post before the briefing. You're going to have to hurry."

Whoever he was, the guard apparently wasn't going to argue with his principal in public. They took off down the hallway, leaving us in their wake. Alex reached up and patted the breast pocket of her flannel shirt.

"Later," I said. "In the car."

Robert, Dalton, and Jack were waiting with Dale's truck and my Charger. Dalton looked a little glassy-eyed, and his limp was worse. I figured his little escapade earlier had hurt his leg more than a little, and I couldn't blame the man for taking a pain pill or two.

Nobody seemed to be watching us. There were surveillance cameras in the parking lot, but I figured enough time had passed since we'd left Burke. I nodded at Alex and she fished a scrap of paper out of her pocket. She read it and handed it to me.

I read the note.

NOT SAFE. Going to kill me.

CHAPTER TWENTY-THREE

We caravaned to the boat ramp on the Meuller River, about eight miles outside of Lehigh Valley. Robert drove me and Alex in the Charger. Everybody else piled into Dale's crew cab. On the ride over we were silent. My head hurt and I still felt woozy. I just wanted a few minutes to sit in quiet, holding my girlfriend's hand in the back seat of the car like somebody was driving us on a date.

When we got out at the boat ramp, I looked over at the spot where Alex and I had been parked. It felt like a lifetime ago since we'd been sitting there making out like a couple of teenagers.

We all huddled in a big circle. I looked everybody over. Henry clearly was hurting. His face was covered in bandages and he leaned against the truck. Dalton looked pale and sweaty. I hoped he hadn't popped something loose in his leg in the process of trying to block Lyle's approach to the ranch. Robert and Dale both looked pissed. Alex stood next to me, with smears of other people's blood on her, and smelling of explosive residue and burnt plastic.

I felt the absence of Eddie and Bolle keenly. Eddie and I had never been close. I had been close with only a handful of people in my life, but I still considered him a friend.

I missed Bolle too. I never liked him, but I always wanted to believe he had some insight into the murky world of spooks and criminals we swam in. He'd always known more than he told me, which had irritated me to no end, but at least he'd known it. Now whatever was in his head was all gone.

I realized everybody was looking at me. I would have given anything to look over my shoulder and find Al, Alex's dead father standing there, ready to step up and take charge. But there was nobody there. It was my turn.

I took a deep breath.

"What next?" I asked. "Do we all just walk away?"

"I ain't inclined to quit now," Dale said. "These assholes have hurt two of my children."

I looked around the circle and saw heads nodding, including Alex. If she'd bowed out, I probably would have gotten in the car with her and just kept driving.

"Ok. Looks like we're in," I said. "What have we got for gear?"

"Whatever we're carrying, and whatever is in the vehicles," Dalton said. "The FBI made it real clear that if we tried to get back into Rudder's Ranch, they'd throw us in jail. Wouldn't let us take anything."

I looked at Jack.

"The Little Bird is still there?"

He nodded. "Gassed and ready to go. Unless they have somebody who can fly the damn thing, there it sits."

"We've got a couple of rifles and some camping gear in the back of the truck," Dale said. "Other than that, most of our gear was in the trailer."

I remembered that we'd left my shotgun and Alex's rifle in the gravel at Rudder's. My .308 was still in the trunk of the Charger, along with two sets of body armor, so that was something.

"We need a place to stay," I said.

"You mean other than the accommodations the Federal government have so thoughtfully provided?" Dale asked.

"Yeah. The ones with the listening devices and surveillance," I said.

"We're gonna need money," Dalton said. "Cash. Not plastic."

"And vehicles," Robert said. "They know these plates."

"And we need to ditch our phones," Henry said.

"We need Casey," Dalton and I said at the same time.

As if on cue, Alex's phone buzzed. She pulled it out of her pocket.

"She says to check the vehicles for GPS trackers, dump our phones, and pick her up at these coordinates. She says to bring a truck or van."

She showed me the screen, which had a latitude and longitude on it.

"Where the hell is that?"

Robert took the phone and punched the numbers into the GPS unit in the truck.

"That's about a tenth mile off a lonely ass gravel road about fifteen miles north of Rudder's."

"Huh," I said.

We pulled a GPS tracker off the pickup and the Charger. I wanted to do something clever with them, but in my mental fog I couldn't come up with anything. Henry pulled a cooler out of the back of Dale's truck, put our phones and the trackers inside, and duct taped it securely. Then he walked over to the boat ramp and chucked it all in the river with a splash.

"It might take them a while to figure that one out," Henry said. He looked at Dale. "I assume the roadside assistance and satellite tracking in your truck is turned off?"

Dale looked like he'd been asked something rude. "Son, I cut all that shit out before I even hung the fuzzy dice from the mirror and put on my nekkid lady mudflaps."

"Ok," Henry said. "We should be as dark as we can get."

"Let's go get Casey," I said. "I'll feel better when the band is all together again."

Dale, Robert, Jack and I rode in the truck, while everybody else rode in the Charger. We left them behind when the road got so rough the Charger was in danger of bottoming out. I could tell Alex wasn't happy about it, but I had no intention of subjecting Dalton's leg to this ride. Henry didn't look like he felt too hot either.

I could have applied the same reasoning to myself. I was continuously queasy, and the rocking of the truck didn't help. I'd had my bell rung more times than I could count, but this one seemed worse than most. I wondered if it was because I was getting older.

"Should be right over there," Robert said, pointing out his right window. I raised a night vision monocular to my eye and was rewarded with a faint flash. It was gone when I took the monocular away, and back when I looked through it again.

"She's using an infrared light," I said. "Stop here."

We piled out, and now Casey was close enough I could see her picking her way through the sagebrush in the dark with a pair of night vision goggles strapped to her face.

"You ok Case?" I didn't even think before I picked her up in a big hug. She was kinda weird about being touched, and I wondered if I'd made a mistake, but she hugged me back enthusiastically.

"I'm fine."

I set her down and she grabbed my hand.

"Come on. This way. I've been busy while I've been waiting for you guys."

She led us to a little swale, where one of Dale's ATV's was parked. It had plastic equipment cases strapped all over it. The ones in front were stacked so high I wasn't sure how she'd seen over it to drive. A small satellite antenna on a tripod was pointed at the heavens, and her laptop was hooked up to it with the screen brightness turned almost all the way down.

"What's all this?" I asked.

"I had some equipment stashed in a line shack on Rudder's ranch in case something like this happened," she said. "I've got some computer hardware, radios, that sort of thing. A couple of guns. Also some money," she said.

"Wow," I said."How did you get out?"

"When the explosion happened, it blew me off the roof of the trailer. I busted my nose," she said and fingered the bridge of her nose. She already had a pair of raccoon eyes started, and there was blood all over the front of her shirt.

"I knew with Bolle gone we'd be cut off. I'd always been worried about that, so I had a little contingency plan."

"What do you mean cut off?" I asked.

"Did you ever stop to think where the money came from Dent?"

"The money? It came from Iraq. The reconstruction funds."

She looked at me like I said something stupid.

"Not that money. Our money. Our operational budget. The money Bolle used to buy stuff like guns, cars, and helicopters?"

"Uhh… No. I guess it came from the Department of Justice?"

"It doesn't. Our salaries come from the DOJ. That's it. All the operational money gets funneled through a series of blind trusts and corporations. None of it is federal money. If you follow the trail, it all leads back to Bolle."

"You mean he's been bankrolling this himself?"

She nodded, and in the weak glow of the red light on my headlamp, I realized she didn't look good. Her eyes were sunken and her movements were quick and jittery. She pointed at the satellite dish.

"I managed to get connectivity two hours after the explosion. By then it was all gone. The funding channels are cut off. All of our access to law enforcement and intelligence databases like NCIC was severed. I'm not even sure we're technically federal agents anymore. We were on contract, which can be severed at any time."

"We had to give Burke our badges. So we've got nothing," I said.

"I've spent the last couple of months figuring all this out," she said as she shook her head. "I put in some backdoors. We've got a bunch of cash, and I siphoned some operational funds through a series of corporations in the Seychelles. I also made separate access accounts into NCIC and the Homeland Security databases. Nobody shut those down, but they might not survive a routine audit."

She pointed at the cases. "I've also got stuff to make fake identification and backstop it in DMV databases and stuff."

"Casey, I could kiss you right now."

"Don't," she said. "My nose hurts. I've spent the last hour booking a vacation home outside Ontario. We've got the rental for a week. Also, I got us some vehicles from a commercial leasing facility out of Boise. I got two trucks, a sedan, and a van. Since we did a bulk order they drove them to the house for us."

This time I did pick her up and hug her. She was shivering.

"I can't believe Eddie is dead," she said.

"Me neither."

She pulled back and collected herself.

"Can you guys help me pack this stuff up and drive it over to the truck?"

The four of us packed up all the gear, along with some energy drink cans and PowerBar wrappers. Dale drove the ATV over to the truck and we loaded it into the back. Despite the rough road, Casey fell asleep in the back seat, wedged between Jack and Robert. I managed to stay awake until we hit the paved road, then the hum of the tires lulled me into a restless sleep fraught with dreams of explosions.

I was out for about an hour and a half. The sun was rising just as we rolled into Ontario, Oregon. It was a small city, maybe 15,000 people, but compared to Lehigh Valley, it was a metropolis, so we hoped we could find some anonymity here. Even though it was small, it sat right on the interstate highway, and the town saw plenty of transient traffic.

We stopped for gas, and fast food then journeyed on. We wanted to get out of these vehicles as quickly as possible. The rental home was a big ranch house several miles outside the city limits, right on the Snake River. The nearest neighbor was several hundred yards away. Perfect. The rental vehicles were already there, and when I entered the door code into the sedan, I found the keys to all four in the glove box.

We all stood in the yard, basking in the early morning sunlight. If we hadn't been dirty, bloody, and exhausted, I could have believed we were a group of friends vacationing together. Dale's truck and the Charger fit in the garage, out of sight.

Casey started digging through the shipping cases we piled in the living room.

"First let's get the antenna set up," she said, her words slurred. "Then I can get us up and running."

I put a hand on her arm.

"Uh uh," I said. "Sleep first."

She shook her head. "But they've got Burke."

"If you go poking around in a computer system and fuck up because you're tired, could that lead them straight to us?"

She stared through the front window for a minute. Her face was swollen and puffy around her busted nose, and like the rest of us, she smelled like stale sweat, explosives residue, and dust.

"I guess," she said.

"Sleep," I repeated. "Eight hours. Then I'll help you set up whatever you want."

She didn't argue, didn't even say anything else, just shuffled upstairs like a zombie.

Alex grabbed my arm.

"C'mon," she said. "You need to take your own advice."

"Somebody has to be on watch," I said.

Fueled by giant cups of coffee, Dale volunteered to drive one of the new vehicles into town while Jack stayed on watch. I handed the pilot the case with my .308 rifle and followed Alex upstairs, where we squeezed into a tiny bedroom. We didn't have a change of clothes or even a toothbrush between us, so we just stripped down to our underwear and climbed into bed.

"I can't keep watching you almost die," she said, without preamble.

"You almost got blown up yourself," I said.

"Somehow that doesn't bother me as much," she said. "Weird."

While I was trying to figure up a reply to that, I heard her breathing slow and she started to snore lightly.

I guess I slept myself because when I woke up again, the sun was at a different angle. I found myself standing in the middle of the bedroom, pistol in hand, blinking. I realized I'd been woken up by the sound of an engine, and looked out the window to see Dale pulling up and climb out with sacks of groceries in his arms.

I dressed quietly, so as not to wake Alex, and went downstairs. Casey was awake, and looking slightly less worse for wear as she hooked up cables to computers.

"I slept four hours," she said defensively.

I gave her a thumbs up and walked into the kitchen, where Dale was unpacking a dozen pre-paid cellular phones.

"I've been all over town buying these damn things," he said. "Didn't want to buy them all at one place."

I nodded. Dale wasn't the most technically savvy of our little bunch, but he had a good head for tradecraft. He'd also picked up food, laundry detergent and a bunch of generic sweatpants and t-shirts in different sizes so we could clean our clothes without embarrassing each other.

There was pizza on the counter. I grabbed a slice and started feeling like a human being again.

The sound of keys clicking on a keyboard drew me back into the living room. Casey was hard at work on two different computers hooked up to four different screens she'd set up on the dining room table.

"I found Burke's cell phone," she said. She pointed at a dot on a map of Ontario. It was right next to an interstate on-ramp.

"What's there?"

"Holiday Inn Express," she said.

"That's where her phone is. Is she with it?"

Visions of Burke being shot in the head and dumped in the middle of the desert filled my head.

"Let's find out," Casey said. She walked into the kitchen and returned with one of the burner phones. I looked over her shoulder as she started tapping a text message.

Hi Anna! It's Dr. Pace. You mentioned my fee from the consulting case. I'd like to get that resolved so I can start closing out my books for the year.

We both stared at the phone as if we could will it to respond. Alex padded down the stairs barefoot. She picked up a slice of pizza, made a face, but ate it anyway.

Finally, the phone buzzed.

Good to hear from you, Alex! I'm all tied up right now and don't have my laptop with me. Was that the Mendecker case or the Paisely case?

"What's she getting at?" I asked.

Casey's fingers flew across the keyboard.

"The Mendecker case is probably a reference to an unsolved homicide from last year. A woman named Mendecker was found in the desert near here, bound and shot in the head. There's a US vs Paisley case pending right now in Portland that is some sort of white-collar crime deal."

I let out a whistle. "She's taking some chances here. Tell her Mendecker."

Again we had that long wait for a reply.

That's what I'm afraid of. I don't have all the details of the billing at my fingertips. My new assistant isn't very helpful. Can I get back to you when I get back to Portland?

Sure, Casey replied, and added a bunch of smiley faces.

"There's no way I would use that many smiley faces," Alex said around a bite of pizza.

Casey rolled her eyes. "I'm trying not to make them suspicious in case they are looking over her shoulder."

Casey and Alex had a sort of frenemy thing going on that I couldn't quite understand, but I didn't want it to derail the conversation, so I shifted the topic.

"She's pretty cagey," I said. "Notice how she said 'that's what I'm afraid of' I think she's afraid of being murdered like that woman."

"Now what?" Casey asked.

"We need a plan," I said. "Then we're going to bust her out."

CHAPTER TWENTY-FOUR

Casey and I checked into the hotel, using clean identification, and a credit card that hopefully hadn't been compromised. We'd stopped for new clothes on the way, and I kept itching. At the front desk, Casey asked for a room on the third floor, so she could have a view, and the woman behind the counter rolled her eyes, cracked her bubble gum, and gave us our room assignment.

Inside our room, she cracked open her laptop and went to work, while I checked out the balcony. Each room had a sliding glass door that led out to a little patio that was only a few feet wide. We were on the top floor, facing the interstate. The sound of semi-trucks barreling their way to Idaho was almost deafening until I slid the door shut again.

Casey was bent over her computer, making little humming noises. She'd tried and failed to find Burke's name in the guest records. No surprise there, as the room was unlikely to be in her name. She told me she wanted to try a few other ideas. I fought the urge to ask her how it was going and instead turned on the TV with the sound almost all the way down. I was halfway through an episode of *Storage Wars* when she leaned back and pumped her fist in the air.

"They use an IP based wireless video system and didn't even bother to change the default password."

"English please," I said. I turned off the TV, disappointed because the last storage unit had revealed a bunch of guitar cases, but I was eager to hear what Casey had to say.

"Instead of using wires to hook up their security cameras, they use wi-fi," she said. On her screen, I saw a surveillance camera picture of the outside of the hotel.

"So we can watch the cameras and see if she walks by?"

She gave me a look like I was proposing we listen to a vinyl record or something.

"Since I have the password, I can just look through the recordings and see if I see her."

"Oh," I said. "Let's do that."

The hotel was in the shape of a capital "L," with the short end running east-west, and the long end north-south. There were cameras in the ends of the hallways, and in the middle. Casey scrolled through them, getting a feel for what camera covered what part of the hotel, then started watching the feeds in fast replay. People appeared to run up and down the hallways.

"There!" we both said at once. Burke popped out of an elevator, flanked by the two guys we had seen at the hospital. Burke and one of the guards walked into one room, the other guard walked into the door right next door.

"That was nine this morning," Casey said. "Those are adjoining rooms."

Burke didn't reappear. Around lunchtime, one of the guards left and came back a short while later with bags of food.

"Which room is that?" I asked.

"315."

There was an emergency evacuation placard on the back of the door with a floor plan. We were on the east end of the short arm of the L. Burke's room was on the southern end of the long arm. We were both on the third floor, which made one of our potential plans much easier.

We spent the rest of the afternoon and evening watching the cameras. Everyone else was in various vehicles, circulating from restaurant to restaurant and store to store in the immediate area, trying to keep a low profile. As long as Burke was in the hotel, she was probably safe. It was extremely unlikely they would kill her here. I didn't know what they were waiting for, but apparently for the moment at least, she was supposed to remain alive.

Our problems would begin if they tried to move her. That's why everybody else in our group was in or near a vehicle. They would pick up the tail while Casey and I scrambled to follow.

It turned out they were settled in for the night. Around six o'clock one of the guards left. We all debated making a move then, but the odds of getting into the hotel room without attracting attention were low, and the odds of getting Burke shot were high. So we all gritted our teeth and watched as the guard came back with more food, hoping we'd made the right call.

Casey and I took turns napping and watching the purloined video feed. It was boring duty, sitting there watching a hotel room hallway on the screen, but we had to stay focused. They could be out the door and into the elevator or stairwell in a few short seconds. We couldn't even go to the bathroom unless the other person was watching the screen.

Finally, at two in the morning, we decided it was time. I opened a back entrance, and Dale and Robert slipped in, carrying duffel bags. Dale and I stepped out on the balcony.

This was the part I'd been dreading. I stood on the balcony rail, then turned so I was facing the building. The overhang of the roof was behind me, and I tested the gutter, hoping it wouldn't tear away. The fall was just high enough to make me a paraplegic, but probably not kill me. I grunted and pulled up, hearing the creak of the gutter as it took my full weight.

I was grateful for all the time I'd spent in the gym. I managed to pull myself up and over the lip of the roof, just as the gutter gave an alarming groan. I went prone and hung my arm over the side. Dale reached up and put the handles of a duffle bag in my hand.

The roof was shingled and had a mild pitch here. I had little trouble walking up to the central, flat part, and found a hefty looking air handler to use as an anchor for the rope. I tied it off and lowered it to Dale. He used the knots we'd tied in it to shinny up like a man half his age.

We were effectively invisible. Nobody in the parking lot would be able to see much over the edge of the roof. It was possible somebody whizzing by on the interstate would see us, but by the time they could do anything about it, this would be over, one way or another. We walked across the roof until we were over the balcony of room 315.

In our gear back at Rudder's ranch, we'd left all sorts of hi-tech cameras and other equipment. The stuff Casey had saved had been a godsend, but she hadn't been able to grab everything, so we were improvising.

Out of my jacket pocket, I pulled a length of parachute cord. Duct taped to the end was a cell phone. I turned the video function on, made sure it was recording and lowered it over the side for about thirty seconds. I pulled it up and checked the playback. I had to do it a couple more times before I got the view I wanted.

The room was lit by the glow of the TV screen, and the light in the bathroom, near the doorway. Burke was sleeping on the bed, fully clothed with her shoes off. That would make this easier. One of the guards sat in a chair on the other side of the bed, awake and watching TV. The connecting door to the room next door was open, and I guessed the other guard was sleeping in there.

Dale and I looked at each other, and we both nodded. We retrieved the rope and tied it off on this end of the roof, but didn't throw it down onto the balcony just yet. During our shopping spree today, we'd both bought heavy canvas work jackets. We zipped them up to our throats and donned clear safety glasses and thin work gloves. Then we each put on a baseball hat and turned it backwards so the bill covered the back of our necks.

I gave Dale a thumbs up and he whispered into the radio microphone clipped to his jacket.

"Ready."

We received two clicks in reply. Then we waited. Robert would be walking down the hallway from the room I'd booked with Casey. Dale and I perched on the edge of the roof, the coiled rope between us.

"Knocking." Robert's voice said in our earpieces.

I flipped the rope over the edge and slid down onto the balcony. I drew one of the dart guns in my left hand, and my pistol in my right, reminding myself not to get the two confused. There was a chance these guys were actual Federal agents, and shooting in the head wasn't likely to further our cause.

The guard was standing facing the door, hand on his gun. I didn't see any sign of movement from the door to the other room.

Dale slid down the rope and pulled a spring loaded center punch from each pocket. He jammed them both against the glass door, and it crazed and shattered, leaving big pieces clinging to the frame. I simply pushed forward, trusting the heavy canvas to protect me from getting cut.

The guard started to turn, his mouth an "o" of surprise, and in that a peculiar slow motion that happened at times like these, I saw the gun starting to come out of the holster just as I put the sights of the dart gun on his chest and pulled the trigger. He crumpled to the ground.

Behind me, I heard the cough of Dale's dart gun from the other I cuffed up the guard, then opened the door. Daniel slipped in, saw I had my man well in hand and ran to the other room to help his dad. I heard a couple of muffled thumps then all was quiet.

"Hello, Dent," Burke said as she sat up in bed. "That went well."

I grunted by way of reply and wrapped some duct tape around the guard's mouth. His jaw was already swelling. His eyes were open but they were glassy and unfocused.

Dale and Robert came in, dragging the other guard trussed up like a turkey. They dropped him on the floor, away from most of the broken glass. I finished wrapping some tape around my guys legs and searched him. I came up with a wallet, pistol magazine, knife and cell phone. I stuffed it all in my pockets and stood up.

"You search your guy?" I asked Dale. He looked up from where he was busy cutting the cord to the room telephone and nodded.

"They each had a black bag," Burke said. She dumped the glass out of her shoes and pulled them on.

I unzipped the black bag on the floor by the chair and saw a silenced Heckler and Koch machine pistol on top of some other gear. Very James Bond. I decided to keep it. Robert went next door for a second and came back with an identical bag.

"Ready to roll?" I asked Burke.

"Please."

Dale and I turned our caps the right way, and took off the glasses and gloves before we stepped out into the hallway. A woman's head poked out of a doorway down the hall.

"Sorry," I said. "I tripped and broke a mirror. Seven years bad luck for me I guess." I gave her what I hoped was a charming smile.

Casey walked up, her laptop bag over her shoulder, and we took the stairwell down to the first floor, then went out the back exit. Jack was waiting with the van. We'd taken the seats out so we could all just jump in quickly. Jack pulled away before the door was even shut.

Alex was waiting with her medical bag.

"How are you?" she asked Burke.

"Fine. Thank you." In the dim light from the street lamps, I could barely see her hands shake and her lip quiver. I looked out the back window. Aside from Dalton in the bland rental sedan, there was no one behind us.

"Please tell me you were actually being held against your will, and we didn't just dart and assault two actual feds," I said.

Burke took a sip from the bottle of water Alex offered her and shook her head.

"They weren't federal agents. They were hired guns. The one in the bedroom was professional, nothing personal. The one in the chair scared me."

She shuddered, and I didn't feel so bad about breaking the guy's jaw.

"Do you know who hired them?"

"I'm guessing the people that helped Marshall steal all that money. I think Hubbard is deeper into this than any of us realize."

I nodded.

"I think you're right. He's CIA, so I don't know how to touch him."

"Well, he just kidnapped a US Attorney, so I'm about to make life living hell for him."

For the first time since the explosion, I was beginning to feel like things were looking up a little bit.

CHAPTER TWENTY-FIVE

Laughlin agreed to meet with us, but not at the command center, so I suggested the boat ramp. We spent the night at the safe house, then the next morning we drove back down to Lehigh Valley. The hour and a half drive from Ontario to Lehigh Valley was one of the many things on my list of worries. It was a miles-long funnel we had to traverse. There were no good alternate routes.

Eastern Oregon was refreshingly devoid of automated license plate cameras and similar systems that were common-place in more populated areas like Portland, but I was still nervous about my team traveling the same stretch of road in the same vehicle more than once. These days, fears of electronic surveillance weren't just for the tin foil hat crowd. Big Brother really was watching. A city in Arizona had disguised license plate readers in fake cactuses. Cities like Baltimore routinely vacuumed up information about thousands of cell phones without a warrant and stored it on a server indefinitely. In cities all over the United States, millions of license plate numbers were routinely recorded by cameras, often with an accompanying shot of the driver.

We were being careful with our burner cell phones, only turning them on when absolutely needed. Ideally, we would have been replacing them every few days, but there were only so many places you could buy them for cash in a place like Ontario. If we bought too many of them, that would attract attention, not just from the store staff, but potentially from someone watching the store's electronic inventory. Somebody like Hubbard could have one of his technological gnomes creep their way into national databases and watch for sudden spikes in pre-paid phone sales in the local area. From there, the store's digital video surveillance records could be searched at the times the phones were sold. Nobody would need to leave Langley, Virginia to do it. Hell, they wouldn't even need a real person. The computer could be instructed to run facial recognition software and report back any matches.

Even with all the precautions we were taking, it was only a matter of time before Hubbard found us if we stuck around. The smartest thing to do would have been to scatter to the four corners of the earth, as individuals or in pairs and lie low until we weren't interesting anymore. We all knew it, but none of us were doing it.

Laughlin was waiting for us when we pulled into the boat ramp. The FBI agent was alone and looked pissed that he was waiting on us. Ordinarily I would have been the first one to arrive at a meeting like this, even if it meant I had to get there hours ahead of time, but in this case, I had an ace in the hole. Dale was across the river, snuggled up to his favorite rifle and doing his best impersonation of a piece of sagebrush. He'd been there before sunup and had given me the go ahead before we pulled in.

Likewise, Casey and Henry were in the rental van. It wasn't quite as well equipped as our old one, but she assured me they had everything she needed to spot lurking ambushers by their radio and cell phone transmissions. Just in case we were all wrong, Dalton, Jack and Robert were standing by a mile or so back to come in guns blazing.

Not for the first time, I thought about how I didn't want to live this way forever.

Burke had recovered nicely from being kidnapped. It was either that, or it just hadn't hit her yet. She got out of the car and strode up to Laughlin like she hadn't been worried about being shot and dumped in the desert only hours before. On the other hand, I couldn't help looking around as we walked up, eyeballing places for potential ambushers to be hiding.

Laughlin looked like a changed man. He looked thinner and haggard. His eyes had the look of a man who realized his life was over and was just waiting for the hammer to fall.

"I don't have much time," he said. "I'll be missed."

"That's fine," Burke said. "I'll get right to the point. I want to know what directions you've been given regarding securing Henderson Marshall when he's eventually arrested or surrenders."

A look passed across Richard's face like he'd been stabbed in the abdomen.

"I don't think you understand. This is all going to be over day after tomorrow."

"What? How?"

"That morning there's going to be an assault on the compound."

"That's stupid," I said. "You've already lost enough men. You'll win eventually, but you know they will fight back and there will be bodies stacked three deep."

He shook his head. "It's not my people. There's some sort of DHS team that's going to lead the assault. My people are just going to be back up."

"What DHS team?" I asked. This didn't make sense to me. There were only a handful of law enforcement special operations teams that were capable of assaulting a position like Freedom Ranch, and I'd heard of all of them. DHS had many arms, but they were mostly investigatory, and they didn't have a team on the same level of FBI HRT.

"I don't know," Laughlin said. "I've never heard of them."

That alone spoke volumes. Laughlin had been in charge of HRT for several years. The thought that there was some secret DHS team out there he'd never heard of was bullshit.

"Hubbard," I said and looked at Burke. "They're going to kill him. Hubbard has enough deniable shooters at his disposal to take the house. They will have their bloodbath, and blame it all on the FBI."

Laughlin turned paler. I wasn't saying anything he didn't already know, but hearing it out loud probably didn't help.

"Shit," Burke said. It was the first time I'd ever heard her curse. "What do we do?"

I'd been turning a plan over in my head for a while now. It was probably stupid, but it was all I had. I looked at Laughlin.

"If I can get inside the house, can you promise your people won't interfere."

He shook his head. "My people only control the inner perimeter. We're in the four Stryker vehicles and a couple of observation posts. The outer perimeter is all State Troopers and a bunch of outside agencies like Customs, ATF, people like that. We tightened up after that pilot escaped. I don't control those folks."

"I can get inside the outer ring. I just need you to look away when I actually enter the house."

Burke was looking at me like I was crazy. I probably was.

"When we get him out, I want to hand him directly to you," I said. "On camera. This guy can't disappear. He can't be shot trying to escape, and he can't have a mysterious heart attack."

Laughlin nodded. Either he was just trying to salvage his career, or maybe he was a straight shooter, I didn't know, but right now I needed him.

"Ok. I'll do it."

We left it at that. Burke peppered me with questions on the drive back, but I asked her for time to think, and to explain my idea to everyone at once. Finally, she relented, and I had nothing but long miles of highway to keep me occupied.

It was late morning by the time we got back to the safe house, thanks to the long surveillance detection routes we all drove. I had many worries about what we were planning, but right now my biggest one was that we wouldn't have time to assemble everything we needed.

We all gathered in the living room. Burke and I explained our meeting with Laughlin and everyone looked at me.

"What's your plan?" Dale asked.

"We're going to need an airplane, some parachutes, and some explosives," I said.

CHAPTER TWENTY-SIX

I sneaked back to Rudder's by myself. Part of it was because everyone else had a job to do. Part of it was a single person was less likely to attract attention if the place was still being watched.

If I was going to be honest, part of it was because I just wanted to be by myself for a while. For months now, I'd been living in close proximity to the others, and it was starting to wear on me. I was by nature a solitary man. I'd lived alone for over twenty years and I was feeling more than a little stifled.

It didn't help that Alex was back in one of her pensive, quiet moods, keeping me at arm's length and not talking. We'd argued about her role in the events of the next 36 hours, and she'd finally crossed her arms over her chest, blew her hair out of her face, and told me she was going to do whatever the hell she wanted, regardless of what I said. She'd reminded me of her dad so much in that moment, it had hurt, physically. I'd felt a pang in my gut like a stab from a phantom sword.

So I'd jumped at the chance to drive the ATV for miles on bad roads, then infiltrate on foot a few more through the sagebrush and lodgepole pines until I finally hit the borders of Rudder's place. I had one more field to cross and I'd be at his house. I paused for a few minutes, checking out the scene through my night vision goggles and feeling my sweat dry in the cool night air.

The place looked deserted. It was after midnight, and the usual glow of his big screen TV was absent. I wondered if he was even home, or if he'd gone to stay somewhere else in the aftermath of the explosion. I would be disappointed to find him gone, although it wouldn't stop me from filling my backpack with what I hoped he had at his ranch, I'd also hoped to enlist the old guy's aid. Besides, I kind of liked him.

I was pleased to find the latest generation night vision goggles had enough resolution to help me avoid the cow pies in the pasture. As I got closer to the house, I could see the giant hole in the driveway where the bomb had exploded. The vehicles and the twisted wreck of Dale's trailer had been hauled away. I could smell the reek of burnt plastic and explosives though.

I decided to do a circuit of the house before knocking. I crept along, looking in dark windows and seeing no sign of Rudder. I'd gone around three sides of the house when I heard the slightest sound behind me and all the hair on the back of my neck stood up.

When I turned around, Rudder was standing about a dozen feet behind me. In the green image of the goggles, I could tell it was him, recognizing his coke bottle glasses and his britches pulled up almost to the bottom of his rib cage. He had a bayonet in his hand, almost as long as my forearm.

"You sure are quiet for such a big fella. Why don't you take off those Buck Rogers glasses and come on in for a drink."

He walked past me and turned the corner towards his porch. Bemused I followed him inside, doffing the goggles as I went.

He flipped on the light in the kitchen and put the bayonet on the counter, followed by a Smith and Wesson Victory Model revolver he pulled out of his waistband.

"I'm not sure what's worse," he said as he collected a bottle of Pendleton whiskey and a pair of glasses. "When those damn arrogant FBI agents were here, or when they left. That's when all the nutcases and crazies started showing up. Earlier today I had a couple men here giving me a hard time for cooperating with the federal government. I had to explain how you don't fuck with a man that owns 160 acres, a collection of firearms, and a backhoe before they would leave."

He poured two fingers of whiskey into each of the tumblers, then slid one over to me.

"I'm sorry we brought you so much trouble," I said and picked up the glass. The whiskey was smooth going down, and I tried to remember how long it had been since I'd had a drink.

"Hell, our trouble started the minute those assholes Webb and Marshall started buying up land here in the county. I reckon what we're seeing now is the inevitable conclusion to letting the wrong people take up residence."

He looked at through those miles thick glasses.

"What brings you here? I don't figure you sneaked in here wearing a backpack and those fancy glasses for a social visit and a repeat of some John Wayne movies."

The whole time I'd been walking, I'd been debating how much to tell Rudder. Part of me had hoped he wouldn't be here. I had a story cooked up I could tell him, not quite the truth, but not quite a lie either, but as I stood there in his kitchen, drinking his whiskey, I looked at the boarded up kitchen window where the glass had been blown out, and the picture of him in his World War 2 uniform across the living room, and I told him the whole story, start to finish.

Rudder just stood there and listened, and about halfway through he poured another finger into the glass of whiskey I hadn't realized I'd been drinking as I talked. Finally, I told him about our meeting with Laughlin that morning and my plan for getting Marshall out and ran out of steam. I took a gulp of the whiskey.

"That's one hell of an audacious plan," he said. "You're going to need a diversion."

"That's where I was hoping to get your help," I said. "Do you have any dynamite?"

"Of course I have some dynamite," he said. "What kind of rancher would I be if I didn't?"

He led me out to one of the out buildings, and unlocked a metal cabinet. Inside was a wooden box with "Hercules Powder" stenciled on the side. The dynamite was old, but not sweating nitro. I still felt queasy loading half of it into my backpack, along with some blasting caps and det cord. I left the other half with Rudder, along with a burner cell phone we'd procured just for him. It was one of the ones with the big buttons and displays.

Once again he proved to be much sharper than most people would have assumed. Rudder didn't own a cell phone because he didn't want one, not because he was too old and daft to use one. He grasped how to use it just fine, and his old fingers were surprisingly nimble on the buttons.

"Well I have to say this is the most excitement we've had around here in a long time," he said as I hoisted the pack onto my shoulders. "I'll be standing by to do my part."

"Thanks," I said and stuck out my hand. It was all I could think of to do or say.

"You're welcome," he said as we shook. "When this is over, we'll kill the rest of that bottle and swap some stories."

"Sounds good," I said and set out into the night. I had miles to go before sunrise and hoped to be back at the house in time to catch a nap before the next phase of my plan. I worked my way through the pasture, then into the sparse trees, trying not to wonder if I was about to get everyone I knew killed.

CHAPTER TWENTY-SEVEN

It turned out to be surprisingly easy to steal a plane. After a brief rest, my little suicide squad drove to Madras, Oregon, well north and west of Lehigh Valley, but still in the dry, eastern part of the state. Sagebrush Skydiving had its headquarters there, and after nightfall, we proceeded to rob them blind.

After 9/11 there had been a big push to secure even the light aircraft that flew out of tiny little airstrips like the one in Madras. The problem was, there were hundreds of rinky-dink little airfields, and thousands of planes. Over the years, nothing much happened, and predictably, security was walked back. According to Henry's research, they'd gone from 24-hour security, to a night watchman, to the current plan of alarms and cameras, and the occasional drive by from a security company. Each step had saved the airport money.

Right now, the security company was answering a rash of alarms at their various clients, courtesy of Casey and Henry, virtually guaranteeing the roving guard would be occupied elsewhere. The video cameras were showing a loop of last night's footage, with a current timestamp. As long as we were careful with our flashlights, we were unlikely to attract unwanted attention.

It turned out everyone had gone skydiving before except Henry. He'd turned a peculiar shade of green at the very thought, but I'd been planning on leaving him behind anyway. Hopefully, by now he was on his way back to Rudder's ranch. While Jack and Robert got the plane ready, the rest of us were digging through Sagebrush Skydiving's parachute loft, checking labels on packed parachutes under Dalton's supervision.

Even with all our distractions and computer shenanigans, we were pressed for time. We quickly found chutes for everybody but me. With all the gear I needed, I would be pushing 300 pounds, so I needed a big canopy. In the military, I'd frequently been over the weight limit for our chutes and had the landing scars to prove it.

"We may not have a chute for you Dent," Dalton whispered around the flashlight he was holding in his teeth so he could read the labels.

"I'm going even if I have to strip down to my jockstrap and just hold a knife in my teeth," I said as I dug through a pile of chutes.

"Spare us the visuals on that," Casey said and dropped a chute on the table with a grunt. "Will this work?"

"It isn't perfect, but it will do," Dalton said. I scooped up the chute and another we'd picked out for Robert and we all filed down out of the loft and across the tarmac towards a hangar. The night was clear and cold, with a stiff wind out of the east. Not the best skydiving weather.

Jack was crawling all over the plane while Robert loaded gear into the back. The Cessna 208 Caravan could accommodate twenty skydivers, so our little group had plenty of room. While Jack did his pilot thing, the rest of us strapped on our chutes, under the watchful eye of Dalton. He wasn't jumping tonight, the impact with the ground would probably blow his barely healed leg apart, but he had more jumps than the rest of us combined, and was a qualified jump master. So I did what he told me and tried not to think about how long it had been since I'd done this.

The mood was somber. I kept trying to catch Alex's eye, but she avoided me. We'd had the worst argument of our relationship a couple hours ago. I wanted her to stay behind. She insisted on coming. Short of physically restraining her, there hadn't been anything I could do.

I didn't mind dying anymore. I felt like I'd been running on borrowed time since the minute I responded to that homicide call so many months ago, but I didn't want to watch Alex die.

Rather than dwell on it, I concentrated on my gear. I was carrying too much stuff, but I wasn't willing to cut anything else. I had my .308 rifle with scope, suppressor, and half a dozen magazines. I was wearing one of the two body armor carriers that hadn't been seized by the FBI. My pistol was strapped to my thigh, and I had Dale's wicked Gerber Mk2 knife strapped to the other side of my belt. He'd insisted I take it since my part of tonight's festivities was likely to be up close and personal. I also had a rucksack with the dart gun we'd seized from Diana and some other party favors.

When I'd been in the Army, we'd jumped with heavier loads than this, but we'd also had the equipment to deal with it. The Army had special bags to carry weapons and other gear that would dangle below us as we descended. Civilian sport parachutists usually just jumped with a Go-Pro and a big goofy grin on their faces.

So we had to improvise. I made sure the chamber of my pistol was empty, and used some cordage to tie it into my holster. Likewise, I made sure the straps on my knife and extra magazines were taped shut, then ran some zip ties through the zipper on my backpack. My rifle went into a simple soft case, one of a bunch we'd picked up at a sporting goods store, and tied the zippers together before attaching it to a line hooked to the front of my armor.

"Five minutes," Jack said. "Everybody on the plane."

We all shuffled aboard, poking each other with rifles cases and almost tripping over our own feet. Jack started the engines with the hangar doors still shut, to keep the noise down for as long as possible. It was deafening inside the plane. Finally, after they were warmed up, he gave Dalton a thumbs up and he opened the doors before climbing in the back with us. As the plane lurched forward, he fell into a seat by the door and plugged in a headset.

The inside of the plane was dark, and Jack had the instrument panel lights turned down as low as they would go so they wouldn't interfere with his night vision goggles. We were taking off without the benefit of runway lights or any of the other niceties of modern aviation. I shoved my fear of dying a fiery death firmly to the back of my mind and told myself this was exactly the sort of thing Jack was good at.

We taxied out to the dark runway, and I debated whether to turn on my own night vision or not. Was it better to see the end coming, or to be blissfully unaware? Finally, my own compulsive need for a feeling of control took over and I slipped the goggles on. In the eerie green, I could see the runway ahead of us as the plane picked up speed. We weaved back and forth, and for one heart-stopping moment I thought one wheel was going to go off the runway, but Jack finally got the plane straightened out and we were airborne.

He didn't climb very high. A key component to this little scheme was for nobody to know we were coming, so we were staying under a thousand feet above ground level. The problem was ground level varied pretty drastically between us and Freedom Ranch. There were plenty of mountains along the way. I'd looked at Jack's laptop, where he'd plotted a zig-zagging course that took us around, and occasionally over various terrain features, and promptly looked away.

Dalton plugged in a headset and handed it to me.

"So far so good," Jack said. "I haven't heard any chatter that makes me think we've been detected yet. Although our first clue might be when an F-15 flies by."

That was not a comforting thought. They would probably hail us on the radio before they shot us down, I guessed. Dalton had a laptop hooked up to a GPS, and was using it to vector Jack onto our course. He had the screen turned way down, but it was still too bright for my goggles so I shut them off.

After the burst of activity back at the airfield, I suddenly found myself with nothing to do. I was in the back of the plane, near the door. Alex was on the other side, near the front, and still wouldn't look my way. Dale looked like he was already asleep with the case for his long barreled .300 Winchester Magnum cradled in his arms like a baby. Robert was staring out the window, and Casey was looking at her cell phone, scrolling through what I strongly suspected was an ebook.

I'd been here before, only in the Army I'd been packed into a C-141 with 120 other Rangers. Sometimes we'd sit there, shoulder to shoulder and knee to knee for five or six hours. We'd take pills to keep us from having to defecate and try not to drink too much, but we'd still wind up trying to piss in a bottle with out getting any on our gear or our neighbor. Guys would sleep, or read, with the bible and Playboy equally represented.

When I left the Army, I swore I'd never do anything like this again, but here I was. Only in the Army, I'd had a thousand other guys jumping with me, and little things like air support from fighter planes and gunships. Now there were just the five us and whatever gear we had managed to scavenge.

I leaned my head back against the vibrating skin of the airplane and promptly went to sleep. I had crazy, restless dreams, almost like I had a fever. None of them made sense. I was treated to a long parade of the dead: men I'd shot, victims of homicides I'd investigated. Finally, I found my self sitting in Al Pace's study, just like the night I'd met Bolle. Al was sitting there behind his desk, wearing his goofy looking sweater with a tumbler full of scotch in front of him, only his head was ruined by the bullet that killed him. He sat there staring mutely out of his one good eye, trying to make his mouth move.

I jerked awake to Dalton's hand on my shoulder.

"Fifteen minutes," he said over the intercom.

I nodded. I felt hot and tired, and I had a foul taste in my mouth. I took a drink of water from a bottle I'd shoved in my cargo pocket and swished it around. I set the bottle aside, then did a final check of my gear.

I flipped the goggles over my eyes and turned them on, being careful not to look at the computer screen. Out the front windows of the plane, I saw a mountain pass underneath, heart-stoppingly close. I gulped.

"Ten minutes," Dalton said. "Hook up and stand in the door."

We were jumping from a low altitude, thus were using static line parachutes. A wire cable ran lengthwise down the plane, attached to the ceiling. I grabbed my static line, clipped onto the wire, and gave it a tug. Then I unhooked my headset and stood so I could duck waddle over to the door. Behind me everyone else stood and clipped in. I turned my goggles off and checked my gear with a red flashlight, then checked Robert's. He looked mine over and turned to check the person behind him.

Dalton gave everyone a final once-over, then held up five fingers. Five minutes out. He clipped himself to the plane's bulkhead and opened the door. A cold wind and the roar of the engines filled the interior of the plane. The night was clear, and the half moon gave plenty of light for my night vision goggles to show the terrain below us. I recognized the highway that ran outside Freedom Ranch.

Suddenly the sky was lit with a brilliant flash. The compensators on my goggles cut in, keeping me from being blinded. That was Rudder and Henry detonating their first gasoline and dynamite bomb, right on time.

Dalton slapped me on the ass, and it was time to go.

Fighting all my better instincts, I hurled myself out the door of the airplane.

CHAPTER TWENTY-EIGHT

I'd never really liked parachuting, but it had been the price to pay for being a Ranger. Despite the Army's other faults, I had to give them credit for one thing: they excelled at training people to do things that their rational minds knew were absolutely insane.

One second the plane's engines roared in my ears, but they faded rapidly and there was just the wind. I let my body assume the right attitude and started counting automatically. Right on schedule, my chute popped and I was treated to a massive jerk that felt like I was being pulled upwards. That was an illusion. I was still falling, just not as fast.

I looked up and saw that my canopy was inflating nicely. At least one thing was going right. I didn't waste time looking for the others. They were behind me and above me, directions I couldn't see because of the three hundred square feet of nylon canopy over my head. Of the five of us, only Dale and I had night vision goggles. My job was to pick a place to land, in the hopes that everyone else would be able to follow my white canopy in the darkness. Dale was last in line, and in addition to getting himself on the ground safely, he was supposed to keep track of everybody else in our little chain of fools in case anyone wound up off course.

I undid the snap link attached to my gear, and my rifle case and backpack dropped to the end of their line. They would hit the ground first, a second or so before me.

The ground was coming up fast. I risked a look at the GPS strapped to my wrist. It looked like I was going to land right in the middle of the drop zone we'd picked by looking at satellite images. Over to the east, a big column of fire lit up the sky, courtesy of the gasoline bomb Rudder and Henry had detonated with a healthy charge of dynamite.

No doubt people on the ground had heard the plane, but since we'd been flying blacked out they'd probably not had time to see it before the bomb went off, and hopefully, nobody would see us falling from the sky, thanks to their night vision being shot from the explosion.

I picked a spot between clumps of sagebrush and made a slight correction. I hit the ground running, hoping to "run out" my landing, but wound up falling anyway. I was ready for it, so I didn't do too bad, although it hurt worse than I remembered from when I was eighteen. I hit the release and my chute deflated. There was no wind so I wouldn't have to chase it all over the desert.

Spitting out grit, I rolled to my knees. Robert landed not twenty-five yards behind me and stuck his landing like a pro. Behind him, I could see three more canopies still in the air.

I patted myself down real quick. All my gear was still attached to my body. No mean feat, all things considered. I turned on the little radio mounted on my vest and was greeted with a burst of static in my earpiece.

"Sagebrush," I whispered into the microphone. That was our brevity code that meant we'd landed safely. Technically some of us hadn't landed yet, but I figured it was close enough.

There was silence for several long seconds. I watched as the person behind Robert hit the ground and the canopy deflated. That would be Casey. She was too far away to see how her landing went. Alex and then Dale were still in the air, at least for a few more seconds.

Finally, my radio broke the silence.

"Crystal," Laughlin whispered. That meant the FBI commander hadn't heard any reports from either the inner or outer perimeter that anyone had sighted our chutes, so hopefully a posse of federal agents wasn't about to descend on us. I breathed a sigh of relief. We'd all agreed that we weren't going to resist if the FBI or the State Police showed up. There hadn't been much discussion really. We all wanted Marshall, but none of us were willing to shoot at the cops to do it.

We were in a little depression that ran east-west, with a line of trees on either side. Nobody could see us from the house, and as long as we didn't shine any light around, none of the cops on the outer perimeter would see us either. The little zone of dead ground gave us some breathing room to assemble and get our act together before the hard work started.

I pulled my chute in, wadded it up, and set a rock on top of it, then shucked out of the harness. After donning my backpack, I racked a round in my rifle and my pistol, then busied myself peeling off all the tape and string holding my various pouches closed, as I walked over to Robert. He had his chute squared away and was tending to his own gear. I jogged across the desert to Casey, who had a big grin on her face.

"That was fucking awesome!"

I slapped her on the ass, just like I would have one of the guys in my old platoon. I think it surprised both of us, and I wondered if I'd made a mistake. Then she stifled a laugh and went back to pulling in her chute. I decided to just keep jogging, back to where I'd seen Alex land.

She was sitting on her butt, pulling in her chute.

"I don't ever want to do that again," she said.

I helped her get her gear squared away. Out of the corner of my eye, I kept watching Dale's chute. It was still on the desert floor, stark white in the moonlight and I didn't see any sign that he was reeling it in. I felt a cold feeling in the pit of my stomach.

I decided to wait until Alex had her medical gear strapped on. By then Robert and Casey had joined us and we all ran to Dale together.

He hadn't landed well. The lanyard attached to his rifle case had wrapped around his leg, tripping him as he landed. We found him on his side, holding his hip and moaning.

Alex knelt down beside him. Without even being asked, Casey and Robert each took a knee and faced in different directions, scanning for threats.

"Landed bad," Dale said. "I think my hip's out."

"You mean the one you had replaced?" Robert asked.

"Yup. That's the one."

"You parachuted with a prosthetic hip?" Alex asked.

"Seemed like a good idea at the time," Dale said through gritted teeth.

I felt helpless standing there while Alex examined him. One unanswered question in our little plan was how we were going to handle a wounded teammate. I figured the odds of us all making it out unscathed, and one of us getting hurt at the drop zone had been a huge worry. Like many things, we'd just glossed over it in our planning.

"There's nothing I can do here," Alex said. "You need surgery."

"Just haul my ass up to the top of the ridge and leave me my rifle," Dale said.

"You've got a fractured hip!"

"Well, it isn't my trigger finger. Come on time's wasting."

"Dale..." I started to argue.

He cut me off.

"Miller, I've let you lead this little shit show until now, but if you don't get your ass in gear and start hauling my ass up to that ridge, I'm going to pull rank on you. These sons of bitches have injured two of my children, and I intend to blow thirty caliber holes in them until they're either all dead or I am."

He rolled over and started pulling himself with his hands. Robert and I looked at each other and we both shrugged. We handed our rifles to Casey and Alex, then picked up Dale.

We didn't have far to go, but the slope was steep and rocky. We picked our way up as carefully as we could but it had to hurt like hell. Still, he didn't make a sound. We stopped just before the crest and set him down. Robert and I crept up the rest of the way. He'd liberated Dale's goggles and we both scanned the area.

We were about three hundred yards from the ranch house to the northeast and the runway and hangar to the northwest. One of the Stryker vehicles was between us and the house. Inside the ranch house, I saw the occasional burst of light. The power had been cut not long after the shootout, and an FBI sniper had put a round through the backup generator.

One of the Strykers was equipped with a loudspeaker. They kept it aimed at the house and blasted noise all night long. Heavy Metal. Gregorian Chants, you name it. We'd climbed the hill to the dulcet tones of AC/DC's Back In Black. If I'd been in a better mood, it would have struck me as funny. There were a few minutes of silence, then an unearthly wailing sound started coming from the speaker. It made the hair on the back of my neck stand up.

"The fuck is that?" I whispered.

"Sounds like a rabbit distress call," Robert said. "They make a surprising amount of noise."

All of this was supposed to keep the people inside from sleeping. The rabbit noises were a particularly sadistic touch. After a couple minutes, they were making my teeth hurt.

We hauled Dale the rest of the way up the slope and got him set up in a place where he could see. Alex gave him just enough of a dose of painkillers to take the edge off, but not enough to knock him out. His rifle had a night vision scope attached. I kept one pair of night vision goggles, and Casey took the second.

"Ready?" I asked everyone. They all nodded, so I keyed my radio.

"Ballgame," I said, our brevity code that meant we were going to start sneaking towards the house and hangar.

Laughlin was quicker coming back this time.

"Field goal." We were clear to start. Not for the first time, I thought about the fact that when you let dudes pick brevity codes, half the time they were sports references.

Robert and I were going to the house. Casey and Alex were going to the hangar. With a whispered "good luck" we started out for our respective destinations. Through the goggles, I saw Alex look back at me like she wanted to say something. I forced myself to shove it out of my mind. If she'd wanted to say something, she'd had plenty of time to say it earlier. Part of me wanted to be angry with her, part of me wanted to beg her to go back into the gully and wait until all this was over. Either way, it was too late now.

We picked our way carefully, trying to avoid noise. Laughlin was supposed to tell his people to "unsee" us. The official explanation was we were the advance recon party for the DHS team that was officially taking over tomorrow. Apparently about half the FBI HRT guys were upset the operation was being taken away from, while the other half, mostly older guys, were glad to let somebody else lead the way on what was sure to be a bloody, near-suicidal assault.

There was a drainage ditch that led to a point only a dozen yards from the house. The area was dry most of the year, but in the late fall and early winter, massive thunderstorms could dump water faster than the parched earth could soak it up. The ditch was only about three feet deep, but when I slid into it, I was effectively invisible to anyone that wasn't standing right on the edge and looking down.

It was bone dry right now, and full of stones, which didn't feel too good as I crawled. I hadn't been looking forward to this. During my Ranger days, a two hundred yard low crawl in a ditch filled with sharp stones would have been a point of pride. Now I was just thinking about how much it hurt.

The ditch ran well past the house, so I kept an eye on the GPS strapped to my wrist. Designed for the military, it had a night vision mode that illuminated it just enough for my goggles to pick it up from a couple feet away. We hadn't had all this nifty shit when I left the Army. Back then the night vision goggles had weighed three times as much and were like looking through a soda straw.

It was amazing how at times like this, things could settle into a boring monotony. I'd crawl forward a dozen feet, and pause to listen and rest, then crawl some more. We were absolutely vulnerable here in the ditch. All someone would need to do would be to walk up to the ditch and empty a magazine into us. Game over. Dale was keeping an eye on us through the scope of his rifle, assuming he hadn't passed out from pain or medications.

The night was cool, but I was sweating as we crawled. Every time I would stop for a while, I would start to get chilled. The dry air had me feeling parched, and I wished I'd brought some water, but I'd left everything behind that wasn't an instrument of mayhem.

I kept wondering how Casey and Alex were doing. I hadn't heard any screaming, or bursts of gunfire, so that was good I guessed. I wanted to call them on the radio, but our plan was to maintain strict radio silence. The FBI technical people had a whole array of frequency scanners and spectrum analyzers deployed, and the more we transmitted, the more likely they were to detect us. They couldn't decrypt our transmissions in real time, but we still needed to be careful.

After crawling one last leg, I checked the GPS. We were there. I rolled onto my side and looked back at Robert. He gave me a thumbs up. He was ready. I tried to stretch out my kinked muscles as well as I could before pressing the transmit button on my radio.

"Jumpshot," I whispered.

Henry didn't have to answer on the radio. The explosion spoke for itself. The rest of Rudder's dynamite went off with a deep boom that I felt through the ground under me. The sky lit up for a few seconds as the fuel cans they'd placed next to the dynamite went off in a big Hollywood ball of fire, then subsided to a faint orange glow. That was our cue.

I pulled myself up out of the ditch, expecting to catch a round in the face at any second. We ran over to the side of the house. The sky was still lit up by the burning gas. Rudder and Henry had detonated their second bomb a few miles from the first, so hopefully they would be able to evade the state troopers that were no doubt looking for them.

The cold part of my mind realized that even if they did get caught, it wouldn't matter. They had already played their most important part in this little drama.

Robert and I hugged the wall against the side of the house. So far no one seemed to have noticed us.

The ground sloped from the front to the back of the house, so the basement actually had ground level access in the rear. Before we'd let him go, we'd picked Stuckey's brain about the layout of the house. He hadn't spent much time there and had no clue about the layout of the upper floors. But he'd told us the basement had been converted to office space for the ranch manager and was used for storage.

Richard and I stopped by a plain white door. In my night vision goggles, I could see that the door handle was on the left, and I couldn't see the hinges, so I knew it opened inward. I turned so Richard could reach in my backpack and pull out the dart gun, then he turned and I pulled a tool called a FuBar out of Robert's pack. It was a demolition tool that had become a favorite of firefighters. It wasn't as good as a fullsize sledgehammer and crowbar, but it was much more portable.

I jammed the claw end of the tool into the door frame right by the doorknob. The dying rabbit noises broadcast by the loudspeaker mostly drowned out the noise. I pushed on the long end of the bar, and with a crack, the door opened a few inches and stopped.

Fuck. It was barricaded. We'd been afraid of that. It was inevitable that sooner or later this was going to turn into a loud, furious, and probably suicidal gunfight, but we'd hoped to at least get inside the house first.

Somebody on the other side of the door said: "What the fuck?" I put my shoulder against the door and it gave a few inches, then a few inches more. I heard something sliding across the floor. Through the gap, I could see a couch was on the other side.

Robert was one of those not-too-tall guys that were almost as wide as he was tall, with thick muscles and a bull neck. He put his shoulder against the door too. We heard a thump that sounded much like a body hitting the floor, and the door got much easier to push. We got it halfway open and Robert squatted down, grabbed the bottom edge of the couch and flipped it over.

I heard a grunt from the other side, and we both piled in the door. There was a guy half under the couch, trying to crawl out. Robert aimed the dart gun at the base of his neck and pulled the trigger from a few inches away. He thrashed around for a few seconds, then stopped.

Robert started zip tying his hands together, while I stepped over the couch. There was no one else in the room. It was full of desks and filing cabinets.

"Earl?" I heard a man's voice come from a doorway off to the left.

Robert abandoned trying to restrain the sleeping man, and turned his attention to the dart gun. It was slow to reload. First, you had to put a dart in the chamber without pricking yourself, then you had to pump it up like an old-fashioned pellet rifle.

"Earl?" The man said again. I heard the sound of a toilet lid falling.

"Earl, answer me." Next came the distinctive sound of a rifle round being chambered.

My own rifle had a suppressor screwed to the end of the barrel. If this had been a movie, I could have shot somebody in one room, and it would be quiet enough that the people in the next room wouldn't know. Real life didn't work that way. Firing a .308 rifle, even with a suppressor would be painfully loud, and everyone in the house would hear it.

I crossed the room in a couple bounds, slinging the rifle across my back as I went. I pulled Dale's leaf-shaped Gerber knife out of it's sheath and stood with my back to the wall next to the door.

The door swung open and the guy stepped out. In the goggles, I could tell he was in his fifties, not very tall, balding and a little chubby. He had a rifle in his hands. I had just enough time to register that he must have had some training because his finger was straight along the receiver of the rifle.

He had just enough time to say "what..." then I wrapped my left arm around his face, covering his mouth with the crook of my elbow, then jammed the knife in my right into his throat.

I held on to him as he thrashed, and slammed the knife in again. I knew instantly that I would never be able to change my own oil again. The hot, viscous blood on my hand and arm felt just like oil draining out of the pan from a warm engine. I heard a wet gurgling sound, a little like water going down a drain, as his lungs pulled air in through the giant gash in his throat.

He fought me and almost managed to get loose. He dropped the rifle and tore at my arm with a strength I wouldn't have predicted. He bit at my arm, and headbutted the night vision goggles askew. I jammed the knife into his chest, and fell backward, bringing him down with me. I landed painfully on the rifle and wrapped my legs around him as he whipsawed around trying to break through. I quit stabbing and just held on with my right arm.

Finally, he stopped thrashing. His heels drummed on the floor for a few seconds, then he gave a final, gurgling rasp and was still. I held on for a little longer, I doubted that he was faking, but I didn't want to have to do this again.

I rolled out from under him and took a second to collect myself. I realized my left forearm was bleeding from where he'd bit me. My nostrils were full of the coppery, meaty smell of blood, and before I knew it I was being sick on the slick linoleum floor of the office. I tried to puke as quietly as I could.

I let it all go. Took a deep breath, wiped my face off, and drove on. Fortunately, puking had destroyed my sense of smell, so that made things a little easier. After I settled the night vision goggles back into place, I could see that Robert was covering the other doors and the stairwell. I made myself retrieve the knife and wipe it off on the dead guy's pants. I still had hot sticky blood all over me, and my stomach lurched again, but there was nothing left in it. I checked my rifle. The flashlight was switched off, and the infrared laser was switched on. I hit the pressure pad with my left hand and a green dot appeared in my night vision goggles. Invisible to the naked eye, it was the only way I could effectively aim the gun with the goggles on.

Robert glanced back at me and I gave him a thumbs up. Over by the back door, the guy we'd darted was snoring loudly. We both listened for a minute, straining to hear anything over the dying rabbit noises coming from outside. Apparently, we'd managed not to disturb anyone else. So far so good.

Robert pointed at the stairs, then the other doors in the room we were in, and shrugged. He was asking if I wanted to clear the whole bottom floor before we moved up. Ideally, we'd clear all the rooms down here before we moved upstairs, lest somebody walk up behind us. Ideally, we'd also have about twelve other people for this little operation.

I pointed at the stairs. He nodded and started moving. The stairwell was narrow. We kept our feet near the junction of the stairs and the wall, to minimize any creaking. Robert went up slowly, gun pointed at the door at the top of the stairs, while I went up backward, gun pointing down.

At the top, he put his hand on the knob right as the dying rabbit noises stopped. We both froze, straining our ears. An indistinct mutter came from the other side of the door. I couldn't tell if it was somebody talking, muttering in their sleep, or even a snore. After a few more seconds, we both jumped at a blare of music. It was some kind of strident classical music piece, with high pitched violins that set my teeth on end. Jesus. I bet the FBI probably employed somebody full time to do nothing but find disturbing shit to play on loudspeakers during sieges.

For some reason, the classical music made me think of my old girlfriend, Audrey. She was a classical cellist and had dropped me like a bad habit when I'd been framed for trying to kill my old partner. I wondered what she was doing right now.

I shoved that thought out of my head. It was weird what came to mind at times like this. Robert looked back at me and held up five fingers. He wanted to wait five minutes, probably to give whoever was sleeping on the other side of the door a chance to settle back in after the change in music. Laughlin had sent us a bunch of daily intelligence summaries via an anonymous Internet account. FBI snipers had been watching through the windows for days now, and the unwashed masses who had showed up unannounced were forced to bed down on the ground floor, while Marshall, Webb, and their goons had the top floor.

So we waited, even though neither one of us were keen to spend any more time in the narrow stairwell. One person at either the top or bottom could take us both out in short order.

While we waited, my earpiece crackled to life.

"Homerun," Jack said. That meant he and Dalton were airborne in the Little Bird. They would keep the helicopter low, playing hide and seek in the canyons to keep their noise and visual signature low. It meant the clock was now ticking. The Little Bird only carried so much fuel, and it was our ride out.

"Fieldgoal." Alex's voice came next in my ear. It almost hurt to hear it, but I was glad she and Casey had made it safely to the hangar and were ready with their part of the plan.

After one song reached a crescendo, Robert moved forward. He opened the door and stepped to his left, so I hooked around the door frame and looked right.

The house had a big central living room with a vaulted ceiling and big glass windows, with smaller wings that came off either side. We stepped into the huge, restaurant-style kitchen, guns up and ready to fight, but there was no one there. The refrigerator stank, thanks to the power being cut off days ago, and there were dirty dishes and flies all around. We moved slowly through the kitchen to the set of double doors that led to the living and dining room. He looked through the gap, shook his head and motioned me forward. I stuck my goggles through the gap.

There were people all over the place. There had to be twenty people sleeping on couches, on chairs, and piles of blankets on the floor. Off to our right was the stairwell up to the top floor. It was the only way up.

As I watched a man with a rifle slung over his back walked around the room, looking out the windows. Apparently he was the sentry on duty. It was pretty shitty security, but most of the sleeping figures had a long gun next to them.

I pulled my head back in the door.

Robert leaned close to whisper in my ear.

"He doesn't have night vision," Robert said. "You reckon we can just brazen it out, act like we belong here?"

I thought about it. Aside from charging through the door and just pulling the trigger as fast as we could, it was the only thing I could think of.

I nodded.

"You need to lose the goggles," Robert said.

He was right. Even in the moonlit living room, the bulbous goggles would give me away. I took them off and slid them into a pouche. I flipped a switch on the powerful-light clipped to the handguard of my rifle. Now pressure on the pad would turn it on.

"If it goes to shit, you run for the stairs, I'll cover you," Robert said and stepped through the door.

We both had our rifles down by our sides, ready to come up. The sentry saw us and cocked his head. I gave him a wave, but didn't make eye contact. We both just headed for the stairs.

He walked towards us, hesitated to look around the room, then walked towards us again. He was tall and skinny, and brought the rifle up across his chest but not pointed at us.

This isn't going to work, I thought.

"Who are you?" he asked. The voice cracked. He sounded young. The intel reports had said there was nobody under 18, but if this kid was older, it wasn't by much.

"We need to go upstairs and report to Marshall," I stage-whispered.

"You... You need to stop."

He started to bring the gun up. Out of the corner of my eye, I saw Robert bring up his rifle. He activated the white light and suddenly the guy was illuminated like a deer in headlights: stick thin, hair like a scarecrow, scruffy attempt at a beard. Robert shot him twice and he dropped. Robert shut the light off and the room went dark again, but people were sitting up.

I sprinted for the stairs, knocking over an end table and a vase along the way. I had a vague impression of expensive furniture, rugs and wall hangings, then I was taking the stairs two at a time. Behind me,

Robert was firing. His light would go on for half a second, he would fire two shots, then it would go out. I realized he was probably shooting people that were still lying down. It was a cold, murderous thing to do, but I understood why.

The stairwell was exposed to the living room. I saw a muzzle flash down below and a bullet blew out a section of hand rail, spraying me with wood splinters. Another whizzed by my head, then I was on the upstairs landing.

I stopped and poured some rounds into the living room, giving Robert some cover to run upstairs. I blipped my light on just in time to see two guys shoot at each other down below. One of them dropped and I shot the other. Hopefully, that would just add to the confusion.

Robert ran up the stairs changing magazines as he came. I dumped the rest of my magazine into the room below, hoping I was doing the right thing. The volume of fire coming back at me fell off, so there was that at least.

Two hallways stretched off from either side of the landing. I picked one, hoping I was guessing right, as I probably wouldn't get a second guess.

"Moving," I said as I finished changing magazines.

"Move," Robert said. He pulled one of our two smoke grenades off his web gear and chucked it down the stairs.

I started down the hallway. A door opened to my left and a guy stepped out, wearing just his boxer shorts, but he had a rifle. In the glare of my light, I had a brief glimpse of a muscular dude with a beard and a bunch of tattoos before I planted two rounds in his chest and one in his head. He dropped, half in and half out of the door to his room. I shined my light inside and saw another guy picking up a rifle. I shot him too. Behind me, I heard Robert firing down the hallway.

More firing came from down the hall. Drywall dust filled the air and a piece of doorway trim flew off. I vaulted over the dead guy in the doorway and dove into the room, hoping there wasn't a third shooter inside. Fortunately, it was empty. There were a couple rifles leaned in the corner and some boxes of ammo on the floor. I wanted to replenish my rapidly dwindling supply, but didn't have time.

The firing was constant. It was a roar so loud it was hard to pick out individual shots. I peeked out of the doorway I was in, and the guy in the doorway of the next room down the hall nearly took my head off. I jerked back in, spitting out more drywall dust, and was glad for the goggles I was wearing.

I took aim at the wall across from me, and pulled the trigger a few times, guessing where the guy would be standing. The heavy .308 rounds would go through drywall without even slowing down.

My answer was some rounds fired right back at me. A trio of shots blew through the wall, narrowly missing me. I dove to my left, and some more bullets passed through the space I'd just occupied. I grabbed one of the rifles leaning against the wall and ran the charging handle. It was a smaller caliber than mine, but it would do.

I dumped the whole magazine through the wall, hammering my already abused ears into oblivion. The bolt locked back and I dropped the rifle. The hot barrel scorched the carpet and I smelled burnt plastic. I thought for a second it had worked, then a couple of bullets came through the wall.

"Shit!" I screamed. This was exactly what I hadn't wanted to happen. Our advance was bogged down, and we were fixed in place. Some of the gunshots were louder, from across the hallway, so Robert was still alive, but it was just a matter of time before we were overrun by Marshall's loonies, or Hubbard's hit squad stormed the place.

"Dent, turn on your strobe." I could only faintly hear Dale's voice in my earpiece.

There was an infrared strobe attached to my body armor. I didn't know what Dale wanted, but rather than wasting time, I just flipped the switch.

There was a lull in the shooting, then I heard glass break and a meaty thud.

"Guy that was shooting at you through the wall is down," Dale said. "Ok to go down the hall."

I realized Dale had been looking through the windows. He'd wanted me to turn on my strobe so he could be sure he was shooting the right guy. It was good to work with professionals.

I stepped out in the hall. Robert was in a doorway, firing back towards the stairway landing. The guy who had been shooting at me was slumped in his doorway, I saw a dark spray of blood all over the wall opposite him.

I shined my light toward the end of the hall. A man stuck his head out of the doorway on the left-hand side, then quickly jerked it back in. He'd been exposed for a fraction of a second, but there was no doubt in my mind who it was: Marshall.

I wanted to run forward, smash my way into the room and grab him, but I forced myself to slow down.

"Bullseye. Bullseye. Bullseye," I said into my radio. Code for Marshall. "Northeast corner, second floor."

Now if I went down, Dale and everybody else would know where to shoot.

I moved forward, rifle up, with my light turned on. As much as I wanted to put that little red dot on Marshall's forehead and stroke the trigger, I reminded myself we were supposed to take him alive.

A pale yellow light came out of the doorway. As I moved so I could see around the corner of the door frame, I saw a Coleman lantern sitting on the floor. Marshall stood in the middle of the room. He held a woman in front of him as a shield. I didn't recognize her, but even through the goggles, I could tell she wasn't Mrs. Marshall. She was young, with long curly hair and wore only a t-shirt. She struggled, but Marshall had an arm wrapped around her neck. He held a pistol in the other hand, pointed down at the ground.

"Federal Agent! Drop the gun!" I yelled as I brought my rifle up. There was no way to sneak a shot around the girl. She was almost as tall as Marshall, and the way she was flailing around, I was more likely to shoot her than him.

"Get out of here!" Marshall screamed. "We have an arrangement."

That was interesting.

He raised the gun. I stepped back out of the doorway in time to not get hit by the bullet that came through. Robert and I backed into each other.

He pegged a couple of shots down the hallway, then changed magazines.

"That's my last rifle mag," he said. "We can't keep this up for much longer."

"I'm going to bang the room," I said. We'd managed to salvage two flashbangs from our gear. One was clipped to my vest, the other to Robert's.

"Give me your smoke," he said. Down at the end of the hallway, I saw movement. I handed him the smoke grenade, then pulled the flashbang off my vest. I yanked the pin, then released the spoon.

"Bang out," I said, and looked away. I slung my rifle around behind my back.

When the bang went off, it was oddly muffled. I charged through the door, empty-handed, hoping I wasn't about to walk into a hail of gunfire. A smell like cooked meat filled my nostrils.

The sound of the grenade had been muffled because Marshall had pushed the girl down on it. She was dead. There was little doubt about that. He sat on his haunches with his hands over his ears, with the pistol on the floor beside him. I rushed forward and soccer kicked him in the chest, partially to get him away from the girl, and partially because I just fucking felt like it. He hit the opposite wall with a thud, and I straddled him so I could put flex cuffs on him.

Robert shut the door and wedged it shut. He walked over to the girl and checked her for a pulse.

"She's gone," he said. "The hallway is full of smoke. That should hold them off a couple minutes. You call the girls yet?"

I keyed my microphone. "Searchlight. Searchlight. Searchlight."

"On the way," Casey answered almost instantly.

"Five minutes out," Jack said.

I looked at my watch and was astounded to find only twelve minutes had passed since we entered the basement of the house. It felt like hours.

"You're making a big mistake," Marshall said.

Unbidden, Dale's wicked Gerber knife appeared in my hand. The handle was tacky with the dried blood of the man I'd killed downstairs. I pushed the blade under his nose.

"You want to talk about mistakes? I'm the Portland cop that you framed. Remember me? Remember the detective your son beat so bad she almost died? That's her brother over there. Now you tell me who fucked up?"

Marshall was very still.

"I have money."

"I don't care about your money. I'm supposed to leave you alive and able to talk, but that doesn't mean I can't slice parts of you off. You can talk without a nose."

He went silent, but I didn't make the mistake of thinking he was cowed. Marshall was used to being in control, and I figured he would do anything to get that control back.

"We need to get rigged up," Robert said. He reached down and plucked the FuBar tool from my back pack. Then he turned so I could take the rope bag and a nylon harness that was attached to his bag.

Robert took the harness and started strapping it onto Marshall. The bedroom had an attached bathroom. I walked over to the common wall and used the FuBar tool to bust a hole the size of my fist all the way through the wall near the floor. I pulled the rope out of the bag and pushed it through the wall. I walked in the bathroom and tied the end of the rope around the tool, and set it on the floor. Now when tension was placed on the rope, the FuBar would jam across the wooden studs in the wall.

"They're coming," Robert said.

I looked out the window. The doors to the airplane hangar were open and an old farm pickup truck was bouncing across the sagebrush, headed right towards our window.

"Smashing," I said.

"Dent. Robert," Dale's voice crackled over the radio. "Confirm you are all in that corner room?"

"Yes."

I heard a thump, then a scream from out in the hallway.

"They're getting close," Robert said.

As if on cue, a pair of shots splintered the room's door. Robert pivoted and started dumping rounds right back.

I opened the window and tossed the rope bag out. The pickup executed a three-point turn on the lawn below, and backed up right under the window. Casey and Alex bailed out of the cab and pointed their guns toward the house.

Robert's rifle ran dry.

"I'm out," he said.

"Go." I pointed my rifle at the door but held my fire. Robert's fusillade seemed to have given the opposition pause, so I decided to conserve my ammo. Marshall was squirming around on the floor, so I put my booted foot on his ankle and bore down.

"I need you to talk, not walk. Hold still or I'm breaking it."

He went still, for the moment.

Robert and I were both wearing nylon harnesses around our waists. He clipped onto the rope with a carabiner, wiggled through the window and rappelled down right into the bed of the truck, just like we'd planned. I hauled the rope back into the room.

Somebody pushed on the door, which now had enough bullet holes in it I was afraid it would fall apart. I shucked my pistol, fired two rounds to give them something to think about, then holstered it.

I clipped a carabiner to the nylon webbing wrapped around Marshall. He started squirming.

"I'm not doing this!"

Instead of arguing, I punched him in the temple. The gloves I was wearing had hard plastic over the knuckles, so it didn't even hurt. He wasn't exactly limp, but he didn't struggle either as I lifted him and stuffed him through the window head first. He dropped a few feet and smacked against the siding, but I caught the rope and lowered him down. He started screaming halfway down.

Somebody banged on the door again, and I heard wood splintering. I forced myself to ignore it, and lowered Marshall the rest of the way, the muscles in my back screaming. He wasn't a light man.

Robert caught him and unclipped the rope. I turned, drew my pistol and dumped the magazine at the door. There were holes in the wood the size of my head now. I re-holstered, clipped on to the rope and struggled to get through the window. Between the rifle and the bulky vest, I wasn't sure I was going to make it.

I managed to get my legs through and was hanging onto the window sill when somebody started shooting. A bullet hit the window sill right next to my hand and splinters hit my cheek. Another round hit my goggles and everything went black.

Instead of doing a proper rappel, I just slid down the rope. Even with the gloves, my hands burned. I dropped into the bed of the truck on my ass hard enough to send a shock all the way up my spine. I pulled the goggles off.

Casey hit the gas, and I stood back up again. I was still clipped into the rope that was tangled in a mess around me.

"Stop! Stop! Stop!" I yelled, and she stood on the brakes. A gun barrel poked out of the window I'd just left and a shot bounced off the cab of the truck. Robert started shooting his pistol as I frantically tried to unclip from the rope. It was a hopelessly tangled mess.

I grabbed Dale's knife and just cut it. I flopped back into the bed of the truck when the rope parted.

"Go! Go! Go!"

Casey stomped on the accelerator and we bounced across the lawn. I managed to get the knife sheathed without stabbing myself or anybody else. So far, the only people shooting at us were inside the house. Star-shaped muzzle flashes winked from the windows, and occasionally I would hear the hiss crack of a bullet passing overhead. I got to my knees and looked over the cab of the truck. The Stryker vehicle was moving to intercept us, but at the breakneck speed we were going, I didn't think it would catch us.

Casey zigged and zagged across the sagebrush, swerving to avoid the bigger clumps that could hang up on the undercarriage. She drove to the north, up the slope where we'd left Dale. The old truck fishtailed and bucked, and it was all I could do to hang on. Marshall nearly bounced clean out of the truck bed as we went over one particularly nasty bump. Robert and I both grabbed a fistful of his harness with one hand and the bed rail with the other. I knew if I lived through this, I was going to be sore.

"I see his strobe," Casey said as we crested the ridge. She slewed the truck around and stopped. Dale blinked a red light at us from fifty yards or so away.

"Babysit Marshall," I said, and Alex jumped out of the cab.

She drew her pistol and pointed it at Marshall.

"If you move I'll shoot you in the knee cap," she said. "I'm a doctor so I can keep you from bleeding to death, but it'll still hurt."

She scared me sometimes.

Robert and I scooped up Dale and carried him to the bed of the truck.

"Nice shooting," I said as we loaded him up.

"Thanks," he said, then groaned. "Fuck this hurts."

Behind us, I heard the heavy diesel engine of the Stryker full of FBI agents as it flattened brush. I also heard the sound of the Little Bird's rotors.

"Our ride is coming. Let's go," I said.

Alex hopped back in the cab and Casey stomped. She drove over the top of the ridge, working her way between trees so close they scraped both sides of the truck. I figured it was a matter of time before we got stuck, but we popped out in the open. Casey pointed the nose of the truck down the steep slope and gunned it. The back end of the truck hopped around, and for a second I thought we were going to turn sideways and roll, then she got it pointed down again. We were headed towards the flat open area where we'd parachuted in.

The ride smoothed out for a few seconds and I thought we were home free. Then with a bang, the truck stopped so quick the back end lifted up in the air, pitching me, Dale, Robert, and Marshall into the back of the cab. I saw stars and tasted blood.

Over the sound of the hissing radiator and Dale moaning, I heard Casey say "I totally did not see that rock. I'm sorry."

"Everybody out!" I yelled. Everything hurt, but I forced myself to move anyway. I picked Marshall up and dragged him out of the truck. Casey and Alex each grabbed one of his arms and started marching him toward the drop zone, while Robert and I carried Dale, stumbling and cursing through the sagebrush.

The Little Bird dropped into a hover. Dalton was strapped to one of the bench seats on the side, and lowered a rope that was attached to the bottom of the aircraft. Six glowing chemical lights were attached to it. Each marked a heavy carabiner looped into the rope. I helped Robert lower Dale next to one, then ran over to where Alex and Casey were struggling with Marshall. Even though his hands were tied behind his back he kept twisting and turning as they tried to hook him up.

I walked up, put a hand on each shoulder, pulled him forward, and kneed him in the belly. He sat down on his ass and I clipped the D-ring onto his harness. Then I checked that Alex and Casey were clipped in properly. Alex surprised me by giving me a quick peck on the lips.

Next I ran down the line and checked that Robert and Dale were hooked up, then attached myself to the last ring.

The Stryker appeared on the ridge top, like some kind of squat, angry beast. A searchlight lit us up, but so far there were no incoming bullets.

I was wearing a harness made of nylon webbing around my waist, two straps running on the inside of my thighs. I reached in my pants, adjusted my testicles so they weren't trapped under the webbing, and gave Dalton a thumbs up.

What we were doing was called a Special Patrol Insertion/ Extraction or SPIE for short. It had been developed as a way to get recon teams out of thick jungles of Southeast Asia. I'd trained this in the Rangers and actually enjoyed it. Now I would be happy just not to die.

Jack pulled the helicopter straight up, and all in a line, our feet left the ground, our weight suspended from the harness and the three-inch thick rope hanging from the bottom of the helicopter. Jack had the touch, I left the ground gently, then when Dalton told him we were all off the ground, he poured on the power, gaining altitude and speed.

We rotated slowly clockwise, and I stuck out my arm, trying to stabilize the group with a little bit of success. The harness wasn't comfortable exactly, but it didn't hurt too bad.

I realized the first rays of the new rising sun were breaking in the east. I looked up the rope at the rest of my team above me, and it finally sunk in that nobody had died. I laughed out loud, partially out of relief, partially out of manic exhaustion.

CHAPTER TWENTY-NINE

We landed in Rudder's pasture, scaring his cows one last time. Jack set us down easy, but Robert collapsed as soon as his feet touched the ground. In the waxing dawn light, I saw the bottom of his left pants leg was soaked in blood.

"You're hit, man," I yelled over the racket of the helicopter.

"Don't mean nothing," he said and pulled his pants leg up. There was a neat hole on one side of his calf and a neat hole on the other side. Blood oozed out.

"Didn't tumble," he said and pulled a combat dressing out of his vest. I helped him get it wrapped up, and pulled him to his feet. Now that we were all safely on the ground, Dalton detached the rope from the Little Bird, and Jack flew over to the barn. Casey was casually pointing her pistol at Marshall, while Alex bent over Dale.

"Is it wrong that I really want to shoot him?" Casey asked as I passed.

"Nope," I said. "Just try to hit him in a spot where we can control the bleeding."

Marshall was still hooked up to the SPIE rope and had his hands flex cuffed behind his back, so I figured he wasn't much of a threat at the moment. There was vomit all over the front of his shirt. Apparently, the ride hadn't agreed with him.

Rudder's old farm truck bounced across the pasture towards us. We loaded everyone in the back for the short ride over to the bunkhouse. Dale looked ashen and tried to stifle a moan every time we went over a bump. As soon as the truck came to a halt, Alex rolled up his sleeve and gave him an injection. He relaxed almost instantly. We picked him up and carried him inside where Alex had set up a makeshift infirmary before we launched this little adventure.

Alex went to work with Dalton's help. He was a competent medic in his own right, so I was a third wheel.

I walked back out to the truck, where everyone was eyeballing Marshall.

I nodded at Henry and Jack. "Will you guys keep an eye out for Burke? I'll take Marshall where he needs to go."

They nodded and walked off. I took Marshall's arm, and lead him through another door in the long, low bunkhouse. We'd shoved the mattresses against the walls. There was a single chair with a video camera pointed at it, and a desk off to the side.

"Is this where I'm supposed to confess?" Marshall asked with a sneer.

I handed my rifle to Casey. She slung it over her back and kept her own rifle at hand.

I forced Marshall to the ground. I replaced the zip ties with a pair of metal handcuffs and methodically cut his clothes off with a pair of EMT shears. I took his shoes off, then stood him up.

"You're all going to pay for this," he said. He looked at Casey.

"Make sure and get a good look," he said.

"It's no big deal," she said, and held her thumb and forefinger up, about an inch apart.

Marshall gave her a dirty look, and I pulled him towards the other door in the room.

"Hey, what's that?" Casey asked from behind us. I turned and saw her bend over to pick up a USB thumbdrive off the floor.

"My insurance policy," Marshall said. "I had it in my underwear."

Casey put the thumb drive on the chair, and wiped her hand on her jeans.

"It's encrypted," Marshall said. "You can't get into it."

"Challenge accepted, nasty old dude, as soon as I find some disinfectant."

I opened the door and marched Marshall through. This room was smaller. We'd covered the floor and walls with clear plastic. There was a chair chained to a ring screwed into a stud in the wall and a small table. On the table were various things we'd rounded up around the farm: branding irons, a cordless drill, a small propane torch, rusty pliers, and the *piece de resistance*, a Henderson cattle castrating tool.

It was all for show, or so I told myself.

"You think you're going to torture me?" The note of bravado in his voice was false.

I forced him into the chair, and put a ratchet strap across his chest, tight enough to not be comfortable, but he could still breathe. Then I zip tied his legs to the chair legs.

"I want a lawyer," he said.

"I don't give a shit," I answered, and walked out the door.

Casey was sitting at the desk and cleaning off the thumb drive with a disinfectant wipe when I walked into the next room. Her laptop was open, and I could see the feed from the camera mounted high up on the wall in the next room. Marshall was looking around wildly and struggling against his bonds. I didn't think he would be able to get free, and even if he did, I was in the next room, so I wasn't too worried about it.

"How long are we going to give him?" Casey asked. She finished cleaning the USB drive and slotted it into the computer.

I shrugged. "Until Alex is done with Dale and Robert. We need to get this show on the road. Burke should be here soon, and I doubt it's going to take the FBI too long to figure out what's up."

A bunch of complicated looking stuff flashed on the laptop screen. I couldn't follow it. It just made me want coffee. Casey grunted.

"Was that a good grunt or a bad grunt?" I asked.

"It's complicated. If I'm going to get into this it will take some time. It's not a sure thing, and it might be trapped to erase the data. It would be best to just get the password."

I shrugged out of my combat vest and enjoyed the feeling of being twenty pounds lighter. I set the vest and my carbine over by Casey, who was tapping away at her keyboard.

"Have Alex knock before she comes in," I said.

"Will do," Casey said without looking up from her screen.

"And turn off the video recording," I said.

She looked up at me, but didn't say anything. She scrolled through some menus on the other laptop on the desk and clicked on a box.

"Done," she said.

I took a deep breath and walked back in the room. I'd interrogated people more times than I could count, but this was the one that would matter the most. A voice in the back of my head was telling me I should wait for Alex to show up with her magic truth serum, but I ignored it.

"I want a lawyer," Marshall said again, as soon as I entered the room.

By way of reply, I kicked him in the chest, not too hard, just hard enough to tip the chair over.

I stood over him and resisted the urge to start stomping until my legs got tired.

"I think you're misunderstanding your predicament Henderson," I said. "Remember those girls your son kidnapped and sold? They didn't get lawyers, why should you?"

"They were trash," he said from the floor.

That was exactly the wrong thing to say to me. I was, by nature, an angry man. I suppose one day I'd need to sit down with a therapist or something and deal with it. I'd grown up surrounded by anger, and violence, in a Tennessee trailer home that stank like cheap whiskey most of the time. My time in the Army had been characterized by testosterone-fueled violence and my police career after that had given me plenty of reasons to feed my anger. So I was no stranger to red-hot rage.

There was another level beyond that though, a cool, detached calm anger that made me feel like I was outside of myself, floating around and looking over my shoulder. The last time I'd felt it, I'd been in a highway rest stop in Oregon, looking at Henderson Marshall's son. Now I thought of a young woman named Heather Swanson, killed by Gibson Marshall and dumped in the weeds like so much trash. Her death had started all of this.

I jerked the chair back upright. A thin trickle of blood was running out of Marshall's nose.

I took a step back, shucked my pistol out of the holster and put it on the floor. Then I opened my folding knife. Marshall flinched when I walked up to him, but I used the knife to cut the zip ties from his hands and legs. Then I put the knife away and undid the ratchet straps.

I stepped to the side. All Marshall had to do was stand up, take three steps and the pistol would be in his hands. His eyes were on it, and I could almost hear the gears turning in his head as he calculated his odds.

I leaned over so my lips were inches from Marshall's ear. The room was full of the stink of his fear sweat.

"You want to talk about trash? Let's talk about your son. He was kidnapping women and selling them. I think you knew that. I don't think you wanted him to do it, but I think you didn't do anything to stop him."

He didn't say anything, just sat there looking at the gun on the floor, and the closed door. A bead of sweat popped out of his forehead and ran down his nose.

"Now you've got something those girls didn't have Marshall, a chance to fight back. You want a lawyer? There's something better than a lawyer. All you have to do is get that gun, and get through me, and you've got a fighting chance."

His hands were down by his sides, and in my peripheral vision, I saw his fingers flex, but he still didn't make any move to get out of the chair.

I leaned in closer. My lips almost touched his ear.

"Your son is dead Marshall. I killed him. I shot him in a bathroom that smelled like piss, then I dumped his body in the forest for the coyotes to eat."

One truth and one lie. I'd certainly killed his son, but his body was somewhere in the Willamette River weighed down by chains.

Marshall still didn't move. He made a little sound, halfway between a grunt and a whimper.

"There was something about your boy that wasn't right. I'm no psychologist, but I'm guessing it stemmed from early childhood trauma. You have a thing for little boys Marshall? Maybe your own son?"

He wasn't looking at the gun, or the door anymore. Now his eyes were closed and he was shaking.

"In a little while, a US attorney is going to come in here. You're going to waive your right to an attorney and tell her everything you know, on video. If you don't do that, she's going to get up and walk away. She'll deny that she was ever here, and then you'll be left with just me to talk to."

The knock at the door made Marshall jump, and a thin stream of piss ran out of him and onto the floor. I picked up my pistol and holstered it.

I let Alex in. When she saw that Marshall was unrestrained, she gave me a quizzical look.

"Henderson has decided to cooperate," I said. Marshall stared at a corner of the room.

She pulled out the syringe and checked it.

"What's that?" Marshall asked. His voice was flat like he was asking about the weather.

"Something that will help make you a better man," I said.

Alex didn't say anything, but I saw her hands shake a little as she injected Marshall.

It took effect quickly. His breathing slowed and he relaxed.

"Let's have a show of good faith," I said. "Tell me the password to the thumb drive."

He had his eyes closed. His breathing was so deep and regular that I thought for a moment he was asleep. Then he stirred.

"You should get something to write with."

CHAPTER THIRTY

We got Marshall cleaned up and into a pair of paper coveralls. He was pliant and docile the whole time. You could tell he was stewed to the eyeballs on something, but hopefully, he'd be convincing on video. Casey tried the password he'd given us and gave me a thumbs up. I looked over her shoulder and saw a directory with thousands of files. She started opening them at random. There were emails, contracts, audio recordings, video recordings. I had no idea if any of it was valuable. It would take days to go through all of it.

I heard the crunch of tires on gravel outside and looked out the window. Burke was here. Dalton met her in the parking lot and walked her in the door. When she came in she looked me up and down. I realized I probably looked like hell, covered in blood and dirt.

Burke didn't waste any time. She sat down across from Marshall and presented her credentials.

"You can either decide to tell me everything, and we'll turn on the camera, or I'm going to walk out of here and forget I was ever here."

His eyes slid over to me, then went back to Burke.

"I'll tell you everything," he said.

Casey turned on the cameras. Burke explained who she was, and asked Marshall to sign a form waiving his right to counsel. I was watching the video over Casey's shoulder. I didn't think Marshall looked obviously stoned. He wasn't slurring his words or rambling.

Burke primed him with a couple of questions, and then he was off to the races. He explained the plan to divert billions in Iraqi reconstruction cash and smuggle it back into the US. Along the way, he sprinkled references to documents on the thumb drive. Casey found them and nodded to Burke as Marshall talked.

Marshall started naming names, and I started getting scared. I recognized some of the names. I recognized them from the evening news. They were political figures, military officers, business leaders. I felt a sinking feeling in my stomach. This was bigger than we'd imagined. Marshall had apparently decided, with the help of the chemical cocktail, that if he was going down, he was going to take all his buddies with him. The problem was, the longer he talked, the harder it was for me to imagine a way that we would get out of this alive.

At one point, Casey looked over at me and mouthed the words "holy fuck!" She seemed excited by all this, more than scared. Sometimes I wondered if Casey had some type of gene that made her fearless. As she made note after note on her yellow legal pad, Burke looked paler and paler, and I wondered if she was having second thoughts about this.

Finally, Marshall trailed off and stopped talking. Burke blinked a couple of times and flipped back to the first page of her notes.

"Ok," she said. "Let's go back to the beginning, I have some things to clear up."

Somehow, Burke had managed to keep the whole narrative straight in her mind. She would ask Marshall a question, which would lead to three more questions and so on. After a while, the sound of their voices just became a drone, like a bee buzzing in my head. I stumbled and realized I'd almost managed to fall asleep on my feet.

I glanced over at Casey. She gave me an "ok" sign and jerked her head towards the door. Marshall was handcuffed, and shackled to an eye bolt in the floor. I knew Casey was carrying a pistol, and figured Burke probably would be too. I grabbed my vest and rifle.

I stepped out of the bunkhouse, glad to be away from the smell of Marshall's sweat. The bunkhouses were long low structures, divided into three or four rooms that each had an exterior door. The rooms where we stashed Marshall were at the end of one building. We'd set up Alex's makeshift clinic at the other end of this building and the room in between was empty.

The other bunkhouse ran perpendicular to this one. We'd set up our living quarters in there. In its heyday, the ranch had employed almost a dozen men, so there was plenty of room for us.

I looked in the infirmary. Dale was asleep, probably enjoying whatever righteous drugs Alex had administered via his IV line. Robert was lying on a bunk with his bandaged leg propped up, reading an issue of *Guns & Ammo*. I gave him a thumb's up and moved on, not wanting to disturb either of them.

As I turned from the doorway, I heard the crunch of a foot on gravel, and my hand dipped automatically towards my pistol. It was Henry, looking vaguely ridiculous in his plate carrier with a carbine slung around his neck.

"Dalton wanted me to stand watch? While he and Jack fueled the helicopter?" It came out as a question. Henry was out of his element and he knew it. I gave him a nod and headed towards the other bunkhouse.

I was most of the way there when I thought of something. I looked over my shoulder at Henry.

"Hey Henry, good job last night."

His face lit up like a kid's, and for a second he reminded me of a young PFC I'd had in one of my Ranger squads. I gave him a wave.

I saw Alex over by one of the fences a hundred yards or so away. She was petting one of the horses, and from the looks of things sneaking it a treat or two from her pocket. I stood and watched her for a second. She looked happy and I decided not to bother her.

There was a mirror inside the bunkhouse and I caught a glimpse of myself. I looked like something out of a horror movie. I dumped all my clothes in the corner and climbed into a shower stall. We'd bleached the hell out of the place, but it was still filthy from years of neglect, and decades of transient male occupation before that, so I didn't linger.

Fresh clothes were a godsend. I still needed food and coffee, but it was a good start. I was strapping my pistol back on when Alex came in the door. I noticed her rifle was in the corner, next to her vest and her pistol was still strapped to the holster on the front of the vest. I almost chastised her for going unarmed but decided to let it be.

"How did it go?" she asked.

"He rolled," I said.

"That's good, right?"

"I don't know," I said. I explained what Marshall had told us, how far the conspiracy went. I started naming names and she sat down on the bed.

"Holy shit," she said. "What now?"

"I don't know. Some of it is up to Burke."

"I thought it would end after this," she said.

"It's just getting started."

"No. No more. I'm done."

She walked over to the corner of the room and pulled out the Hill

People Gear backpack she'd been wearing during the raid. She unzipped it and showed me what was inside: stacks of $100 bills.

"You cleaned out the plane," I said.

"We barely made a dent in it. There was so much money in there. Casey filled up hers too."

We'd debated taking some of the money, and had agreed we'd try if there was time. The money was untraceable, so oddly it had very little value as evidence. In all the other excitement, I'd forgotten to ask them about it.

"How much is it?"

"I don't know. I haven't had time to count it. Casey did some math and she thinks it's over a million dollars, maybe closer to two."

I hefted the backpack in my hand. It was heavy. Thirty? Forty? pounds? I realized it probably contained more money than I'd made so far in my life.

"Casey and I had plenty of time to talk while we were in that hangar, waiting for you," Alex said. "She learned a bunch from Bolle about how to hide money, set up offshore accounts and corporations, that sort of thing. She thinks we should take the money in our bags and create an escape plan for ourselves."

"I think that's a good idea," I said slowly. I once again had that familiar feeling of things happening quicker than I could keep up with them.

"I think we should just leave Dent, just scatter to the four winds with the money."

I shook my head.

"I told Burke we'd help her get Marshall to safety. After he gives his statement, we're going to fly him straight to FCI Sheriden. Once he's booked, and the evidence is recorded, we've got leverage. They can't just make that vanish."

That was the plan anyway: to create enough of a paper trail, a big enough official record that it couldn't be easily erased. Once we had Marshall's statement recorded, it wouldn't be the end of the world if he died of a sudden illness or slipped in the shower, but our case would be much stronger if he remained alive. The Federal Corrections Institution at Sheriden would be under the microscope if something happened to him.

"I want to be done with this Dent," she said. "How many names are on the list Marshall gave you? How long will it take to build a case against all of them? We could spend the rest of our lives doing this."

I sat down heavily on the bed. The room spun a little for a second. I was bone tired and just wanted to lie down, pull the covers over my head, and wake up when all this stuff had gone away and I didn't have to worry about it anymore.

"The question is," I said slowly. "Are we safer trying to bow out of this and fading into the woodwork, or seeing it through to the end? What's that saying? 'Once you ride the tiger, you can never get off?'"

"I don't think it will ever end, Dent. What are we going to do? Arrest everybody in the federal government? The military? Every contractor?"

I held my head in my hands.

"Let's do this," I said. "I'll help them get Marshall to Sheriden then we go. We'll take some of the money, get a vehicle and just take off."

She sat down next to me and put an arm around me.

"God, what will we do?"

"I don't know, but we should probably buy a place big enough for you to have a horse."

She leaned against me.

"That sounds nice."

She kissed me then, and despite my fatigue, and the fact that every time I breathed through my nose I still thought I could smell blood, I enjoyed it. She put her hands on the sides of my face, just the way I liked and kissed me harder. I made a little noise in the back of my throat.

Before I even realized I was doing it, I slid a hand under her shirt. It felt so good to touch her skin.

She laughed. "Easy there, tiger."

"I don't have anywhere I need to be," I said.

"This isn't exactly private."

I immediately started running through the options there on the ranch. It was nice to have something to think about besides impending death.

From outside, I heard a sound like a book slamming shut, then the crunch of gravel. I almost dismissed it, but something tickled at the base of my brain, some alarm bell that I was only half conscious of.

I was up and moving toward the door before I even thought about it.

"What is it?" Alex asked.

"Not sure," I said. "Stay here."

I stepped out into the gravel. It was quiet outside, and I didn't see anyone.

Still, I couldn't shake the feeling that something was wrong. I saw something between the parked vehicles and walked over to where I could see, my hand automatically going to my pistol.

It was Henry. There was a neat hole in his forehead, and a spray of blood, skull fragments and brain matter all over the cars on either side of him.

"Dent?" Alex called from behind me.

I turned to look back at her, and that's when the bullet hit me.

CHAPTER THIRTY-ONE

The bullet hit my upper left arm. It felt like I'd been smacked with a bat. I half fell, half dove for cover between the two vehicles. Another bullet hit the fender of the car to my left. I rolled under the SUV to my right. The ground clearance was just high enough for me to fit.

A guy in combat gear was out in the pasture, holding a stubby little carbine with a suppressor screwed to the barrel. He moved and I lost sight of him because of my limited field of view under the car.

There was blood all over my arm and chest. I felt detached from what was happening. There was blood pouring out of my arm. I found an entrance wound on the outside of my bicep, and an exit on the inside. There were no jagged shards of bone poking out which, I took to be a good sign, despite the fact that my arm was limp and lifeless. I felt a tingle like a mild electric shock but no pain yet.

I took a deep breath and realized my chest hurt. The bullet had gouged across the front of my pectoral muscle after it exited, leaving a bloody and wide but shallow wound. Oddly, it hurt more than my arm.

There was a combat dressing in the cargo pocket of my pants. I squirmed to find it. The front differential of the SUV dug into my cheek as I contorted myself.

"Dent?" Alex yelled from inside the bunkhouse.

"Take cover!" I yelled. "There's a guy out here with a rifle."

A couple of shots hit the ground, spraying me with gravel but not hitting me. The guy was trying to skip rounds under the SUV. If it had been a paved lot, it might have worked.

I felt cold and sick to my stomach. It felt like my arm was waking up. It wasn't so much that it hurt, as I could tell it was going to start hurting any second now.

I managed to get the bandage unwrapped, and around my arm. I pulled it tight with my teeth, and that's when the pain hit. It was like that extra little bit of stimulation was all it took to open up the floodgates.

"Ahhhh," I said. I wasn't even articulate enough to curse.

I heard rounds hit the sheet metal of the SUV, and more skipped into the gravel. I saw a pair of legs run by but had no idea who they belonged too. I had to get out of here, no matter how much it hurt.

The SUV was parked with its nose towards the bunkhouse. If I could squeeze out under the front bumper, I'd be in the dead ground between the SUV and the bunkhouse. I had no idea what was going on. The firing would slacken for a few seconds, then more rounds would go off.

Every time I moved, it hurt so bad I couldn't breathe for a second, but I pulled myself forward under the SUV. I slithered out from under it right as a bullet smacked into the ground beside me, spraying my face with grit.

I stood up and finally got my pistol out of my holster. I recognized one of Marshall's thugs over by the combine, and fired at him, but missed. I was a bit unsteady on my feet.

I realized someone was screaming "Stop! Stop!"

I turned and looked back at the bunkhouse door. There was a guy standing there in combat gear. He had a full plate carrier, a helmet, goggles, the whole outfit. He also had a rifle. It wasn't pointed at me, although I wished it was. It was pointed inside the bunkhouse.

At Alex.

"Drop the pistol or I'll smoke her," he said.

They tell you in the police academy, you should never give up your gun, even if your partner is taken hostage. The right thing to do would have been to try to swing around, and as off balance, and in a state of shock as I was, try to plant a bullet in the guy's face. There was no way he could get both of us. If he shot Alex, I could kill him. If he shot me, that would give Alex time to get to a gun and shoot him.

Fifty-fifty.

I should have gone for it.

Instead I sat the 10mm down on the hood of the SUV in front of me.

"Step back away from it," he said. "You, step out, don't get close, I know all about that Aikido bullshit."

Alex came out, her hands over her head. She looked at me.

"I'm sorry," she said.

I shrugged. It was done.

I turned to see Hubbard walking up with a gun screwed to Burke's head, followed by Diana leading Casey at gunpoint. Behind them all walked Henderson Marshall, looking worse for wear and barefoot, but free with a smug expression on his face that made me want to kill him even more.

"John Smith" the computer guy from Hubbard's safe house drove up in one of the big bro-dozer pickup trucks. He climbed out of the rig and vanished inside the interview room for a minute. When he came out, he held Casey's laptop with the thumb drive still sticking out of the side.

Robert was led out of the infirmary at gunpoint, blood streaming from a fresh cut on his forehead.

"The old guy's out cold. I took his gun," Marshall's operator said. I saw Dale's battered old Combat Commander tucked behind a strap on his vest. That pissed me off even more. The old guy had bought that gun for himself as a present for surviving Vietnam and had carried it ever since. This punk had no right taking it from him.

Then came Dalton, lead by the last pair of Hubbard's goons. There were still Taser barbs in his back, connected to the Taser one of the mercenaries was carrying.

Dalton caught my eye. He looked like hell.

"Jack?" I asked.

He just shook his head.

Casey saw Henry's body and gave a low moan. Hubbard and Diana pushed Casey and Burke towards us. Casey stumbled into me and surprised me by sticking out her tongue. I got the briefest glimpse of an SD card on her tongue before she pulled it back in again. I tried to keep my face neutral and watched out of the corner of my eye. Her jaw worked slightly as she tucked the card into her cheek.

There were six of them. Hubbard, Smith, Diana, and the three thugs, along with Marshall who still had a shit-eating grin on his face. Hubbard managed to look aristocratic, even in combat gear. He had a chromed Browning Hi-Power in his hand, not quite pointed at Burke.

"Now how should we play this?" Hubbard said. "It's rare that I get an opportunity to solve so many problems at once."

Smith was balancing Casey's laptop on one hand and typing with the other.

"There's no sign they uploaded the file anywhere," he said.

"I heard her say the connection wasn't good enough, and she

needed to adjust something," Marshall said with a nod towards Casey.

"Excellent," Hubbard said. He holstered the Hi-Power, then pulled Dale's .45 out of the front of his lackey's vest. He turned, pointed it at Marshall's face, and pulled the trigger. Marshall dropped like a puppet with cut strings. The sound of the shot echoed off the hills beyond the pasture.

"Now the money is all yours," I said. I was glad to see Marshall dead, but I wished I'd been the one to pull the trigger.

"Now everything will be all mine," Hubbard said. "One loose end down, seven more to go."

"I'm a US Attorney," Burke said. "What are you going to do? Murder me? That's a bit much even for you."

Hubbard smiled expansively. "No my dear. This group of criminals and psychopaths is going to murder you, and then kill each other in a dispute over the money you squirreled away from the airplane. We were never here."

Around me, everyone tensed. It was all I could do to stay standing. I felt sick and weak. Big drops of blood were dripping off my fingers and leaving quarter sized stains in the gravel. Every time I breathed, I felt like someone was running a red-hot poker through my arm and into my chest.

"This isn't going to work," Burke said.

"I'm wiling to bet it will," Hubbard said. "You saw those lists of names. No one is going to be particularly enthused to investigate your death too closely. We'll construct some kind of narrative that fits. People will swallow it like children taking their medicine. Within some number of weeks, some new atrocity will capture everyone's attention."

I still had a gun. My little five-shot Smith and Wesson rode in my right front pants pocket. There were six of them, seven of us. But Robert and I had both been shot recently. Dalton and Dale could barely walk. I didn't know if anybody else had a hideout gun, but even if they did, it didn't look good.

"Go get the old guy," Hubbard said to the youngest of his three mercenaries. "Drag him out here if you have to. We have to set this up just right."

The guy let his rifle hang around his neck and turned to walk off. I felt a sick feeling, both from my wound, and the realization that this was it. As soon as the guy walked off to get Dale, there would be one less gun pointed at us. I wouldn't get a better chance than that.

Mentally, I rehearsed the mechanics of getting the little revolver out of my pocket. I'd shoot Hubbard first, I decided.

I tried to shove Alex out of my mind. She was about to die, and I was going to have to watch. I tried not to think about it.

I took a deep breath and flexed the fingers of my right hand.

"Stop," Diana said. She brought her gun up and pointed it at Hubbard. "We're not doing this."

I felt a wave of dizziness pass over me. If nothing else, it was good to see Hubbard's facade crack, even if it was just for a second.

"What's this?" he said. The three goons, all brought their guns up, realized they were pointing them at their boss and lowered their muzzles.

"We're not doing this. We're not committing mass murder and walking away," Diana said.

"Growing a conscience? Or do you just want more money."

"Give me the thumb drive," she said. She held out a hand. Smith pulled the thumb drive out of the computer and looked at his boss.

"I really don't think you'll shoot me," Hubbard said. He jerked his chin towards the three men with rifles. "They'll cut you down before I hit the ground."

"The FBI is on its way," Diana said. "I sent the message as we were sneaking onto the property."

A flicker of understanding and annoyance crossed Hubbard's face.

"I see. So Mack wasn't the only turncoat."

She sneered. "I'm not a turncoat. I was never yours to begin with, you piece of shit."

"I can only guess who you are really working for," Hubbard said. He turned towards her slowly, careful to keep his hands up. "We've got quite the impasse. If you shoot me, my boys will cut you down. If we wait for the FBI, we all have much explaining to do. I don't care who you're really working for Diana, you're not blameless. I've got video. On a secure server."

Diana looked past him, at the three goons. "Put your guns down. You guys are just contractors. You can surrender to the FBI when they get here and you'll be fine."

The leader brought his rifle up.

"Or we could just smoke you in the head and take our chances that your finger won't pull that trigger once your brains hit the gravel."

He had a point. A rifle bullet to the head had an excellent chance of destroying the centers of the brain that would send a nerve impulse to her trigger finger. I'd trained for that shot, and there was no doubt he had too.

Diana was pale, and sweat ran down her face. Out of the corner of my eye, I saw Alex turn her head, look at something behind us, and quickly turn back again. I realized the mercenaries were all focused on Diana, not on us. I wondered if we should try to make a move.

I was unsteady on my feet, and a bone-tired lassitude was creeping its way through my body. I just wanted to lie down for a while and sleep.

Something sailed through the air and landed between us and Hubbard with a thud. I had just enough time to realize it was a flashbang grenade. Alex pulled some kind of Aikido move on me and swept me to the ground. She turned me so I landed on my right side, instead of my injured left arm, and fell so her body was covering my head.

The blast was still like getting hit in the head with a hammer. My hearing shut down and I saw stars. Pieces of gravel stung my skin.

Alex rolled off me, and I sat up, digging in my pocket for my little revolver. One of the mercenaries was on the ground with his hands over his ears. The other two looked dazed but were on their feet. Smith was on the ground in the fetal position. Diana was running, seemingly unaffected by the grenade blast. Hubbard, swaying on his feet, pegged a couple of shots at her.

One of the mercenaries seemed to be recovering quicker than the other. He started to raise his rifle towards Diana. I brought the revolver up to eye level, wiling my eyes to focus on the front sight. His head exploded in a spray of gore and he dropped. I saw Rudder standing there with his old Garand that looked as long as he was. He charged forward, his mouth open in a scream I couldn't hear and rammed nearly a foot of bayonet through the second mercenary's throat. He pulled the rifle back, and butt stroked the guy across the face.

Alex, Robert, and Dalton all dove for the third guy. They pinned him to the ground and Dalton struggled to get the rifle away from him. Out of the corner of my eye, I saw Dale sitting in the doorway of the infirmary with Rudder's old Victory model revolver in his hands. We had thrown Robert's vest in the corner when we tended his wounds. Dale must have pulled the grenade out of the webbing.

Hubbard turned and aimed at the knot of people struggling on the ground. I managed to get the front sight of the Smith and Wesson on his chest and jerked the trigger. It was a poor shot, and I realized the light wadcutter round probably just flattened on the ceramic plate of his armor, but it got his attention. Hubbard turned, vaulted over Burke who was still on the ground and ran.

I squeezed off another shot, aiming for the back of his head this time. When he didn't hit the ground, I knew I'd missed.

The world spun as I fought to my feet. Rudder circled the pile of people on the ground, blood dripping from his bayonet. Alex smashed a hammer fist into to the guy's face and he went limp.

I lurched after Hubbard. I felt like I was moving in slow motion, and expected to hit the ground with each step I took. He ran to the door of the big bro-dozer pickup truck and yanked it open. He saw me coming after him and fired a couple of rounds at me. I didn't even try to get out of the way, just kept shambling towards him. I didn't feel anything slam into me, so I figured he missed or I was past the point of feeling pain. He looked scared and I took a grim satisfaction at that.

I squeezed off another shot while he was behind the open door. The window shattered, and I saw him stumble. Dale's pistol hit the ground, but Hubbard kept climbing into the truck. The wadcutter rounds in the Smith and Wesson were soft lead, and low velocity, so I knew they weren't likely to make it through the thick auto glass of the windshield. I tried to run, but only managed a fast shuffle.

My vision narrowed to a dark tunnel. The only thing I could see was Hubbard. His left hand was pressed to the side of his neck, and blood welled from around his fingers. I made it to the front bumper when the engine roared to life. I could barely hear the big diesel over the whooshing sound in my ears. Out of desperation, I fired a shot, but I was moving and it hit the door pillar. A piece of trim blew off and hit Hubbard in the forehead, but other than that, it had no effect.

I reached for the doorframe with my bad arm, cutting my hand on the broken glass. I stuck the little gun through the window. I was focused on his left eye, but Hubbard batted it away just as I pulled the trigger. The gun went off, and the truck lurched backward in reverse.

I fell down, narrowly avoiding getting run over by the massive front tire.

The truck backed up in a circle. I could see Hubbard sitting upright in the driver's seat, but the truck didn't accelerate past a walking pace. The rear end swung around in a lazy arc, plowed into a piece of farm equipment and stopped.

The driver's side was facing me. Lying on my side, I raised the gun, took careful aim and squeezed the trigger. The hammer fell on an empty chamber.

I made myself kneel and transferred the empty gun to my blood slick left hand. I promptly dropped it. I picked it back up with my right hand and swung out the cylinder. I managed to hit the ejector rod with my numb left hand and a couple empty cartridge cases popped out. I stuck the gun in the waistband of my jeans, dug a speed strip of new ammo out of my pocket and shoved a pair of fresh cartridges into the cylinder. Hopefully, that would be enough.

I pushed myself up, and pitched forward, skinning my face on the gravel. I took a couple of breaths, and with a scream, got to my feet. It was hard to walk in a straight line because everything kept spinning, but I continued my zombie shuffle forward with the gun pushed out in front of me. I tried to keep the front sight on Hubbard, but it kept waving around in a wide figure eight, so I just kept walking forward.

Hubbard was thrashing around in the driver's seat. He threw the truck into drive, but the bumper was hung up on the old cultivator, and the wheel's just spun. He gave up on that and pulled his pistol. The muzzle of the Hi-Power spat flame, but apparently he was in no better shape than me, because the bullet threw up a spray of gravel in front of me.

I pulled the trigger, but the hammer fell on one of the empty chambers. He fired again, and I felt something brush past my ear. I was close enough now to see the Browning was jammed. A spent shell casing stuck up out of the half-closed slide like a stove pipe. He looked at it owlishly. There was a big hole in the left side of his jaw and cheek, where one of my shots had connected, and blood ran from his neck.

Just a few feet from the window, I stopped, raised the gun, and willed the front sight not to move. The shot broke right when the sight was over his ear. Hubbard's hand's flew up, and the Browning dropped from his fingers. He thrashed spasmodically. I knew he was probably done, that the movement was just random brain activity, but I wanted to be sure. I took a couple more steps and pulled the trigger again. Click. Another empty chamber. Then another.

Finally, the hammer fell on a live round, and Hubbard was still. The last round had hit just under his left eye. Before, at the end of a gunfight, I'd felt a savage thrill of triumph. Now I just felt tired.

I turned around. The only people standing were my people. Burke had scooped up a gun from somewhere and was pointing it at Smith. All three mercenaries were on the ground, unmoving. I stumbled towards them, taking stock, and looking for Alex. Finally I saw her walk from around one of the vehicles with her medical kit slung over her shoulder.

The sun was so bright it hurt my eyes. We locked eyes across the parking lot and I stumbled towards her. My arm and chest suddenly hurt terribly, and I gritted my teeth to keep from throwing up. I looked down at the leg of my khaki colored pants. They were soaked from the waist to my knee with blood from my arm. I tried to remember how much blood a person could lose before it became a serious problem, but my recall was a little fuzzy.

I realized I'd stopped walking, and was standing there staring mutely at the ground. I looked up and saw that Alex was running towards me now.

It seemed unfair to make her do all the work, so I decided to move towards her. I took a step and the ground came up and hit me in the face before everything went black.

CHAPTER THIRTY-TWO

When I woke up, I was on my back on a table, looking up at an x-ray machine. The room smelled strongly of dogs. I realized there was an IV plugged into my arm and a bag of blood hung from a hook over my head.

"Where the hell are we?" I asked.

Alex's face came into view. Her hair was tied back. She looked exhausted and beautiful.

"We're in a veterinary clinic. It's Sunday so it's closed. We broke in. I need x-rays of your arm to figure out if you're going to the hospital."

"No hospital," I mumbled. I thought about the people on Hubbard's thumb drive. Once I was in a hospital, it would be way too easy to make me die in surgery or something.

"I'm trying," she said. "This is the second time I've had to patch you up like this. I don't want to do this again."

"Ok, I'm in." I heard Casey's voice from across the room. I craned my neck to look at her. It hurt to move. She was sitting at the computer that controlled the x-ray machine. There was a heavy gauze bandage wrapped around her hand.

"The password was the clinic address, how lame is that?" Casey said. Her speech sounded a little slurred, and she looked glassy-eyed. I wondered what Alex had given her.

Alex sat down behind the terminal.

"Ok. How the hell does this thing work?" She started clicking through windows.

That did not fill me with confidence. There was a TV mounted to the wall over Alex's head. The sound was muted but the screen showed an aerial view of Freedom Ranch. Both the ranch house and the hangar were burning.

"Ok," Alex said. "I think I can make it take an x-ray."

"Shouldn't I have something to cover my, you know…" I made a vague gesture at my groin.

Alex looked irritated. "Casey?"

Casey rummaged around the room and finally came up with a lead-lined vest.

"I think the person running the machine is actually supposed to wear this?" Casey asked.

"Just put it on his balls," Alex said as she clicked through menus on the screen.

Casey sat it down, none too gently and I exhaled.

"I got shot," Casey said, holding her bandaged hand out. "Took my pinky off. I guess I didn't use that one much." Now that she was closer, I could tell she was thoroughly stoned on something.

"Where's everybody else?" I asked.

"Dalton is driving Burke and that IT guy to Portland so she can hand him over to the US Marshalls. He's singing like a canary. It's all about Hubbard though."

"And Hubbard's dead," I said. "Shit."

"I copied the USB drive though," she said. "It's in the cloud now. I uploaded it."

Something occurred to me. "Wait a minute. Dale's hip is busted, and me, you and Robert have all been shot. Alex is the only person who isn't hurt."

"Well, her eardrum is busted, but I think mine is too."

I realized we were all talking really loud.

"Ok Dent," Alex said. "I need you to hold still while I get x-rays of your arm."

I took a deep breath and sat back. I looked at the bag hanging from a hook.

"Hey, you aren't giving me dog blood, are you?"

"Oh for fuck's sake, Dent." I knew it was a stupid thing to say as soon as it came out of my mouth. She walked over to her bag, took out a syringe and stuck it in the port of my IV line.

"What's that?" I asked.

"Good night, Dent."

For the second time that day, everything went black.

CHAPTER THIRTY-THREE

The cabins at Oregon's Silver Falls State Park weren't bad, all things considered. I sat inside, looking out the window and trying not to worry about Alex. The sun was going down, and despite the heat of the day, I felt a chill. I pulled a blanket over my lap, both to keep warm, and better hide the pistol in my lap. Since I'd been shot, I'd had trouble feeling warm.

My arm was still in a sling. The bullet had barely nicked my humerus, causing some hairline fractures. If it had plowed right through the bone, I would have needed extensive reconstructive surgery, probably a metal rod and a long hospital stay where I would have been easy to find and vulnerable. Still, I should have received more attention than Alex had been able to give me. She'd kept the wound clean and let it heal, and now we were tentatively starting some physical therapy exercises she'd dug up off the internet. My chest was mostly healed, although I'd bear a nasty scar there as well.

It had been a long month. We'd moved from place to place all over the Pacific Northwest, going as far south as Northern California, and as far east as Montana, staying in campgrounds, state park cabins, and more often than not parked on some obscure forest service road. Our new home was parked out front: a ten-year-old camper van. We'd bought it off an aging hippie in Eureka California for cash. The inside smelled strongly of patchouli and faintly of burnt marijuana. We'd left the Grateful Dead stickers on the back as a form of protective camouflage.

Alex had been excited. I'd been dubious, but soon realized it was much better than crawling in and out of the tent with my busted wing.

The worst part of all this was the amount of time I'd had to think. We would drive for six or eight hours a day, with Alex spending most of the time behind the wheel, leaving me with nothing to do but scan the mirrors, looking for anyone who might want to kill us and ruminate. I'd had plenty of time to replay the events of the last few months in my head and plenty of occasions to sit and wonder what I could have done differently. It was rare for me to get more than a few hour's sleep at a time. I'd wake up screaming, grasping at the blankets, or at Alex. My dreams were full of death and mayhem. I'd replay things that had actually happened: getting shot, cutting a man's throat, being framed for trying to kill my partner. Sometimes my dreams would take real life and give it a twist. I lost count of the number of times I'd watched Alex die in my dreams. Sometimes I'd wake her up, just to make sure she was really alive.

The events at Freedom Ranch had been in the headlines for a few days. Congressional hearings were threatened. The FBI stonewalled. Through a series of leaks, press releases and fluff journalism pieces, a narrative was constructed where Marshall and Webb had only a peripheral association with the US Government, that had been terminated when they went off the reservation.

No mention was ever made of the money.

The Freedom Ranch raid first started to slip out of the headlines in favor of a scandal involving a US Senator and an intern, then there was a mass shooting in a shopping mall. I remember the first day I heard no coverage about the raid at all and started realizing it was going to go down the memory hole. After a few more days it was done and over with, mentioned only on Internet sites frequented by conspiracy theorists and other cranks.

I shifted in my chair, trying to get comfortable. I'd tried to get back in the habit of reading, although it was hard to concentrate for more than a few minutes at a time. Most thriller novels seemed laughably unrealistic to me, I'd thrown more than one out the window of the van, thanks to a horribly unrealistic gunfight or something similar. I'd finally settled on old classic science fiction novels, stuff I'd read as a kid. Right now, it seemed like too much effort to get up and go across the room to get one.

At the crunch of tires on the gravel outside, my head jerked up. I'd been unaware that I'd dozed off. The pistol was still in my lap. I took it with me when I went to look out the window. Alex got out of a pickup truck and pulled on her right earlobe, our sign that everything was ok. She'd walked out to the main gate of the park to meet everyone. An SUV and a sedan pulled in behind the truck.

Everyone filed in and we all shook hands. Dale was walking, albeit with a cane. Robert had a limp but otherwise looked fit and healthy. Casey looked older somehow. She was wearing her trademark jeans and hoody, but her hair was now a nondescript shade of brown. There were lines around her eyes that hadn't been there six months ago. She held her left hand close to her body, careful not to bump the still healing scar where her pinky had been.

Dalton didn't look well. He still moved like an old man, thanks to the metal rod holding his leg together, and his face was puffy. I wondered if he'd been drinking. He shook my hand but didn't quite meet my eyes.

Last, there was Burke. She'd lost weight, and she looked older too. She wouldn't quite meet my eyes either, and I knew that was a bad sign.

We made the rounds of greetings, then all looked at Burke expectantly.

"I'm just going to get this over with," she said. "There aren't going to be any prosecutions."

"The thumb drive?" Alex said.

Burke shook her head. "I've shown the Justice Department the data. They've let me know in no uncertain terms they aren't going to prosecute."

"Maybe a new administration?" Alex asked.

"Maybe. These people are embedded like ticks. I'm not sure that really matters."

She looked around the room.

"We need to watch ourselves," she said.

"That's where I come in," Casey said. She flipped open her laptop.

"The contents of the thumb drive are encrypted in over a thousand locations on the web. Starting right now, at least three of us need to go to this website once a week and type in a unique password, or the file gets decrypted and sent to all the major news outlets in the world."

"Do they even care?" Dale said. "It seems like these people are bulletproof."

"I think they'd rather the information doesn't get out," Burke said. "It could be… inconvenient."

I thought about the trail of dead bodies we'd left behind us: Henry, Jack, Bolle, Eddie, the dozens of people who burned to death at Freedom Ranch. The best we could hope for would be to inconvenience some people.

"I need everybody to pick a password," Casey said, and turned the laptop to face us. One by one, we each typed a password in twice.

"Can they hack this?" I asked.

"Maybe. I've also got encrypted USB drives for everybody," Casey said.

That left the money. We'd entrusted most of it to Casey. She'd moved it into precious metals, bearer bonds, offshore accounts, and from there set up various dummy and shell corporations. We'd lost a significant amount of value in the process, but the money was now as clean as we could make it. Some of it she'd invested, and we'd all be able to draw a small amount every month under assumed names as employees of a dummy corporation. The fake identities she'd set up for us while using all of Bolle's connections seemed to be holding up.

"Just don't get arrested and fingerprinted," she said. "And you really want to avoid facial recognition software."

One of the few constructive things I'd done over the last few weeks was learning more about the surveillance state. We needed to stay away from major cities, but there were still vast, ignored swaths of the country where we could operate.

Casey had also set up ways for us to communicate: anonymous computer bulletin boards, shared email accounts where we could leave messages in the draft messages folder, classified ads, things like that.

"So that's it," she said. "I guess now we scatter."

There was silence in the room for a minute. I felt a lump growing in my throat. I felt like I should say something, but I had to force myself to get the words out.

"I'm sorry it worked out this way," I finally said.

"We got some licks in," Dale said. "That matters."

"We have a couple million dollars," Casey said. "And I didn't get thrown out of a plane over the Pacific Ocean. Thanks for that dude."

Dale pushed himself up out of his chair with his cane. "Well, I reckon we'll head back to the ranch. My to-do list has been getting longer while I've been off on this little adventure."

Of all of us, Dale and his family were the ones most at risk. He'd declared that he wasn't leaving his ranch. He wouldn't be hard to find. I was worried about him, but there was nothing I could do. I knew better than to try to change the old guy's mind.

We all filed out of the cabin. Alex and I had spent one night there, so it was time to move on. Dale pulled a long, tweed-covered case out of his truck.

"Reckon I better give this to you, since it might be a while before we see you again."

It took me a moment to realize it was my old Fender Stratocaster guitar. I'd stashed it at Dale's house after my house was blown up.

I took it from him. "Thanks for everything Dale."

He clapped me on my good shoulder. "You're welcome. I'm going to give you some unasked for advice. You look like shit. Get some sleep, quit chewing on the past, and enjoy your time with that woman over there. You've got to know when to hang up your guns and walk away from the war."

"Ok," I said.

Then the old geezer did something I would have never expected. He hugged me, careful of my busted arm. It was quick, but he squeezed me hard before letting me go.

"After you get that arm healed up, and take a little vacation, come by the ranch. I'll teach the two of you to ride a horse."

"I'll do it."

With that, he maneuvered himself into the pickup. I put the guitar in the back of the van and climbed into the passenger seat.

Alex started the engine. "Where to?" she asked.

"Wherever you're going."

Did you enjoy Rose City Kill Zone? Please leave a review!

Visit www.dlbarbur.com to join the Dent Miller Army Mailing list. We'll send you a link to a free Dent Miller short story! We promise not to spam your inbox. We'll email you a few times a year, when there is a new DL Barbur book release, or we have something interesting to say.

You can also check out the Dent Miller community on Facebook: www.facebook.com/dlbarbur

Made in the USA
Columbia, SC
09 December 2022

73263120R00143